IN SECRET SERVICE

MITCH SILVER

POCKET STAR BOOKS
New York London Toronto Sydney

Pocket Star Books
A Division of Simon & Schuster, Inc.
1230 Avenue of the Americas
New York, NY 10020

This book is a work of fiction. Names, characters, places, and incidents either are products of the author's imagination or are used fictitiously. Any resemblance to actual events or locales or persons, living or dead, is entirely coincidental.

Copyright © 2007 by Mitch Silver

All rights reserved, including the right to reproduce this book or portions thereof in any form whatsoever. For information address Touchstone Subsidiary Rights Department, 1230 Avenue of the Americas, New York, NY 10020

First Pocket Star Books paperback edition May 2008

POCKET STAR and colophon are registered trademarks of Simon & Schuster, Inc.

For information about special discounts for bulk purchases, please contact Simon & Schuster Special Sales at 1-800-456-6798 or business@simonandschuster.com.

Design by Jae Song

Manufactured in the United States of America

10 9 8 7 6 5 4 3 2 1

ISBN-13: 978-1-4165-3795-3
ISBN-10:   1-4165-3795-3

Packed with "twists and turns worthy of a James Bond novel" (*The Mystery Bookstore*), Mitch Silver's stunning debut novel deftly links Ian Fleming's world of sex, intrigue, and treason to today's headlines. Peopled with characters including Winston Churchill, Princess Diana, the Duke and Duchess of Windsor, Anthony Blunt, and FDR, and illustrated with authenticating documents, this unique and imaginative page-turner reinvents the espionage thriller!

Acclaim for
IN SECRET SERVICE

"A great thriller, worthy of Ian Fleming himself—and the story might ever be true."

—Lee Child, bestseller author of *Tripwire*

"Silver creates a dizzying and yet undeniably fascinating tale."

—*Richmond Times-Dispatch* (VA)

"A monarchy in trouble, muderous treason, and a World War II betrayal that resonates into the present. The real thrill of *In Secret Service* is watching this contemporary and historical tale recounted through the fun house mirror. Enjoy the ride."

—Brad Meltzer, bestselling author of
The Book of Fate

"Mitch Silver impressively overlays speculative scenarios atop actual historical events. . . . Locating where fact bleeds into fiction is half the fun here."

—*The Washington Post*

This title is also available from
Simon & Schuster Audio and as an eBook

"This smart and breezy reprise of the spy stories of the 20th century is slyly plotted and bolstered with clever evidence and a winsome heroine. Winner of the beach-read sweepstakes, it will have us teasing facts from fiction."

—*Library Journal*

"Entertaining. . . . [Silver's] high spirits are so contagious that readers will happily go along for the ride."

—*Publishers Weekly*

"[A] fine thriller. . . . Fast-paced. . . . *In Secret Service* will fascinate readers."

—*MBR Bookwatch*

"This story that harks back to the best of the Cold War thrillers is at home in the past and the present—and compelling in both. It's one Ian Fleming himself would have enjoyed."

—*Rocky Mountain News* (Denver)

"Fun."

—PoisonedPen.com

For my mother and my father and
the very wonderful Ellen

Friends, Romans, countrymen, lend me your ears;
I come to bury Caesar, not to praise him.
The evil that men do lives after them;
The good is oft interred with their bones.

—William Shakespeare, *Julius Caesar*

PROLOGUE

1936

The trim little man did the thing he always did with the palm of his hand, running it over his yellow hair to flatten it down. He inched his chair a little closer to the microphone. The BBC people were still adjusting whatever they adjusted in the minute before a broadcast, giving the King just enough time to reconsider his words. He smoothed the typewritten page on the desk with the flat of his hand just as he had done with his hair. He put his right hand in his trouser pocket and scratched his leg through the material. Of all the things that had happened to him up to now, all the things he had been given and all the things he was now giving away, trouser pockets suddenly seemed immensely important. His father had had all of David's pockets sewn up when he was a boy, to teach him to keep his hands out of them. If only Father had been a little more understanding.

Ten . . . nine . . . eight . . . The man on the other

side of the desk was counting down from ten with his fingers. How had the poem gone? "Give crowns and pounds and guineas, but not your heart away." The man had run out of fingers.

"At long last I am able to say a few words of my own. I have never wanted to withhold anything, but until now it has not been constitutionally possible for me to speak. A few hours ago I discharged my last duty as King and Emperor, and now that I have been succeeded by my brother, the Duke of York, my first words must be to declare my allegiance to him. This I do with all my heart."

The words poured out of the sleek new Bakelite radio in the darkened drawing room of the Villa Lou Viei. The villa's owner, the tall, patrician American Herman Rogers, stood at the window, smoking. It was ten o'clock, too dark to make out the Mediterranean on a moonless night. His wife, Katherine, sat on the sofa, holding her houseguest's hand.

"I want you to understand that in making up my mind I did not forget the country or the Empire which as Prince of Wales, and lately as King, I have for twenty-five years tried to serve. But you must believe me when I tell you that I have found it impossible to carry the heavy burden of responsibility and to discharge my duties as King as I would wish to do without the help and support of the woman I love."

With that, Wallis Simpson let go of Katherine Rogers's hand and picked up one of the little Ming figurines from the table next to the radio. Calmly, she dropped it on the stone floor. Herman Rogers turned back from the window at the sound. Without looking up, Wallis said, "I'll pay for it, of course."

Meanwhile, in New York, a group of men was gathered around the large mahogany DuMont radio in the place they called The Room, at 34 East Sixty-second Street. They were dressed in evening clothes, though it was only four in the afternoon local time. The voice speaking from the Augusta Tower in Windsor Castle was a familiar one. Many had golfed or ridden or sailed with him.

"I want you to know that the decision I have made has been mine and mine alone. This was a thing I had to judge entirely for myself. The other person most nearly concerned has tried up to the last to persuade me to take a different course. I have made this, the most serious decision of my life, only upon the single thought of what would in the end be best for all."

Vincent Astor, the old-money New York financier, poured the Krug '28 for his fellow members of The Room: Winthrop W. Aldrich, president of the Chase National Bank; Nelson Doubleday, publisher; William Rhinelander Stewart, philanthropist heir to a department store fortune; Marshall Field, journalist, whose family had even bigger department stores; David K. E. Bruce, sometime diplomat; and Kermit Roosevelt, Theodore's son, among others. They raised their glasses.

"I now quit altogether public affairs, and I lay down my burden. It may be some time before I return to my native land, but I shall always follow the fortunes of the British race and Empire with profound interest, and if at any time in the future I can be found of service to His Majesty in a private station, I shall not fail. And now we all have a new King. I wish him, and you, his people, happiness and prosperity with all my heart. God bless you all. God save the King."

Astor proposed the toast. "God save the King! And . . . to hell with the Duke!" The men laughed and clinked their glasses and congratulated one another on a job well done.

1997

It had been a beautiful summer day, but now it was after midnight and the well-known couple just wanted to get back to the apartment for a few hours of sleep before returning to London.

The paparazzi were waiting in front of the hotel

on the Place Vendôme, so they hurried out the back, she in light-colored trousers and a dark blazer, he in jeans and a leather shirt. Instead of their usual limousine they were bundled into a less conspicuous Mercedes 280S. The security man from the hotel drove the car. The bodyguard, a former member of the Parachute Regiment who had done two stints in Northern Ireland, got in next to him and fastened his seat belt.

As always, time was of the essence. A couple of photographers on motorbikes were already alerting their colleagues to join the chase. The driver quickly pulled out into the rue de Rivoli but found a car stalled in the lane for the Champs-Élysées. So he made for the Seine and the tunnel under the Place de l'Alma, just as the men who had blocked the exit knew he would.

Nothing had been left to chance. The closed-circuit video cameras en route and the speed-enforcement ones in the Alma tunnel had all suddenly "malfunctioned" at the stroke of midnight. The man with the brake box was waiting behind the tunnel's ninth concrete post for his cue, the moment when the Kawasaki motorcycle would come into view.

At exactly twenty-five minutes after midnight, the two stuntmen on the Kawasaki came tearing through the concrete maze ahead of the Mercedes and the recently painted white car, weighted down with cement blocks in the trunk, that was poking along in the right-hand lane. When the driver of the white car suddenly turned his wheel full to the left and rammed the Mercedes, the piercing screech of shearing sheet metal filled the tunnel as the two cars went door to door. The driver of the Mercedes was fighting to regain control when the man on the back of the Kawasaki—the one wearing the special goggles— turned in his seat and aimed his weapon. The American-made SureFire Dominator high-intensity light flashed its 460 blue-white lumens directly into the driver's eyes, forcing the reflex known as optic shutdown. Later, the first paparazzo to reach the scene would report a blinding light coming from the tunnel half a mile ahead of him.

Now the man crouching behind the pillar hit the switch on his "Boston Brakes" box—a misnomer, really, as it was the drivetrain and steering wheel on the Mercedes he was now controlling, not the brakes—and moved the joystick violently left, then right, then left again. The 280S jerked to the left, crossed to the right ahead of the white car, and then came back across the road toward oncoming traffic, smashing into the thirteenth concrete pillar and coming to a stop, facing the way it had come.

In the back seat of the wreck, the boyfriend was

dead and the woman who knew too much would soon be joining him. It was simply a question of injecting the dying driver with the syringe of alcohol and chemicals, detaching the shortwave receiver from the Mercedes drivetrain, and, to sell the white car story, salting the crash scene with a few broken Fiat Uno parts. The white car had already driven away, followed into the night by the men on the motorcycle. Another car that had been traveling behind the Mercedes now slowed just enough so the man with the brake box could get in. Then it too sped away before the first of the photographers reached the crash.

CHAPTER 1

2005

Mr. Raymond Greenberg, or his assigns
88 Edgewood Avenue
New Haven, CT 06511 USA

4 April 2005

Dear Mr. Greenberg,

Our information shows you are the holder of record of Box 1007, Ansbacher Bank, 33 Shelbourne Road, Dublin 4, Eire. Pursuant to the recent sale and impending closure of the Ansbacher Bank, we are requesting non-Resident holders of safety deposit boxes to remove all goods and valuables from said boxes by 15 May 2005.

We regret that failure to do so will result in public auction of said valuables, the proceeds, if any, to be credited to the holder's account after payment of required sales and transfer taxes.

Please advise soonest.

Milo Macken,
Vice-President of Private Banking, Rand Bank

Group, Cayman Islands, Dublin, Johannesburg,
London, Munich, New York, Paris, Zurich

Dear Mr. Greenberg,

I regret to inform you that recent adverse decisions of
the Irish Tax Courts have forced us to liquidate all
assets of the Ansbacher Bank. Permit me to express the
holding company's deep regret for any inconvenience
this has caused our customers, especially one of such
long standing as yourself.

Permit me to add my personal regret that we have
never met. If you are coming over, please call on me
personally at the bank so I may assist you in any way
I can.

Milo M.

Amy Greenberg folded the letter and let it drop into
the soft-sided black computer bag that doubled as
her briefcase. The cab had already jolted her over
several thousand of Dublin's finest cobblestones, and
the driver, in his effort to take the longest, most
expensive route from her hotel, seemed determined
to leave no stone untouched. Amy didn't mind. The
city on this morning in early May was just as she
had remembered it from fifteen years before, that

wonderful two months she'd spent researching her dissertation on the *Book of Kells*.

The cab ride had even taken her past the rundown youth hostel on Bride Road, now even shabbier. She'd made the driver stop there while she'd hurriedly sketched it in the converted day planner she always carried in her handbag, drawing a circle around the third-floor window. She would impatiently spend her nights in the room on the other side of that window, counting the hours until the moment the doors to Trinity College Library would reopen in the morning—allowing her back into the presence of the most beautiful illuminated manuscript in the world. She could see it as if it were in front of her now: the four Gospels of the New Testament, painstakingly transcribed by hand onto 680 pages of calfskin in a spectacularly Celtic version of Latin script, the insular majuscule, all elongated letter forms, exaggerated serifs and ligatures. And that was just the calligraphy. Virtually every page was inked in as many as ten colors, with no symbol, illuminated initial, or Celtic knot ever repeated.

If God is in the details, He is in every page of the *Book of Kells*. When her dissertation had been published as *The Book of Kells and the Magical Power of the Truth*, Amy had asked the publisher to enlarge

one square inch from a single initial ornate capital letter that contained over 180 delicately inked interlac-
ings. Sure, the *Lindisfarne Gospels* had its fans, but
for Amy's money those silent and anonymous men living on the island of Iona had knocked one out of the
park when they'd finished the *Book* 1,200 years ago.

The cab came to a stop in front of a Late Georgian
edifice where a yard sale seemed to be in progress.
People were coming and going with shopping bags
and satchels. One woman walking down the steps
lugged a big cardboard box overflowing with a mink
coat. Amy dug into her wallet for the euros her dollars had bought at the airport and handed a wad of
them to the self-satisfied driver.

No heads turned that Monday morning when the
American stepped out of the cab. Not that she wasn't
perfectly nice to look at, she was—possessing her
family's olive skin and the dark, tightly curled hair
she liked to think of as "electric." But Amy knew
hers was the body type people call "angular" as
opposed to the head-turning "womanly." Speeding
past forty, she realized she'd spent most of her adult
mental life in the Middle Ages. It hit her now that
"middle age" was taking on a new, and unwelcome,
meaning.

Making her way up the front steps of the bank,
Amy thought back on what a strange couple of

weeks it had been. She had felt a sort of seismic shift the moment she'd picked up the mail at her Yale post office box and had seen the Irish stamps on the envelope. Her grandfather Raymond's will had made no mention of a Dublin safe deposit box. As his only surviving relative and executor, she was in a position to know. What's more, this Milo Macken person obviously had no idea that Chief had died almost ten years before.

And the letter wasn't even the week's big event. Scott had finally proposed! She was picturing him now, down on bended knee in the middle of the restaurant like some swain of yore, with the borrowed ring in his hand, telling her he loved her in the quaint remnants of an upper-class English accent. He was awfully gangly—was there a height limit on swains?—but cute-gangly, kneeling there even as the waiter was serving the tiramisu.

She'd said yes, of course. Who could turn down an ardent lover in front of all those smiling faces at the other tables, strangers looking on in hushed amusement as they waited for your answer? He'd slipped the ring on her finger and they'd kissed and the place had burst into applause. She took a quick peek at it on her finger now. The jeweler had given the ring to Scott to propose with while hers was being engraved. It had taken every ounce of her discipline not to wave it in every shop clerk's face during the weekend.

Amy pushed on the bank's oversized revolving door and for a moment she could see her reflection in the glass. What *did* he see in her, anyway? Too tall, too flat. It was a lot easier to understand what she saw in him. On the surface, Scott Harcourt Brown had everything Amy had always wanted. Smarts. A sense of humor. And a shared interest in art. In his case, he'd got it from his mother, Margaret Harcourt Brown, who'd made a name for herself in European bronzes and was still going strong doing art history in London. Scott had come over to the States to do his graduate work with Amy's grandfather, the man everyone called Chief. The gawky young Englishman became the star pupil who eventually moved in, renting the spare room on the third floor. He had stayed on after his old professor's death, and now he was really moving in. A rising star in Yale's Renaissance department, Scott was already tenured at age thirty-six—much to Amy's untenured chagrin. Oh, he was a charmer, all right.

And yet. There was something about the way he'd popped the question in public—so she couldn't say no—on the very evening she'd told him about the letter from the Irish bank. She should have known something was up. Galileo's was way too pricey for a couple of teachers. And the way Scott had peppered her with questions on the walk over. He'd started with, "What did they say was in the safe deposit box?"

"They didn't."

"And what's the deadline again for picking it up, whatever it is?"

"May fifteenth."

"And your grandfather never mentioned storing something valuable in Ireland?"

"Scott, sweetheart, I told you all this. I showed you the letter. You *read* the letter. You know everything I know."

"You're sure Chief never discussed—"

"Never. Why all the questions?"

He mumbled something like "Curiosity, that's all," and let the subject drop.

The Ansbacher Bank, now that Amy was standing in the vast lobby, was in its death throes. A century ago it must have been an awe-inspiring cathedral of commerce, reassuring the depositor with its marble and granite permanence. Now it was a mostly empty way station for hundreds of cardboard storage boxes full of valuables or files, Amy couldn't tell which.

Amy's mind's eye was picturing another lobby, though, the one in the Omni Hotel in New Haven. Galileo's, with its romantic nighttime view of the

New Haven Green, is on the hotel's nineteenth floor. But Scott was so preoccupied the night he proposed, he forgot to press the button for the elevator. He'd just stood there, waiting. And then, on the way up, Amy had had to take Scott's hand in hers, giving it an extra squeeze every couple of floors to try to bring his thoughts back to her. To them.

The whole proposal must have been an unsettling thing for him. It certainly was spontaneous: he said he'd picked out the ring that very afternoon. Amy didn't know whether to feel good or put off by that. Who the hell buys a ring these days without asking the woman what *she* wants? So many questions . . . Wasn't marrying the man in your life supposed to put an end to questions? Or was she just having the jitters, a slight case of buyer's remorse? This was one of those times when a girl really needed her mother.

Scott's mother had seemed awfully nice on the phone. He had insisted on waking her up in the middle of the London night to tell her their good news. Then and there Mrs. Brown had volunteered to help Amy "with all the motherly, busybody details" of the wedding. As if she had already known Amy's story, about the death of her parents. Amy smiled. Scott must have been planning it with her all along.

She was already more than halfway across the

marble floor of the old-fashioned bank, her rubber-soled shoes making little squelching sounds with every step. Amy could have chosen the perfectly presentable, and quieter, black flats. But no, she had to wear the not particularly comfortable low heels with their red leather lining—her own secret red battle flag in the cause of individuality. She wished Scott was here with her, despite her misgivings. But he had two final exams to grade and couldn't get away. Her classes had ended earlier than his, so they'd agreed she would come to Ireland alone. And then, when the History of Art Department had asked her to run an errand for them "as long as you're in Dublin anyway" and agreed to pay for her flight—and only *her* flight—her going solo was a done deal.

Nearly everyone else on the plane was coming over for the grand finale of Dublin's yearlong celebration of the one hundredth anniversary of Blooms-day. She had seen many of her fellow passengers again and again that weekend, wearing their ReJoyce buttons as they fanned out from the Irish National Library on Kildare Street, crossing and recrossing the River Liffey as they retraced the fictional steps of Leopold Bloom and Stephen Daedalus. Amy had seen them as she looked out the windows of the lace and dress shops on O'Connell and Grafton Streets. She had decided on the plane that walking down the aisle in a wedding dress of Irish linen was the only way to go. After all, Dublin was a long way to come for what might be an empty safe deposit box, and now she was glad she had found the dress for her big day. A sort of Gibson Girl number, it was trimmed in handmade Irish crochet lace on the high collar, bodice, back, and sleeves, with little bows on the skirt along with hundreds of tiny tucks. Maybe it was already on its way to the States.

Within moments, Amy was shown into the office of the vice-president of private banking. After examining her paperwork, the young but hardly youthful Mr. Milo Macken led her to the elevator. "It's a sad day. A sad couple of weeks, actually." He pressed the down arrow. "For ninety-two years we've been our own little Swiss canton right here in the Republic. Numbered accounts, client confidentiality, and, of course, our little offshore wrinkle. Funds deposited here could be invested in the Caymans without so much as a by-your-leave to the Irish Inland Revenue."

He led her into the elevator and pressed Vault. "Was your grandfather a singer or dancer?"

"A college professor."

Macken sighed. "Pity. We were very popular with your glam entertainers and tax-averse professionals. Until the courts barged in."

The elevator opened onto a reception area of stiff

leather chairs and mahogany end tables and, beyond it, a barred grille through which Amy could see rows of safe deposit boxes. A fortyish woman with unfashionably long, coal black hair sat at a desk across from the elevator.

Macken did the honors. "Miss Greenberg, this is our Mrs. O'Beirne." Amy had thought of piping up with a politically correct "Ms. Greenberg," or even "Dr. Greenberg" (she *did* have her PhD), but well, when in Dublin . . . Mrs. O'Beirne wore one of those skirt-and-jacket business outfits that had been out of style with American women for years. She produced a file of papers and a separate, yellowed envelope. Clearing her throat, she read aloud from the file.

" 'Amy M. Greenberg, born 22 February 1963, parents deceased. Sole surviving relation to Grandfather Raymond Greenberg, died 12 December 1995.' " She looked up at Amy. "Thank you for faxing the testamentary documents to us."

"Colleen O'Beirne wears two hats here," Macken put in. "She manages our private client facility, and in her professional capacity as solicitor is empowered to produce certain articles which have been entrusted to the bank's care."

On cue, Mrs. O'Beirne picked up a letter opener and slit open the envelope, allowing a little silver key to fall into her palm. "All I am in a position to tell

you is this: In 1964, someone other than your grandfather paid for a long-term lease on box 1007 and
put it in the name of Raymond Greenberg of New
Haven, Connecticut. He or she left the key in the
bank's keeping with the stipulation that the box not
be opened until fifty years after the purchaser's death.
Had the bank not been liquidated"—at this, she
glanced fiercely over at Macken—"we would not be
having this conversation for another decade." Mrs.
O'Beirne handed Amy the key. "All right, Martin,"
she said. "We're ready."

A man Amy had taken for another customer got
up from one of the chairs and smiled at her with a
collection of mismatched teeth. "Pleased to be of
service, miss."

Macken turned to go. "I'll leave you here," he
said. "Unfortunately, I have a flight to catch. Martin
will witness the opening of the box with Mrs.
O'Beirne and will certify that it's empty once you
have removed your goods. It's been a pleasure having
you as a customer, Miss Greenberg."

As Macken walked away, the man named Martin
pressed a code into an electronic box and opened the
grille. Then he led them through narrow corridors to
number 1007. Hers was one of the smaller boxes. So
much for gold bullion, Amy thought. Martin inserted
a key into the box. Amy put the one she had just been

given in right below it and pulled on the handle. Thinking it might be heavy, Martin braced his hands under the box as it slid away from the others. No such luck. Amy easily carried it over to a high wooden table nearby. Inside, nothing gleamed or twinkled. All she saw was a thick pile of papers kept in place by two straining rubber bands. Amy glanced up at Mrs. O'Beirne, who was discreetly looking away from the box and its contents. "I should have known," Amy said. "What do you give a college professor? Papers."

Eager to discover if anything of more fungible value was lurking at the bottom of the box, Amy picked up the three-inch sheaf of papers by their forty-year-old rubber bands, one of which immediately snapped, stinging her hand like a scorpion. Amy lost her grip, scattering her inheritance all over the floor.

Right away, Martin knelt down and started to retrieve the papers. "Let me help you, miss." Soon he and Mrs. O'Beirne were handing her fistfuls of what appeared to be a manuscript, with a few handwritten letters thrown in along with official-looking documents in different languages. Mrs. O'Beirne looked up from the pages in her hand. "The typed ones seem to be numbered, at least. That should be of some help." Martin came out from under the wooden table, holding what appeared to be the title page.

It said, "*Provenance*, by I. Fleming."

CHAPTER 2

GRAND HOTEL&SPA INTERLAKEN

DR. RAYMOND GREENBERG   16 January 1964

My Dear Chief,

What were the odds I'd be waiting for my
breakfast, gazing stupidly out the window
at the funicular when you and your wife and
your granddaughter would be boarding? Or
that I'd recognize you from the back of
your head, after not seeing you for almost
20 years? Admittedly, I did spend several
hours that day just staring at the back
of your head as you drove us up the
Kronberger and back down again, but
still . . . I believe myself to be a
phrenologist manqué.

Though we only knew each other for 24
hours at the end of the war, I must say I

found your company a delightful surprise.
An appreciation of the Romantic movement in
German art isn't the sort of conversation I
would have anticipated from a Chief Warrant
Officer in the American army. So it was
most pleasant to have drinks with you and
Marjorie last evening. Though of course,
I'm devastated to learn your return to this
part of the world is such a melancholy one.
To have lost your son and daughter-in-law
to a drunken driver is an unknowable grief.
I can only hope your visits to the clinic
here and the much-advertised mountain air
will work their restorative magic on your
lovely wife's state of mind.

The thing is, Chief, I have something
important to tell you. Or rather, to tell
your granddaughter Amy, as I have no
intention of it being read for a long time
to come. (Though how does one write about
the pure, unalloyed evil in the world to a
one-year-old?)

You see, I've been sitting on a terrible
secret since the war. And so have you,
though you don't know you know it. A big,
fat, ugly, For-Your-Eyes-Only secret. And
it's not the sort of secret one just blurts

out. Not when most of the principals in the story are still above ground and lying and covering things up. One must have facts. Proofs. On the other hand, it's not the sort of thing one takes to the grave, in all conscience. And lately I've had some pretty strong hints of my mortality. Which makes your granddaughter the ideal person to tell it to. The neutral party . . . the innocent . . . the American!

For the last 18 months, I've quietly put all my efforts and energies in service of the truth. Not some nebulous artistic "truth", but the genuine living and breathing article.

And now I intend to press Amy into service as well. What I propose is this, I'm going to put down everything I know, and it's quite a lot really, in the only way I know how to do it. As a story. Only this time, there won't be any Goldfinger or Blofeld or SPECTRE. All the names and dates and places (and as many supporting documents as I can get together) will be the real thing, written in as clear and thorough a way as I can manage. I'm calling it <u>Provenance</u> as I intend to authenticate

what I'm telling you as I go along—in
other words, provide you with the proofs
and how I know them to be the proofs. When
I'm done, I'm going to set the dossier
aside for Amy to read. And to know. After
you and I are long gone.

As you were kind enough to mention, I
have quite a cottage industry going out
of "re-imagining" my wartime experiences.
A lot of Boy's Own stuff for post-
adolescents, nothing to trouble the MI5 and
MI6 Johnnies. But this is different. And
with all the Lords and Ladies and Evelyns
and Noels in my circle, I can't be certain
whom to trust. So I'm going to trust the
innocent bystander to do the right thing.

Don't let me down.

IF

Amy opened the minibar in her hotel room and
helped herself to a miniature bottle of a single malt
scotch. This definitely called for a celebration. Ignor-
ing the upside-down glasses on their doily by the TV,
she swigged her Macallan straight from the bottle.
Ian Fleming. Ian Fleming and Chief. Ian Fleming
writing for her eyes only, for chrissakes.

Amy glanced over at the jumble of papers she had
dumped on the bed, then back at the paper she still

held in her hand. Just the signature alone was probably valuable.

The phone next to the bed didn't so much ring as hum. Amy looked at her watch. Her cell phone wasn't the kind that works in Europe, so she'd left it home. Scott was making his six o'clock call right on time. "Hello, Scott?"

"Sweetie? How'd it go today? Are we rich?" Always the kidder.

" 'No jewels, no gems, no golden diadems.' But, my love, we did score an Ian Fleming original."

There was a pause while Scott processed her last remark four thousand miles away. "You mean a first edition?"

Amy could just reach the box of crackers at the foot of the bed if she stretched out all the way and used her toes. "Better. An unpublished Fleming manuscript."

"Brilliant!" Scott's English upbringing always came out one way or the other. "What's it about?"

"Don't know"—the cracker made a surprisingly loud crunch—"yet. I just got back from the bank."

"So, Amy love, what's keeping you?"

She had always thought of Scott as the bright one. Would she have to reconsider? "You. You're keeping me."

"Well, don't tell me. I want to read it for myself. When are you coming home?"

"Tomorrow. Plane lands at three at JFK. Then customs and rush hour and the train to New Haven. Figure about six."

"Okay, sweetie, I love you. Massively. Take care of yourself and the diary and hurry home to me,"— he did that mock–Sean Connery thing from the movies—"Bond. James Bond."

"I love you too. We have a lot to talk about with our—" Amy stopped. Scott had hung up.

She spent the next twenty minutes cross-legged on the bed, laying out the manuscript pages in numerical order on the yellow bedspread. She wound up with about twenty documents left over, some of them old photocopies on slick paper that had curled. Several were in German. Fortunately they were numbered on the back, numbers that seemed to correlate with Fleming's chapters. She sure hoped so, because the time had come for a little reading in bed.

CHAPTER 3

IMMEDIATE ACTION

HEADQUARTERS THIRD ARMY

VEHICLE REQUEST FORM

WC1 Command Car And Driver/: *Greenberg*

FOR 24 HOURS BEGINNING: *0600 hrs. 5/1/45*

NOT TO BE TAKEN OUTSIDE US THEATER OPS

FOR THE COMMANDING OFFICER:

CHRIS S. SCHOTT,
MAJOR INFANTRY

PROVENANCE

In the week before the Second World War
ended in VE-Day, two officers detached to
Britain's Military Intelligence were driven
into the American theatre of operations

outside Frankfurt before transferring to a
U.S. Army command car. The Brit who made a
show of spreading his handkerchief over the
seat before risking his trousers was
Anthony Blunt, soon to be appointed
Surveyor of the King's Pictures in civilian
life. It would turn out that he had also
been, for the past ten years, spying for
the Soviet Union. Sitting next to him, I
was, my papers said, Owen Morshead,
Librarian to King George VI. While I've
been *in* libraries from time to time, I was
in actuality Assistant to the Director of
Naval Intelligence and the yet-to-be
creator of Agent 007. Yours truly,
Commander Ian Lancaster Fleming.

At the wheel, chosen for his discretion
(and his marksmanship, if needed), was your
future grandfather, U.S. Army Officer Raymond
Greenberg. All he was told of our mission was
the cover story: that paintings looted by the
Nazis had been discovered by advance elements
of Patton's Third Army and were awaiting
authentication by two English art experts at
Schloss Friedrichshof, the mountaintop home
of Prince Christophe of Hesse. And that he
had been chosen to drive us.

What Chief wasn't told was quite another matter: that Prince Christophe had been head of the Forschungsamt, Hermann Goering's intelligence operation; that Christophe's brother was married to the daughter of the King of Italy; and that Christophe's own wife was one of the four older sisters of Philip, the prince of Greek and Danish ancestry who later married our own Queen Elizabeth. So that sitting around this one family's proverbial dinner table were Nazis and Fascists rubbing elbows with auxiliary members of the British monarchy. Nor was your grandfather told that King George VI was keen to get his hands on something in the castle of much more recent vintage than an Old Master.

So for all the secrecy, *mea maxima culpa*. Now, as it happened, the Americans already had the Prince in custody and had evicted the rest of the Hesse family to a small house in the nearby village of Kronberg, so we simply could have presented our credentials to the American officer in charge of the castle. But if we had done, there'd be one of those awkward reports of our visit. I had another idea. (I'd been

given this job because, among other things,
I was in charge of 30 Assault Unit, the
Intelligence squad trained to go into
battle and capture documents the enemy had
no intention of handing over.)

We had your grandfather drive us directly
to the village, where Blunt and I conferred
with the Hesse family. That night we drove
with our running lights off up to the
servants' entrance at the Schloss, carrying
instructions from the Prince's mother for
the loyal family retainers to help us.
Gaining access to the castle's upper
floors, we located the torn piece of paper
we'd been sent across bombed-out Europe to
find. Without the American guards' ever
knowing we had been there, Chief drove us
through the night back to the edge of the
British zone. A week later, a torn document
was placed in royal hands at Buckingham
Palace. It contained a secret that would
not be revealed until . . . well . . . now.

CHAPTER 4

The minibottle of scotch was now history. With only a few crackers on her stomach, Amy was feeling light-headed. She took off her glasses and rubbed her eyes with her two index fingers, a gesture she had inherited from her grandfather. "The researcher's rub," he had called it.

Amy put the papers down and decided to run a bath. She'd probably be up half the night reading, between the excitement of the thing and the jet lag. After the bath, she'd check her e-mail on her laptop and maybe get something to eat.

As the water flowed in, Amy shrugged off her clothes and put her hair up. Maybe she should have kept the perm. Her stockbroker friend Susan had talked her into it; said it did wonders for Amy's face. But $110 every few months? Maybe if she worked in Manhattan . . . Of course, if she'd kept it short, she wouldn't be worrying now about its taking too long to dry before she could make it downstairs to the hotel restaurant.

What's the etiquette with engagement rings, anyway? Do you wear them in the bath? Then Amy remembered hers was a loaner and, with a little difficulty, slipped it off and put it next to the sink. She stepped into the tub and let the water well up around her.

Tomorrow would be hectic. Before her flight, she had her "errand" to run, a meeting her department chairman had arranged with a local antiquarian bookseller named Cedric Shields. "He already knows of you from your writing," her boss had said. "Just press the flesh, let him put a face to the name, and tell him we're interested. Half an hour, no more."

"Interested" was putting it mildly. Yale was drooling. Shields claimed to have unearthed a ninth-century explicit, the afterword that the copyists in a monastery would append to an illuminated manuscript when they had completed their task. In those days, it was a sort of credits page, making "explicit" the names of the monk or monks who had toiled over the text and giving the date of its completion. The Irish bookseller said he had bought several old calfskin books and found the explicit bound together with two later, unrelated texts. And this wasn't just any explicit Shields claimed to have found. It was the lost Explicit of the *Book of Kells*.

He *could* be on the level . . . Many a manuscript

and its explicit had parted ways over the years. Amy
sank back a little farther into the bathwater and
imagined how distressing that fact would have been
had the early Christian monks known it. Those guys
lived for recognition. For starters, the labor of copying manuscripts was considered to be the highest
calling of monastic life. Saint Jerome had copied
books in his monastery at Bethlehem, as had Saint
Benedict, who had established a scriptorium in every
Benedictine monastery. Cassiodorus had gone even
farther, saying, "Every word of the Savior written by
the copyists is a defeat inflicted upon Satan." No
wonder the man who penned an explicit wished, "for
the salvation of my soul," to be remembered in the
prayers of the readers.

Twenty minutes later, she realized with a start that
she'd dozed off, dreaming of fat monks and lanky
Englishmen and—And then she heard the sound
come again—someone was in her room. Suddenly
wide awake, Amy called out, "Who is it?" The bathroom door was open a crack, and she could tell
someone was there.

There was a pause and then a woman's voice said,
"Room service, miss." Another pause. "When you
didn't answer my knock, miss, I thought you were
out. I'm just chilling the champagne for you."

The nearest bath towel was a good six feet away.

Amy tried to calculate the time she'd need to get up, dry off, and go to the door. She went with Plan B. "I didn't order champagne. And anyway, I'm in the tub."

"The card says it's from your solicitor, miss," the voice said.

This private banking thing had its rewards. "Oh . . . all right." Stretching her leg out of the tub as far as she could, Amy eased the bathroom door closed with her wet foot. She was getting very good with her footwork.

She listened to the server bustle around a little more before remembering with alarm that she had left her purse where the woman could see it. Amy started to get up, splashing the bathwater as she reached for the towel. Almost immediately she heard what sounded like the clink of glasses and then the outer door opening.

Amy was too late to see any more than the back of the woman's hotel uniform as she closed the outer door behind her with a hurried, "Enjoy your celebration, miss." Funny about her not waiting around for a tip.

Sure enough, a bottle of champagne was chilling in a bucket near the wing chair by the window. Amy moved over to her purse on the desk and quickly looked through it to be sure all her things were still

there. Her wallet, checkbook, her day planner with
its two new sketches of Macken and Mrs. O'Beirne
that she'd doodled in the cab—even the three tam-
pons she'd brought along were undisturbed. Her
computer and her watch on the desk were just as
she'd left them. 8:55. When did they stop serving
dinner?

Amy's clothes were on the bed, where she'd
thrown them before her bath. No time to dig into the
suitcase for a new outfit. She'd just put them back
on. Something on the bed caught her eye. The manuscript was where she'd put it down. But the other
papers . . . Had she really left the German ones
spread out like that? With the floor lamp that close
to the bed? She didn't think so.

The growling in Amy's empty stomach turned her
thoughts to food. She didn't want to eat here in the
room if she was going to be cooped up with
Fleming's manuscript for the rest of the evening. The
hotel restaurant had looked all right. Hmm, what
could a vegetarian order in the land of corned
beef and cabbage? Cabbage? The thought of it
stirred up a slightly queasy feeling that the scotch
and the jet lag must have brought on. Amy decided
to limit herself to something safe, maybe a salad for
dinner.

She grabbed her things and was about to leave

when she noticed that a card hung from the neck of the champagne. It read, "For a client of long standing. May the road rise up to greet ye, as we say over here . . . Colleen O'Beirne." Amy closed the door to her room behind her, allowing herself to be rather pleased to be anyone's client of any standing.

CHAPTER 5

Just at the moment when Amy Greenberg was closing the door to her hotel room on the way to dinner, or possibly a minute or two later, Colleen O'Beirne was taking the Rathmines Road on that little downhill stretch before she had to turn into Martin's street. He was sitting in the passenger seat, staring out as Dublin accelerated past them.

They had been carpooling for the past couple of weeks, ever since he had started at the bank and she had discovered that his flat was on her way. Martin had a nightly computer report to file on the day's withdrawals, and she had the responsibility for locking the vault area, so they usually finished up together. A widow with a modestly sporty car and male companionship probably should have been thinking of the amorous possibilities, but she just couldn't picture herself kissing a mouth with those teeth. So theirs would be forever a platonic relationship.

Forever arrived at the bottom of the Rathmines

Road when a lorry backed out of a side road at high speed. There was a blinding flash of light, and then the little Fiat 124 slammed into the truck and burst into fire.

Before the police and the reporters arrived at the scene, the lorry driver joined the two men who were watching the flames. The one with the heavy goggles in his hand turned to the driver and, in an accent suggesting the Indian subcontinent, said, "Nicely done."

CHAPTER 6

THE DAILY NEWS   FRIDAY, AUGUST 29, 1924.   5

Here He Is, Girls—
The Most Eligible Bachelor Yet Uncaught

PROVENANCE

Amy, I don't know how much English history
you'll have learned by the time you read
this, so I'm going to give you a little
background on the principal players in our
drama. The year 1925 was the absolute
apogee of the British Empire, and the royal
family were in their glory. I remember that
when I was a teenager, the Hearst papers,
the largest international newspaper
syndicate, ran a heavily publicized contest
inviting readers to vote for the "World's
Most Eligible Bachelor." Rudolph Valentino
finished second. The winner was the blond,

blue-eyed, slightly built young man who had been England's King-in-Waiting for the past dozen years: Edward, the Prince of Wales. Popular? When the Empire Exhibition opened later that year at London's new Wembley Stadium, the most visited exhibit was a life-size statue of the Prince made of New Zealand butter. I recall the guard wouldn't let me touch it.

Of course, it wasn't just his warm manner and charming personality. Wherever he went, and by the end of the 1920s he had travelled to every corner of the British Empire as the King's stand-in and emissary, the Prince trailed an unmistakable aura of power and authority. Trains and planes were held; yachts materialized; the best suites in the finest hotels were flung open— all without the Prince's appearing to notice.

But what the Hearst readers and the butter sculptors never knew was, the Prince felt himself pathetically unworthy. In part, it was simply that he had never done anything to earn the wealth and adulation except be born into it. But there was something else. Goethe had agreed with

Madame de Sevigny: *"Es gibt für den Kammerdiener keinen Helden."* "No man is a hero to his valet." Or his nanny. Mrs. Green, the child's governess and mistress of the royal bath, was only the first of the women in his life to discover that the Prince's sexual equipment was far from princely. Suffice it to say that the adult Prince would spend much of his life trying to disprove an anatomical fact: that he was not fit for a king. Or, even fully erect, for a queen.

Barren, neurotic, and deserted by her husband, Mrs. Green used to pinch her little charge painfully or twist his arm in the nursery before his regular teatime visits to coldly formal King George and his German wife, the former Princess Mary of Teck. The boy's bawling would guarantee he was swiftly passed back to Nanny. And then, once more in the nursery, Nanny would quiet the child by assuring him that, however unlovable and ill equipped he was, she would always be the one woman who truly adored him.

Today, the headshrinkers call it aversion therapy. The Chinese Communists call it brainwashing. I prefer to just call it what it was: sadism. Mix love and pain the wrong way round early enough in life, and the man who emerges will spend his years seeking a cold, cruel mother's love in all the women he meets.

CHAPTER 7

Amy looked out the window of her hotel room at the lights of Dublin. It was beautiful at night. What was Fleming going on about, all this psychological mumbo jumbo? They said he had sex on the brain, but the Duke of Windsor's sex? She thought about cracking open the Widow Clicquot's champagne, but she knew she shouldn't. Not now.

The yawn surprised her. Okay, just a couple more chapters, and then maybe a closer look through the other papers. She'd be flying back to the States tomorrow morning, and there'd be plenty of time to read on the plane. She wanted to have it all finished by the time she saw Scott. Amy picked up the manuscript again.

PROVENANCE

The thing I always keep in mind about the Prince of Wales is that he was Queen

Victoria's great-grandson. That meant that
nearly all the royal families of Europe
were his aunts and uncles and cousins.
Kaiser Wilhelm II of Germany was benevolent
"Uncle Willi" to young David (as the Prince
was called when he was a boy) and to his
younger brothers and sister. On their
summer holidays at Bernsdorf Palace in
Germany, he'd let the children sit in the
cavalry saddle set on a block of wood that
the Kaiser used instead of a desk chair. He
claimed he always thought better on
horseback.

Another handy thing to keep in mind is
that Windsor is a made-up name. The Prince
was born Edward Albert Christian George
Andrew Patrick David, with all seven of
those Christian names (including Christian)
ending in Saxe-Coburg-Gotha. It was the
family name of Queen Victoria's German
husband, Albert. They changed it during the
war when being descended from Huns was no
longer a point of English pride. It
explains why the bilingual Prince often
said he was three-fourths German.

While we're at it, David's first cousin
once removed and godfather was Tsar

Nicholas II of Russia. (In the nursery hung a photograph of the Tsar, the Kaiser, and the King on a hunting trip together in 1903. The three men looked so much alike it was kind of a game for the children to pick Father out of the group.) So when the Great War pitted Englishmen against Germans against Russians, David watched the two sides of his heritage battling to the death while the third, Eastern branch of the family was swept away on a Red tide.

The Prince, just twenty when hostilities began, wasn't wanting for bravery. Though commissioned into the Grenadier Guards, he was prohibited from going to the front himself because his capture by the Germans would require a king's ransom—and possibly an armistice as well—to get him back. But he saw enough to make him all the more determined that "his" two countries would never go to war with each other again.

Two things happened in 1918 that make the events of later years easier to understand. In late summer word reached the Windsors of the execution of the Tsar and his family by the new Communist government. The murder of

his Russian cousins sealed his hatred of
Bolshevism, one he not surprisingly shared
with the rest of Europe's royals, and threw
him over for good to the other side of the
political spectrum. It also threw the
impotence of democratic institutions into
high relief. Years later he noted, "Just
before the Bolsheviks seized the Tsar, my
father had personally planned to rescue him
with a British cruiser, but in some way the
plan was blocked. 'Those politicians,' he
used to say. 'If it had been one of their
kind, they would have acted fast enough.
But just because the poor man was
Emperor . . .' "

The other thing was more personal. While
on leave back in London, David was invited
to a dinner party in Belgrave Square.
Introductions were still being made when
the air raid siren went off. Everyone made
their way down to the darkened cellar,
where they smoked and waited for the all
clear. One of the guests, Mrs. Freda Dudley
Ward, spent the time conversing with the
man standing next to her in the dark. It
wasn't till they were back upstairs that

she realised she had been chatted up by the Prince of Wales.

Within a month, the Prince would be writing her, "My angel!! I can't tell you how much I hated having to say good-bye this morning . . . and my last night in England too." His postscript read, "Please curse me if I have written a terribly stupid and indiscreet letter as I expect this is, darling; but I can't help it, sitting in my room all alone tonight thinking of you, and I'm not caring much or thinking of the consequences. Good night, my angel!!!"

In the next fifteen years, David would write Freda more than three thousand such letters. (I've had a chance to read several of the ones available to the public.) For her part, she made no demands. It was all the same whether he was telling her about his latest fling, *"mais les petits amusements ne content pas,"* or the latest joke. "My dearest, know why the biggest gun they have pounding Paris is called Rasputin? Because it comes every fifteen minutes!" Her presence was tolerated by the

authorities for one reason: whenever the
"dark, dark mist" of depression fell over
him—and it was often—and the Prince
threatened to drop his public mask of
Britain's Jazz Age golden youth, only
Freda's mothering and security made it all
better again.

CHAPTER 8

The Times

Friday, May 25, 1917.

VALENTINE FLEMING.

AN APPRECIATION

"W. S. C." writes of the death of Major Valentine Fleming, M.P., who, as announced in *The Times* on Wednesday, was killed in action:—

This news will cause sorrow in Oxfordshire and in the House of Commons and wherever the member of the Henley Division was well known. Valentine Fleming was one of those younger Conservatives who easily and naturally combine loyalty to party ties with a broad liberal outlook upon affairs and a total absence of class prejudice. He was most earnest and sincere in his desire to make things better for the great body of the people, and had cleared his mind of all particularist tendencies. He was a man of thoughtful and tolerant opinions, which were not the less strongly or clearly held because they were not loudly or ~~equally~~ asserted ~~the~~ violence of faction ~~and~~

PROVENANCE

And now we come to the part where I tell you how I know what I know. Part of it, much of it, is that I have friends in high places. Highest among them, my own godfather—trumpets, please—Winston S. Churchill.

When my father, Valentine Fleming, was killed in the Great War, the First Lord of the Admiralty, his comrade-in-arms and fellow Member of Parliament, was kind enough to write a remembrance (as W.S.C.) in the *Times*. After that, Winston took it upon himself to watch over me, with a usually baleful eye, during my formative years. I can honestly say that at no time did he intervene on my behalf, either with the many teachers I was to disappoint in my many schools or with my several employers as I struggled to "find myself," first as a journalist and later as a banker.

What he did do was to make use of me, and the one or two talents I possess, during what he called his wilderness years between the wars. It is only beginning to be acknowledged that Winston Churchill's personal network of friends and acquaintances was probably the world's third-most impressive intelligence service, after Britain's official one and, in the 1930s,

Germany's. Certainly it was better informed than what the Americans had.

And, as he did with the others who carried out his little "tasks," if he thought I needed to know something, he told me. For instance, when he learned I would be navigating a friend's entry in the Cross-Alpine Motor Rally of early 1933, he asked me to monitor German election broadcasts while we were in Switzerland. Winston wanted to know whose names were mentioned and whose words were quoted by the Nazis, especially any reference to Joachim von Ribbentrop or Rudolf Hess. He told me these two were Hitler's internationalists, and Ribbentrop in particular was cultivating friends in England in the Prince's circle.

The other way I know what I know is through my obsessive reading of the files in Rooms 39 and 40 of the Admiralty, where I was Assistant to the Director of Naval Intelligence during the war. I was not Assistant Director of Naval Intelligence. That was quite another, much more important job. But as Assistant to the Director, I was, among other things, Head Janitor of

the files. So I had access to everything
heard and done by both MI5 and MI6, as well
as our own service. (My godfather once
described our system as "tangle within
tangle, plot and counterplot, ruse and
treachery, cross and double cross.") On
paper, British Military Intelligence (MI)
consists of several departments. MI5—the
service that catches "their" spies—is
responsible to the Home Office. MI6—
officially called the Secret Intelligence
Service—are "our" spies and report to the
Foreign Office. In practice, they function
much as do your FBI and CIA.

We'll pass over the 1920s, most of which
the Prince spent either abroad—reviewing
the troops of whatever colonial outpost or
planting a ceremonial tree or observing the
centennial of some local historical event,
all worked around various safaris to India
and Africa—or at home, going from dinner
party to dinner party and doing everything
he could do to earn the title of Flaming
Youth Number One. As a young man I was
invited as an afterthought to one such
party where the Prince was guest of honour.
We spoke for less than a minute, and he

interrupted even that to remind the
servants to refill the glasses of certain
of the female guests. The encounter left me
with the clear picture that the Prince was
acquainted with the effects of alcohol and
opiates on the human body.

By the 1930s, the Prince of Wales, now
choosing to be publicly called Edward, was
a no-longer-young London society
institution whose head was turned one day
by an extraordinarily beautiful woman. Her
name was Thelma Morgan, the Viscountess
Furness, a fabled South American beauty
whose twin sister had married a Vanderbilt
and produced a daughter, Gloria, the Poor
Little Rich Girl. Thelma—beautiful, exotic,
cosmopolitan, desirable—had first married
the man who ran Bell Telephone. Then she
divorced him and took a second, richer,
titled husband, who spent all his time
playing polo. Supplanting Freda in the
princely affections (and bedroom), Thelma
served the tea and doled out the crumpets
when the Prince entertained at his snuggery
in Fort Belvedere, on the edge of Windsor
Great Park. Her only mistake was
introducing the Prince to Wallis Simpson.

The words on the manuscript page swam up to meet her, and then swam away again. Amy stifled a yawn. Who could she call? She was bursting to tell the Girls about Fleming and the King and . . .

She reached over to grab her purse and flipped open the day planner to her sketch of the Girls, as they had dubbed themselves. Four career women with their arms around each other, lovingly drawn from a snapshot taken at their fifteenth college reunion. Susan, the one with the perm and the balding husband, on the left. Blanche, the brilliant one with the two ex-husbands, on the right. Amy next to her, and Katie making four, still in her short, spiky hair from college and now an "aboriginal archeologist," whatever that was.

Amy couldn't call Katie; wasn't it 5 a.m. tomorrow in Australia? Blanche, who "didn't believe in cell phones," was away at a conference. And Susan would still be busy at work. And then came another yawn, this one too big to stifle. Amy put down the manuscript and turned off the light. The jet lag had won. She'd pack in the morning.

CHAPTER 9

In the morning, Amy decided to carry her own bags and save on the tip. She had her rolling American Tourister overnighter in one hand and her IBM ThinkPad in its soft black carrying case (along with its precious cargo of Fleming's pages) in the other. Her handbag hung from her shoulder. Now, if she could just reach the elevator button . . .

While she waited at reception for her receipt to be printed, a young, already balding man a few feet down the counter turned to her with his bill. "*Sprechen Sie Deutsche,* Fräulein . . . ?" he asked.

"Greenberg. *Ja,* a little, Herr . . . ?"

"Kaltenbrunner."

Amy's sketchy history-of-art German led her to gather that Mr. Kaltenbrunner was unfamiliar with the concept of hotels gouging their guests on long-distance calls. Enlightened if not mollified by her explanation, he zipped open a pocket of the blue rucksack at his feet and stuffed the offending bill inside. "You have been so helpful. Perhaps, if you are going to the Dublin Airport, I might be permitted to share with you my taxi?" Herr Kaltenbrunner smiled and reached out his hand toward Amy's black nylon case. "I could perhaps carry your computer? It must be heavy."

It was an odd smile. The man's lips parted to show his teeth on only one side of his mouth. Amy said, "Thank you, but I'm not going directly to the airport. I have to make a stop first."

Kaltenbrunner seemed unsure what to do with his extended right arm now that Amy wasn't letting him carry her computer case. Finally he dropped it to his side, only to offer it again in the form of a handshake. "Well then, Fräulein . . . Miss Greenberg, I mean—possibly we will meet again."

Amy shook his hand. It was surprisingly calloused. "I hope so," she said, not totally meaning it.

Slightly over an hour later Amy was at Dublin International Airport, standing in front of an electronic board indicating DL 106 to New York was delayed one hour. The stopover at Shields's bookstore had gone well enough, a preliminary meet and greet with a man who might have something extremely valuable to sell, something he was *not* making available for public inspection at the moment. To build up the suspense, Amy supposed. She wouldn't have much to tell them about the visit back at Yale.

Lacking the wherewithal to make any real impact in the duty-free shops, Amy resigned herself to waiting in the boarding area, where the only seats to be had were in the glassed-in smoking section. What was the point of being a vegetarian and avoiding meat if you were going to die from secondhand smoke?

She stepped up to the kiosk, where the Delta agent looked at her ticket and, after punching a few computer keys, tore it up. Aghast, Amy stammered, "Don't!"

Liam Carmody, according to his plastic clip-on airport ID, looked up from his keyboard. "I'm sorry, miss. I thought you knew. You've been upgraded to business."

"Upgraded? I don't have any miles. Or at least not enough."

Mr. Carmody hit a few more keys before saying, "Dr. Amy Greenberg of America, yes? A Mrs. O'Beirne at your bank confirmed the change this morning. Aisle or window?"

In ten minutes, Amy was sitting in the business lounge of Delta's Crown Room, away from the smokers. She was pleased but far from content. First the champagne and now the ticket. Who was she to the Ansbacher Bank that they should care so much about her? She hadn't even been the holder of the

account, and they'd certainly never see her again. In a
few weeks, they'd probably be out of business themselves.

Still, if you had to wait out a delay, there were
worse places. Amy scanned the headlines of the com-
plimentary *USA Today* on the coffee table in front of
her before turning her thoughts to the need for
bridesmaids' dresses. Which inevitably led to the
need for bridesmaids. Katie was halfway around the
world. Would she be able to come back for a June
wedding? Susan and Blanche she could count on. As
a hoot, Amy tried to imagine the look on their faces
when she told the Girls they'd have to wear matching
bridesmaids' dresses. Make that the mutinous look
on their faces. She'd string them along for a while,
describe some burgundy—no, lavender—outfit with
capped sleeves and squared-off neckline. Really make
them sweat.

Amy started to take out her day planner to make a
sketch of those shocked faces when she thought better of it and, instead, popped the little brass lock on
her black computer case and pulled out her now
slightly dog-eared copy of *Provenance*.

CHAPTER 10

MAYFIELD WILLIAMS, M.D.

31 BELVEDERE

BALTIMORE, MARYLAND

October 6, 1911

Dear Mrs. Merryman,

At your request, I undertook an internal
examination of Miss Bessie Wallis Warfield
in my offices on September 29th last. I
herewith set forth my findings, although I
continue to believe it highly improper to
describe the female anatomy in such detail
to any but another physician.

Your niece presented with a failure to
menstruate. While this is not unknown in
girls of 16 years of age, I do not believe
that, given more time, menses will occur.
I am sorry to have to report that Miss
Warfield lacks the requisite anatomical
aspects for female menstruation and reproduction. She has no uterus or fallopian

tubes, a condition described in the medical literature as occurring in one out of
20,000 female births.

Your niece has the external genitals of
a woman, although her vagina extends only
one-third of the length that is normal in
women, ending abruptly in a membrane
rather than a cervix. And, as she will not
ovulate, it follows that she will be
unable to bear children.

I concur in the opinion of Miss
Warfield's own physician, Dr. Neale. And,
if you will permit me, I also agree with
his opinion that it is not well advised to
share any of this information with the
patient. I strongly urge you to reconsider.

Yours respectfully,

Mayfield Williams, M.D.

Mayfield Williams, M.D.

PROVENANCE

A thin membrane separated Wallis Warfield
from the other professional Southern belles
of good name and scant assets whose one
purpose in life was to be married off to

money. Even so, Wallis married for money.
Twice. Once to Ernest Simpson, a middle-
aged Anglo-American businessman who settled
her into the middle tier of London society
in the late 1920s. And later, to the
Prince.

But her first marriage was for love, to
one Earl Winfield Spencer, a dashing airman
training other reckless young men to pilot
the "flying egg crates" that took off with
regularity from Pensacola Naval Air Station
in the years before the War. The Wright
Brothers, having recently invented the
thing, were still ironing out the kinks in
airplane design. But that didn't stop the
Daring Young Men who took to the skies. And
afterwards, at balls and cotillions
throughout the South, they took to the
ladies.

From just looking at her picture, one
might imagine that Wallis would have stood
little chance in such a competition. And
one would be wrong. Though she was anything
but feminine—tall, with a flat chest, slim
hips, and (something you couldn't tell from
the picture) a voice like a rusty gate—
Wallis Warfield knew what men were

interested in. Themselves. Whether it was
the captain of the football team at the
boys' school across town, or the pick of
Baltimore's litter of young men from the
right side of the tracks, Wallis boned up on
them. She would ask her friends, and then
his friends: What song did he favour? What
drink? What play? What scent did he notice?
And then, when she had cornered her prey at
a dance or party, she'd spend the evening
requesting that song, drinking that drink,
and exuding that scent. She'd be totally
taken with the man's wit, or muscles, or
shoe size, whatever was required.

At her 1913 debut held at Baltimore's
Lyric Theatre, her presence was financed by
her guardian, Aunt Bessie, and Bessie's
brother Sol. (Bessie was the paid companion
to a newspaper heiress and Sol just
happened to own a string of railroads.)
Between dances Wallis rested in a theatre
box-cum-bower, decorated during the whole
of the previous night with hundreds of
orchids, roses, lilies, gladioli, and her
favourite white chrysanthemums, more
flowers than are draped over the winning
horse at the Preakness.

And then there was the dress. While all the other girls wore the sort of dresses young girls were expected to wear, Wallis invested the enormous sum of twenty dollars in an exact copy of the white satin Worth gown made in Paris for the society dancer Irene Castle. Though its cinched bodice and modified hobble skirt would prove to be most uncomfortable, Wallis insisted on standing for hours while it was fitted to her wiry frame. And she spent hours more improving her waltzing and learning the new, sensational tango. And then, plain as she was, she was danced off her feet the entire evening. Years later, she would swear she had never allowed one of her beaux "below her Mason-Dixon line." She didn't have to. Good old American ingenuity had made her the twentieth-century Jezebel who turned every head and caught every male eye.

Her love for Winfield Spencer and her marriage proved to be a disaster. Too valuable an instructor to fly in the Great War, he remained stateside, posted to the new naval air station in San Diego. Spencer had hours and sometimes days to kill between training sessions, and an unlimited supply of Officers Club alcohol to kill them with. With the liquor came dinners missed and women met. By the end of the War, Wallis discovered her husband had, if not a girl in every port, a dozen in the same town in which she was living.

The years immediately after the Armistice found the Spencers cooped up together in government housing in Washington, D.C. Wallis took back up with her friends from Baltimore, leaving Win to his bottles. With every bottle came a battle. Before long, Spencer was bringing his bellicose attitude to work, arguing with his commanding officers for promotion and higher pay, alienating one Navy superior after another.

Ironically, it was her husband's insubordination, and not her own upward mobility, that set Wallis upon the road to the throne. Initially, though, it set her upon the deck of the USS *Pampanga* in the South China Seas in the late summer of 1924, a year before her thirtieth birthday.

How she got there we'll come to shortly. But picture, if you will, the arriviste belle from Baltimore climbing aboard the

rusting ex-Spanish Navy relic with great
holes in the hull, put there by the guns of
one or the other of the warring Chinese
factions. Described in a later newspaper
account as "the least shipshape ship in the
American Navy," the *Pampanga* was the only
vessel small enough to slip through the
narrow marshes and estuaries of the Canton
Delta. It had a bucket of water on a string
for a shower, no proper toilet, and no
ventilation at all. It was no place for a
lady. Even if she was America's newest spy.

CHAPTER 11

SECRET ISSUED BY THE INTELLIGENCE DIVISION
OFFICE OF CHIEF OF NAVAL OPERATIONS
NAVY DEPARTMENT

S-E-C-R-E-T

Serial R-5-3-24   Date _16 November_ 19 24

From _Chief, U.S. Naval Intelligence/Pacific at Honolulu, Hawaiian Territory_

To _Captain J. H. Barnard, U.S. Naval Attache, Pekin, China_

Subject _Mrs. Winfield Spencer_

Jack,

Please extend all customary hospitality to the bearer of this note and
accompanying orders. Mrs. Spencer is the wife of Cmdr. Winfield Spencer,
and has been thoroughly vetted. I would appreciate your billeting her
for the duration of her stay, which I estimate at ten days. You and
Gauss may entrust your monthly reports to her for delivery back to me.
Please regard her as you would one of our own people.

Henry

SECRET   Prepared for: _Henry R. Hough_

HENRY R. HOUGH,
Rear Admiral, U.S. Navy, PacFleet

PROVENANCE

The day, more than a year earlier, when
Winfield Spencer's CO had finally had
enough of his drinking and complaining and

signed the orders banishing him to a patrol
boat in the Pacific was the day Wallis
Spencer was liberated. Living in Washington
on a husband's pay without the husband,
Wallis set out to ingratiate herself in the
burgeoning diplomatic world of the post-WWI
capital.

With the German she'd been taught in
school and a smattering of French, she
gained entrée to the embassies and
consulates of Massachusetts Avenue.
Naturally, Wallis would settle for nothing
less than an ambassador. Conveniently, the
forty-five-year-old Prince Gelasio Caetani,
representing Mussolini's new government,
returned her interest. Caetani, who had
marched on Rome with Il Duce in 1922, was
only too eager to believe that every
Fascist word was music to Wallis's ears.
Next came the First Secretary of the
Argentine Embassy, Felipe Espil. Rich,
smooth, a classic Latin lover who danced
the best tango in town, Espil was
everything any woman could want. So what
did he want with Wallis?

As it happened, Wallis had already
learned that her anatomical shortcomings

gave her a double-barrelled advantage in the battle of the sexes: every man felt his endowment had magically tripled when he slept with Wallis. Added to her enormous gifts of flattery and seduction, and her willingness to forgo her own pleasure for the sake of the man's, Wallis Simpson's membrane had them lined up for miles along Embassy Row. Her second advantage was at least as powerful as her first. Knowing she could never become pregnant freed her to pursue her affairs with the independence and creativity of a modern midcentury woman. It left her peers, those post-Victorian "flappers," flapping in the breeze.

Soon, the "Wallis Grip" became the qui vive among the men of a certain set, whispered about in the clubs and described in the locker rooms. Word of it, though in garbled form, even reached President Harding, who asked the pro at Burning Tree Golf Club if he would show him the Wallis Grip. The man broke down in hysterics, leaving the President to hole out on his own.

It came to the attention of the Navy

Department, and more particularly, the
Department of Naval Intelligence, that the
wife of a cantankerous, low-grade officer
had ingratiated herself in the upper
echelons of diplomatic society. As it
happened, they had a very real need for
presentable Navy wives . . . in China. The
Civil War there between Sun Yat-sen and the
regime occupying Peking was boiling over
into indiscriminate slaughter in the
streets, Westerners included. Funded by
Russian ex-revolutionaries and Japanese
militarists, the war threatened not only
life and limb but also the Chinese holdings
of Standard Oil, which the American
government had secretly pledged to protect.

Telegraph lines were cut on a daily basis
by one side or the other. And the only
broadcast tower in the country powerful
enough to reach American bases in the
Pacific was in enemy hands. So the Navy had
to depend on trusted couriers to get
information into and out of the country.
And who was more trusted, with better
cover, than the Navy wives making conjugal
visits to their husbands away at sea?

When she was first approached about going

to China, Wallis demurred. Things were going swimmingly with a high-ranking Rumanian at the time. So a little pressure was brought to bear. The Navy merely started sending Win Spencer's checks directly to him instead of his wife. With the money tree suddenly bare, and at the urging of her Aunt Bessie, Wallis had a change of mind.

A four-month course in the basics of spycraft—in which Wallis learned how to encode messages and use lemon juice as invisible ink, and how to leave messages in "drops" for other agents to collect later—and she was on her way. Ostensibly Wallis would rejoin her beloved husband, but in actuality she was to rendezvous with Lt. Col. Jack Barnard at the American Legation in the Forbidden City.

CHAPTER 12

M iss Greenberg?"

Amy looked up with a start. Was her flight boarding? She put the manuscript in her computer case. She'd lost track of the time.

The man who had spoken was blocking her view of the monitor. "You have a few minutes, Miss Greenberg." He indicated the seat next to hers. "May I?"

She nodded. The man, very English and nicelooking in a dark suit, was balancing a cup of tea with lemon on a folded copy of the *Financial Times*. He managed to place the cup and saucer on the broad arm of the chair, put the paper down on the coffee table, and sit, all in one motion. He'd done this before.

Amy could now see the monitor had DL 106 to New York leaving in thirty minutes but not yet boarding. She turned back to the man and saw that he had extracted a business card from a silver case and was holding it out to her. It read "Brian Devlin,

Publisher" above the company name, "Glidrose." At the bottom was a London address and several phone numbers.

She took the card.

"As luck would have it, Miss Greenberg—or is it Mrs.?" He paused, smiling.

Hmm. Not your usual pickup line. Did engaged count? "Miss."

"Well, *Miss* Greenberg, as luck would have it, my business takes me to New York this morning, and I couldn't help noticing we're on the same flight."

How had he noticed that? And then she followed his eyes to the boarding pass that peeked out from the side flap of her handbag.

It was a little early in the morning for an illicit romance. She smiled back. "Well, Mr. . . ."

"Devlin."

"Well, Mr. Devlin, as coincidences go, it's pretty meager. This *is* the Delta lounge."

His smile broadened slightly. "But I don't have business to discuss with them. Only with you."

"With me? I don't—I'm a college professor. Educational business?"

Mr. Devlin took a moment to return his card case to his jacket pocket and take a sip of his tea before saying, "Publishing business."

Amy's brain struggled to play catch-up. "If you

mean my thesis, I'm published by the Yale Press. You could speak to them about European rights or . . ."

From the look on his face, Mr. Devlin *didn't* mean her thesis. He was straightening the old-fashioned points of the white handkerchief in his breast pocket. "Actually, I'm referring to the manuscript you were just reading."

An impulse, something, made her touch the lock on the black case at her feet.

Devlin turned his body to face her full on. "It's a reflex, really. If someone is engrossed in a stack of pages, I'm interested." Were his teeth capped? They were way too even. All these European men and their strange mouths. Was she developing an oral fixation? Devlin leaned in closer. "*Entre nous*, I've never heard of an Ian Fleming book called *Provenance*."

Amy's radar went up. How did he know what she was reading? She studied his features. He was hardly bookish. About forty, tall, with combed-back dark hair and deeply tanned skin, Mr. Brian Devlin appeared more the very model of a modern global Eurocrat flying back from three weeks in the sun.

She stalled with "What is Glidrose?"

"We're a closely held, um, marketing firm of a sort. Set up to exploit the, uh, possibilities of a select group of novels, screenplays, and films. And, naturally, *defend* those interests."

Where was this conversation going? "You said defend?"

"Ensure the copyrights are adhered to, that all rights fees are remitted, that sort of thing. We can't have some street person marketing *Da Vinci Code* backpacks or 007 perfume, can we?"

Amy tried a girlish laugh. "I thought they did that all the time."

"About your choice of reading material . . . would you be interested in knowing that an original Ian Fleming manuscript, if that's what you have, could with our help fetch in the five or possibly six figures?"

For no earthly reason, Amy decided to derail the conversation. She remembered the title page had for some reason said "I. Fleming." "Oh. You think the manuscript I was reading is by *Ian* Fleming."

Devlin did a kind of mini double take. "Is there another I. Fleming?"

"Ira Fleming. He's a . . . graduate student. Of mine. At Yale." The way Devlin was staring at her, she thought, the word *liar* must be flashing on her forehead. What kind of stupid name was Ira Fleming? "*Provenance* is the working title of his dissertation proving the, uh, presence of the unapprehended deity in German Renaissance painting."

Devlin took out a cigarette and then, as if noticing what he'd done, he put it away. "Really?" was all he said.

Amy regretted her lie. After all, fate had put her in this seat in this airport to be noticed by this man, who just might be able to help her evaluate her inheritance. But alarms had gone off in her brain. There was something about him. What?

Devlin took a sip of what must be very tepid tea. "An art history thesis on, what did you say, the 'unapprehended'? How stupid of me." Something caught his attention. He reached into his jacket and withdrew a cell phone. Amy thought it was turned off, but she must have been wrong because Devlin spoke into it. "Yes?"

He listened to the phone for a moment and then turned back to Amy. "I'm sorry. Change of plans." He listened some more and then closed his phone. "Miss Greenberg, I'm afraid you'll be flying to New York without me." And then, "You're boarding."

Amy looked at the monitor. She was. Mr. Devlin stood and held out his hand. "So nice to have met you." And then he was off.

In a minute, Amy gathered her things and headed out of the lounge for her plane, surprised at the pang the man's sudden departure had caused in an "affianced" woman. What was it with her and Englishmen?

CHAPTER 13

9 O'CLOCK.
DON'T BE LATE.

HONG KONG HARBOUR

PROVENANCE

First, let me give you the "authorised"
version of Wallis's trip to Peking in late
November of 1924. The railroad tracks had
been so badly torn up by warring forces,
the Blue Express couldn't make the journey
from Shanghai. Wallis had to take a
freighter, the SS *Shuntien*, via Weiheiwei

and Chefoo to Tientsin, where she changed
for a train to complete her journey. The
ship was constantly pitching and rolling,
the heat was stifling, and the passengers
all became seasick. And that was the easy
part.

Waiting for her connection at the
Tientsin depot, a ramshackle collection
point for typhoid victims, starving
families, and deserting Chinese soldiers,
Wallis found she was the only American
civilian, and the only woman of any
nationality, making the trip. The eight-car
train, its windows shot out long before,
slowly rolled in. It had been commandeered
by the U.S. Army, but the tracks, lined on
either side by 25,000 of his troops,
belonged to Chang Tso-lin, one of the
warlords besieging the capital. At Pei-
Tsang and every whistle-stop thereafter,
the Chinese boarded the train and paraded
up and down the aisles, trying to provoke
the Americans into a fight.

The American soldiers were no better.
Drunk and disorderly, they fought over
whose turn it was to "protect" the lone
female passenger. The winds of northern

China blew through the unheated cars. The
toilets were holes in the floor. A journey
that should have taken ninety minutes
lasted thirty-eight hours.

Her unwashed protectors were such that
Wallis took to dousing her handkerchief
with perfume and holding it over her nose.
It must have been a relief to see Commander
Louis M. Little of the Marines and his grey
armoured Navy car waiting for her at the
station.

The relief didn't last long. Passing
through the Hatamen Gate on their way to
the fortified Legation Quarter, they drove
beside a line of human heads stuck on
thirty-foot bamboo poles, a none-too-subtle
statement made by Chang's enemy, the
notorious General Feng Yü-hsiang, who held
the city.

Okay, now for the unauthorised story, my
own blend of information from the files of
British Intelligence and the lips of
Winston Churchill. It's much more fun.
Wallis had left Washington in July and
sailed through the Panama Canal to Pearl
Harbor and thence to Manila, arriving for
her reunion with Win on the *Pampanga* in

early September. She's next seen in Peking
the second week of December. What happened
during those missing ninety days? Well,
some of the time Wallis spent on the move.
And some of it she spent on her back.

Her reconciliation with her husband was a
put-up job, a convenient cover story
choreographed by Naval Intelligence.
Ostensibly, Win agreed to once again turn
over to her his Navy pay, in return for
Wallis's playing the role of Navy wife. But
there was a secret codicil to their pact,
one bought and paid for with money from the
government's "black funds." For $10,000,
Win would agree to provide her with two
things: an eventual divorce and, to help
the new spy get started with a bang, an
introduction into the "singing houses" of
Hong Kong.

The singing houses, sometimes called
"singsong" by Navy officers, were luxurious
brothels. Women from the poorest sections
of inland China, chosen for their looks,
were trained from their teens in the arts
of love. The client was entertained with
stringed instruments, delicately erotic
songs, and dances of sinuous beauty. I have

no idea whether Wallis could dance or play
the lute, but I gather her clients left
singing her praises.

The most refined of the Hong Kong
brothels were the "purple mansions." In the
late 1940s I was fortunate enough to have
been a guest in the only purple mansion
that had survived the Japanese occupation,
the one that featured foreign women. A male
slave in a blue cotton robe greeted me,
smiled deeply, and ushered me into a large
square room with green and white draperies
covering the walls. There was no place to
sit down. The elderly Chinese madame who
ran the establishment inquired as to my
racial preference in women. "You choose," I
said.

There were cabinets fashioned of
expensive mahogany, with shelves displaying
valuable china ornaments. It had earlier
been made clear to me that the gentleman
was expected to compliment his hostess on
her collection of knickknacks as he waited
for his "companion" to join him. I did so,
cooing absurdly over each piece in pidgin
Chinese until my escort joined us. Brenda
(imagine!) turned out to be an Indo-Chinese

beauty. We spoke in French as we made our way upstairs past elegantly furnished cubicles. Each had a name, such as "Field of Glittering Flowers" or "Club of the Ducks of the Mandarin." Ours was "Bamboo Meadow."

In Wallis's day there were also the flower boats called *hoa thing*, sixty- to eighty-foot-long barges floating in the harbour. The interior floors were lavishly carpeted and crystal lamps hung from the ceilings. It was customary for the client to hire the entire boat for the evening. His party would begin with a multicourse dinner at 9 p.m. Afterwards, each guest would lead his dinner companion across a small wooden platform to one of the boats tethered by ropes to the mother vessel.

Wallis's "China dossier," as MI6's file became known, was ordered destroyed after the war. I should know. I destroyed it. But I made a few more mental notes: that Wallis Spencer spent ten weeks in these houses is beyond dispute. That she did so with the knowledge, and under the orders, of American Naval Intelligence will, of course, be hotly disputed by the Americans. But in any case, by the time she reached Peking, Wallis was a cum laude graduate in the seductive arts, specifically in the very particular skills of *fang chung*.

Practised for centuries, *fang chung* works by relaxing the man through prolonged and carefully orchestrated massage of the nipples, stomach, thighs, and, after an exquisitely protracted delay, the genitals. The practitioner is taught to target the nerve centres of the body, so that the lightest movement of the fingers has the effect of arousing even the most moribund of men. *Fang chung* is especially helpful in building the confidence of men of, let us say, diminutive stature, as well as those given to premature ejaculation. By the application of a firm, specific touch between the urethra and the anus, climax may be delayed, removing the fear of failure in intercourse that underlies male dysfunction. While I've never required such a service, it sounds like an awful lot of fun.

By November, Wallis was ready for her assignment. But first, Win Spencer had a surprise for her. On the eve of her trip to Shanghai and Peking, he confessed he had fallen in love during their long separation. In the future, any correspondence between them should be sent in care of Robert Leslie, a young painter of some note (and famously little body hair), who lived in Kowloon and was the talk of the Colony. In shock, Wallis bade him good-bye in the morning, never to see him again before his death from alcohol poisoning in 1950.

CHAPTER 14

Vous êtes invités
à un thé dansant
au Grand Hôtel de Pékin
à dix-sept heures,
le 19 décembre 1924

Wallis, avec mes compliments...
de Zara

PROVENANCE

Jack Barnard, the American military
attaché, briefed Wallis on her initial
intelligence target in Peking, a prominent
member of the diplomatic community. (I
mentioned earlier that we had a dossier on
Wallis. Actually, British Intelligence were
compiling dossiers on every prominent

foreigner in China, Barnard among them. I'm
rather disgusted to say that our people
went through the legation's garbage.)

At any rate, we discovered that Wallis
used the entrée she had acquired in
Washington to make the rounds of Peking's
foreign colony—the teas in the afternoon,
the dinners at night, the Sundays at the
dog track—as opposing forces fought in the
sprawling native quarters not three miles
away. She finally met her subject, not at a
private function but at a public ceremony.
Every afternoon at four, the foreigners
shared a communal moment with the ordinary
citizens of Peking when a thousand pigeons
were released from wicker baskets into the
ice-blue late autumn sky. Tiny bamboo
flutes tucked under the birds' wings
created an eerie, plaintive sound and
provided the conversational opening for
Wallis to engage her prey: the blond,
suavely handsome naval attaché to the
Italian Embassy, Alberto de Zara.

Descended from a long line of cavalry
officers, de Zara as a youth had been sent
abroad every summer, where he developed
numerous international contacts. In 1907,

he achieved a boyhood dream when he was
accepted into America's Naval Academy at
Annapolis, Maryland, where he became the
classmate and good friend of—wait for it—
Earl Winfield Spencer.

In his memoirs, de Zara later wrote, "The
role of naval and aviation attaché in a
country such as China, without a navy or
aviation, did not appeal to me." His
passion, somewhat misplaced in a naval
officer, was for horses. So Wallis did what
she had always done. Feigning her own
passion for horses, she got him to take her
to the Peking Horse Show, where she oohed
and aahed over the animals, their riders
(especially the Italians), and de Zara
himself.

What could the thirty-five-year-old
Italian do for the Americans? He was the
one man with the position and the
persuasive powers to marshal support among
the anti-Bolshevik military advisers in
China—which was all of them except the
Russians—for the defence of Standard Oil's
vulnerable supply line. Which he eventually
did.

During her assault on de Zara, Wallis was

"billeted" in the home at 4 Shih Chia
Huting of Mr. and Mrs. Herman Rogers. A
tall, handsome, athletic intelligence
officer at the embassy, Rogers could have
been the model for the Cary Grant character
in *Notorious*. In everything but looks,
Wallis Spencer might have been the woman
played by Ingrid Bergman.

Rogers had grown up in the privileged
world of Crumwold Hall, two estates down
from FDR's in Hyde Park, New York. He and
his wife, Katherine, had the means and,
through friendship, the desire to help
Wallis in every way possible, as they would
continue to do a dozen years later at the
Villa Lou Viei. On weekends they drove her
up to their rented Buddhist temple in the
hills that doubled as a lookout post on
General Feng's army. Wallis joined them for
horseback riding, poker, and the inevitable
Mah-Jongg. (I'm told that she had already
developed her petulant habit of breaking
things when fortune did not go her way: our
service found a receipt describing three
jade replacement pieces for the Rogers'
delicately carved Mah-Jongg set.)

On the twenty-ninth of December, Wallis

left the make-believe world of the Imperial
Yellow City and the Forbidden Violet City,
with their sea palaces built on icy lakes,
spanned by marble bridges and dotted with
frosted lotus leaves. She carried with her
a letter from de Zara introducing her to
another handsome, and much younger,
Fascist. The dark, moody Count Galeazzo
Ciano would later marry Mussolini's
favorite daughter, Edda, and become Italy's
Foreign Minister. For the present he was
the Americans' second target in China
because of who his father was: the Admiral
of the entire Italian fleet and a member of
Italy's ruling clique.

The elder Ciano had also marched on Rome
in 1922 and was one of the plotters in the
murder of Giacomo Matteotti, the Socialist
leader of the opposition to Mussolini.
Together, father and son would be able to
do much to impede or impel America's march
toward world naval supremacy.

Wallis made short work of the twenty-one-
year-old Ciano. She went up the coast to
Qinhuangdao, the summer resort where the
Great Wall of China meets the sea. The
young Count Ciano came down from Peking to

spend much time with her there. A woman
whose husband was one of Win's fellow
officers on the *Pampanga* was none too kind.
"It was the gossip among us Navy wives back
in Hong Kong. It was an open scandal."

For Wallis, almost thirty, seducing the
callow Ciano must have seemed like child's
play. But for him, Wallis Spencer was his
first great passion, the passion one never
gets over. Like Espil, de Zara, and
countless others before him and after,
Ciano would be left in her wake as she
climbed the ladder of social position.

Amy did her two-fingered eye rub and looked to her
left, out of the plane. Clouds and ocean. The same
clouds and ocean a transatlantic traveler would have
seen a century ago. Only the traveler then would
have been sandwiched between white and blue, not
flying high above them at thirty-something thousand
feet.

As she sketched a few misshapen clouds to keep
her hands busy, she tried to understand Fleming's lin-
gering interest in Wallis Simpson. His letter had
promised to reveal something about "pure, unalloyed
evil." The Duchess of boring old Windsor? It didn't
add up. Of course, the woman's *love* life was any-

thing but boring. Dashing Count This, suave Ambassador That throwing themselves at her feet. Amy thought she could handle it if handsome foreigners threw themselves at her and . . . Hold it. Hadn't Scott-the-adorable-Englishman just done precisely that? With a ring?

She looked straight in front of her at the flight monitor two rows away on the bulkhead. Atmospheric temperature: −2° F. Distance to go: 2,940 miles.

She'd never read a James Bond book. She'd seen the movies, of course. They played all the time on TV. She wondered what Fleming's fiction was like, how it played out on the page without Connery and Roger Moore and—who was the current one?—doing the heavy lifting, conning the con men and killing the killers.

Con men. Her thoughts shifted to Shields, the bookseller, and his "find." The man had seemed genuine. But con artists always seem genuine, don't they? And there were a lot of them in this game, because it was so easy to pull off. All you had to do was identify a museum or library with an illuminated manuscript that was missing its explicit. Concoct some "old ink" by scraping it off worthless documents and reconstituting it with linseed oil. A couple of pages of calligraphy on aged calfskin calculated to match that of the chosen manuscript, and bingo! Big bucks.

Amy knew Yale had been burned a couple of times before, in the sixties and seventies. But what if this one was real? Imagine. The actual explicit signed and dated by the men who had created the *Book of Kells*! If Amy could authenticate it and Yale could buy it . . . She could envision her next book: *The Men Behind the* Book of Kells. A tenure-grabber, if ever there was one. Then she and Scott would be on an equal footing.

Whoa! Was that what this was about—pulling even with Scott? Competing with Scott? She wondered, was Scott competing with her? She tried to imagine herself in his place and guessed he didn't give her career a moment's thought. Was that good? Or bad? Susan would know. Her husband was a lawyer at a big New York firm. She'd have to ask Su about competing with your man when she got back. Just then Amy realized that she'd been holding her breath, and she let it out. Men didn't trouble themselves with all this stuff, did they?

Irritated with herself, Amy turned back to the manuscript on the tray table in front of her, reangling the little gooseneck lamp built into the headrest for maximum light. She had to admit it was awfully nice up here instead of in the back of the plane. Some of the people sitting around her had lowered their window shades, anticipating the in-flight movie. Others were reading newspapers from the cart that had come through: the *Wall Street Journal*, the *Economist*, the *Financial Times*. When they said seat 2A was in the business section, they meant it.

2B, next to her in the aisle seat, was a beefy man with a bull neck and an old-fashioned crew cut. Football player? Ex-football player? Scott's only sporting interest was something he called rugger, and Amy had better things to do on Sunday than watch the NFL, so he could be the most famous football player in the world and she'd never know—except for OJ. She'd recognize OJ.

"Looks interesting. Work?" The bull neck had a voice. And a smile.

Amy was not one for plane chat. "Kind of."

The man indicated the *Wall Street Journal* he was holding in his huge hands. "Me too."

A person with any social skills was now supposed to say, "What kind of work do you do?" But all Amy could manage was, "I see," and turned back to her reading.

CHAPTER 15

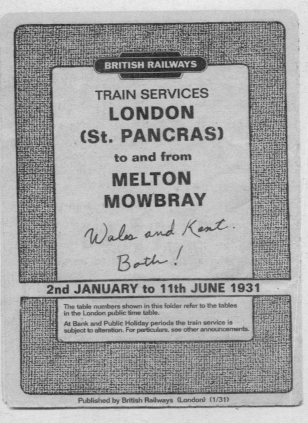

BRITISH RAILWAYS

TRAIN SERVICES
LONDON
(St. PANCRAS)
to and from
MELTON
MOWBRAY

Wales and Kent.
Both!

2nd JANUARY to 11th JUNE 1931

The table numbers shown in this folder refer to the tables in the London public time table.

At Bank and Public Holiday periods the train service is subject to alteration. For particulars, see other announcements.

Published by British Railways (London) (1/31)

PROVENANCE

It was the middle of January 1931, and by seven o'clock it was already night at the Furness country house in Melton Mowbray, in the heart of Leicestershire's foxhunting country. By now, the Prince had thrown over Freda Dudley Ward and installed dark, gorgeous Thelma Furness in her place as "the Princess of Wales." When Thelma strolled through the salon door with her houseguests, the Prince of Wales and his brother, the Duke of Kent, it was the first time another weekend guest, Wallis Simpson, had seen the Prince in the flesh. Here he was, not as the golden personage of the newsreels and magazines but as the somewhat sad-faced thirty-seven-year-old man of real life who was actually saying "Good evening" to her and shaking her hand. She curtsied, looking hard at him with a burning curiosity.

Much later, Wallis would tell me all about it. She had liked the Prince at once. The man who had seemed so unapproachable in photographs, all yellow hair and dazzling smile, had, up close, world-weary blue eyes and an old man's pouches under them. His face was lined from too much sun and too little sleep. Wallis thought she detected a secret pain behind the mask.

Three years earlier, Wallis had got her divorce from Win and had taken up with Ernest Simpson. A friend of mine, Harold Nicholson, had called him a "good-looking barber's block." Married in New York in 1928, they were happy at first. When the Crash came, Ernest was called to London to take the reins of his father's faltering shipbuilding company. Hard times were coming on, but that didn't stop the lovebirds from leasing a flat in Bryanston Court in George Street, on the Savile Row side of Regent Street. The lease came with a cook, maid, butler, chauffeur, and Maud Kerr-Smiley, Ernest's sister, who immediately installed herself as the couple's chaperone and tour guide to London society. And who should turn out to be Maud Kerr-Smiley's best friend in all the world? Thelma Furness.

But right now, this evening, the contrast between her tongue-tied husband and the sparkling conversation of the golden Prince

led Wallis to consider trading in her
current man for a newer, flashier model.
Dinner was served at nine, and Wallis and
Ernest were seated a long way down the
dining table from their hostess, Thelma,
and the royals. Too far for her to engage
the Prince in any of that witty
conversation.

Late the next morning, Wallis walked
downstairs to find the Prince of Wales
chatting with his aide, Brigadier-General
Gerald F. Trotter, known as "G." G. Trotter
had lost his right arm in the Boer War and
had his uniform sleeve pinned to the front
of his tunic. The luncheon table had been
set without place cards, and Wallis,
boldly, sat herself next to the Prince.

For something to say, he observed, "You
must miss central heating, Mrs. Simpson."
To which she replied, "To the contrary,
sir, I like the cold houses of Great
Britain," which she most certainly did not.
Then she added, "I am sorry, sir, but you
have disappointed me." The Prince was
startled by this effrontery. "In what way,
Mrs. Simpson?" The other guests must have
been stunned when she replied, "Every

American woman who comes to England is asked that same question. I had hoped for something more original from the Prince of Wales."

From the moment she had looked into his weak, sensitive eyes, Wallis had known he wanted to be dominated. Her cool, expert calculation paid off. She had caught his interest, and she knew it.

CHAPTER 16

THIS DOCUMENT IS THE PROPERTY OF HIS BRITANNIC MAJESTY'S GOVERNME.

The circulation of this paper has been strictly limited. .

This copy is issued for the personal use of _H R H the P of W_

TOP SECRET   Copy No. _3_

FROM THE PERMANENT UNDER-SECRETARY
TO HIS MAJESTY'S PM, THE HONOURABLE MR. MACDONALD

COPIES FOR

_____ HIS MAJESTY, HRH THE P OF W

_____ HOME OFFICE

_____ FILE

<u>PROVENANCE</u>

Let's jump ahead to 1934. Ramsay MacDonald's government have been unable to pull Britain out of the Depression. In marked contrast, the first anniversary of the Nazi regime finds Germany well on the way to economic recovery. In Russia, the Reds are purging the usual suspects.

Meanwhile, the old King is starting to go downhill. For this reason, red dispatch boxes of state papers begin arriving at the Prince's digs in Fort·Belvedere. It is the MacDonald Government's belief that, if the end should come, it would be better for the future King to be as informed as possible about the day-to-day affairs of state. But the Prince seems congenitally uninterested in the workings of state, and even less in state security. He regularly leaves drafts of treaties lying around for the charwoman to find. One dinner guest used the powder room and discovered a secret memorandum from the Permanent Under-Secretary of the Foreign Office, Sir Robert Vansittart,

expressing alarm over recent remarks by
Herr Hitler, Germany's new Vice-
Chancellor.

Thelma Furness has returned from an
extended winter holiday in America. Before
going, she had put the fox in with the
chickens by asking Wallis, her new best
friend, to look in on the Prince while she
was away, and "see he doesn't get into any
mischief."

Remember, Thelma was movie-star
beautiful. Besides the usual number of
gorgeous breasts and limbs, she had
inherited the lustrous black hair of her
father's Chilean forebears. It was
impossible for her to conceive of any way
in which the Prince would prefer Mrs.
Ernest Simpson to herself. Now add to your
mental picture the irony that Thelma has
returned from her ocean voyage looking ten
years younger than when she left.

Has the rest and relaxation in warm
American climes done the trick? Or the
skill of some New York plastic surgeon?
Neither. Thelma has just come from a month
in the arms of Aly Khan, the lithe,
muscular, twenty-three-year-old heir to an

immense fortune. Addicted to polo, fast cars, and smouldering Latin beauties, Aly had been sent at eighteen to the brothels of Cairo by his father, the Aga Khan. (The things I missed not having a father. Sigh.) There he had become skilled in the art of *imsak*, the Egyptian equivalent of *fang chung*.

By a piece of luck, Thelma had been invited to a boring society dinner at the Hotel Pierre in New York and was seated next to the young Lothario. Before the sorbet they left the table for the suite upstairs that Thelma had taken for the evening. In the morning, she extended her stay for a fortnight. One can only imagine the nocturnal good fortune that led her to delay her return to the "Little Man," as she derisively spoke of the Prince, temporarily replacing him with the inviting presence of a lover whose notorious staying power had caused him to be compared with Father Christmas. "Each comes but once a year."

Thus buffed to a high gloss, Thelma, all fox stole and long legs, arrives at Fort Belvedere for lunch on Good Friday to find

Wallis sitting in her place beside the
Prince. While they wait to be served, he
helps himself to a piece of lettuce from
the salad bowl, at which point Wallis
spanks his hand hard enough to make him
drop the leaf on the table, saying, "Next
time, use a knife and fork." The Prince
gives everyone a caught-in-the-cookie-jar
schoolboy grin. Thelma looks across the
table at Wallis, who returns an icy stare
of triumph. *Vivat Regina*! After that
Sunday's Easter service, Thelma packs her
bags and leaves, never to return.

And that's how Wallis became the queen
bee who would be Queen. But this is also a
history of how and why she wouldn't be
Queen. And why her vassal wouldn't be
King. That's where I come in.

CHAPTER 17

"I would rather be ashes than dust! I would rather that my spark should burn out in a brilliant blaze than it should be stifled by dry-rot. I would rather be a superb meteor, every atom of me in magnificent glow, than a sleepy and permanent planet. The proper function of man is to live, not to exist. I shall not waste my days in trying to prolong them. I shall use my time."

PROVENANCE

Here's all you need to know about me: it's the bit above that I lifted from Jack London and had Mary Goodnight pronounce over James Bond at the end of *You Only Live Twice*. Now for a little of my CV: Though I was schooled for a while at Eton and for a while at Sandhurst, I owe any education I actually absorbed to the Forbes-Dennises and their little school in Kitzbühel in the Austrian Alps. Childless themselves, they had the idea to create a kind of idealistic establishment for boys of good English families (and good English money) who had made a dog's breakfast of their previous education. Ernan was a tall, aristocratic Scot who had been badly wounded in the war. Phyllis was a Quaker with heaps of prematurely white hair who, as Phyllis Bottome, had been a novelist of some repute.

They had taken a large chalet halfway up the mountain called the Tennerhof. It had apple trees and a great interior space that could be adapted to classroom work, dramatic production, or evening soiree. I was consigned to their care by my mother for the summer of 1926, when all else had failed.

So, one bright July morning, I stepped off the Arlberg Express and found myself in a sleepy little Tyrolean market town in the shadow of the Kitzbühler Horn and the Kaiser Mountains, that awe-inspiring range of giant stone teeth that give Kitzbühel its threatening northern horizon. In the mid-1920s, the travel agents and the downhillers and the "glitterati" had yet to discover it, and what visitors there were—mainly the snob set from Vienna—took no notice of the Forbes-Dennises.

What notice Forbes-Dennis took of me on the platform that morning I can only imagine. I was tall for sixteen, tall enough to look him in the eye. I was trying to be cool but probably came off as arrogant, what the French call *difficile*. I had come to the right place: the reason Forbes-Dennis and his wife, and therefore I, were in Austria at all was their total belief in the application of Freudian psychology to education. In the conviction that neuroses grow from the early struggle to assert one's personality against the environment of home and family, Ernan and Phyllis set out to create a second, more loving home and family for their students. I can honestly say my life with the two of them is one of my most cherished memories.

Ernan gave me something to shoot
for, a career in the Foreign Service.
Encouragement came in a hundred
conversations over dinner, in walks amid
the apple blossoms and long hikes up
and down the Kitzbühler slopes. Along
the way, I became impeccable in German,
fluent in French, and even passable in
my native English—all of which I used
to practice regularly on the *Mädchen*
who frequented the Café Reisch in town.

Unlike the English girls I had
known up to then—the great unwashed,
literally—in Kitzbühel the most amazing
girls were available in abundance for
the tall, presentable English boy from
the Tennerhof. Where girls in England
were prudish or mercenary, boring or too
much trouble, with no idea how to
properly make love, in the looser moral
climate of Kitzbühel there were no
hovering mothers to worry about, no
families to offend, no moral codes to
outrage, and no entanglements that could
not be forgotten by breakfast time. I
don't know if it was the mountain air

or me, but I could look at an Austrian girl and she would fall into my lap.

By the time I was twenty, I was enjoying two separate existences. One was up at the school, learning to love German literature. And the other was swimming and skiing and climbing and bedding German-speaking fräuleins. It was this second life that led me to meet Wallis Simpson.

In the years after graduation, it had become my habit as a young working man in the City to return as often as I could to the Tyrol to pay my respects to Ernan and Phyllis and renew acquaintances with as many of the young ladies as I could crowd into a skiing vacation or bank holiday. By February 1935, the thing was fairly routine. I would work quite hard for a month or two and then hop the Channel, jump in a car, and motor down from Normandy. I would ski in the morning, have something to eat, and then wander about a bit and see what developed.

I was doing my wandering on the terrace of the Grand Hotel one afternoon when a grating American voice stopped me. "Was that you skiing past the hotel

an hour ago? You're quite good." I saw
a woman of about forty, playing bridge
with three other women. She said, "I
seem to have mislaid a prince. Have you
seen one schussing about?"

As it happens, I had seen the Prince of
Wales skiing that morning. He was terrible.
I had watched two young Frenchwomen trying
to overtake him. The three of them had
veered off into a snowbank, the Prince by
accident and the mademoiselles on purpose.
Better play dumb.

"I haven't had the pleasure. My name is
Ian Fleming."

She looked dead into my eyes with
hers, a blue that later became known as
Wallis blue. "And I'm currently Wallis
Simpson."

So. Here was someone who put her
cards on the table. She turned to her
bridge group. "Excuse me, ladies, but
I'm going to trouble Mr. Fleming to
find me a Campari."

The woman who was dummy pointed to the
glass Wallis had left on the table. "But
you already have one."

Without looking back, Wallis replied,

"One always desires something fresh. Do you not find it so, Mr. Fleming?"

I walked Wallis into the bar next to the terrace, and Wallis walked me right through it and out into the hotel lobby. We passed a very satisfactory, and rather athletic, hour in the Prince's suite.

When I returned to London ten days later, a note was waiting for me on my desk at Rowe and Pittman in Bishopsgate. It was from Lancelot "Lancy" Smith, one of the firm's senior partners, requesting my immediate presence in his office. Feeling every bit the schoolboy summoned to the headmaster's rooms, I walked in to find two men I didn't recognize waiting for me with Lancy. I took the hot seat across Lancy's desk from the three of them.

"This is our young Mr. Fleming, gentlemen. Ian, may I introduce Sir Edward Peacock of the Bank of England. And Mr. Conrad O'Brien-ffrench of . . . well, more on that later."

Mr. O'Brien-ffrench, being the nearer, shook my hand. "Two small efs," was all he said. Sir Edward remained in his chair. He

wasn't *of* the Bank of England. He very
nearly *was* the Bank of England.

"Am I overdrawn?" was all I managed.

They took me for a wit and laughed.
"Actually, it's rather the other way
round," said Mr. Two-Small-Efs O'Brien-
ffrench. "We think you have an untapped
asset of considerable value."

My face must have looked as blank as my
mind. Sir Edward spoke up. "Your ability to
get on."

The three men looked at me as if that
explained everything. I looked at them as
if I understood nothing. I was the more
convincing. Mr. O'Brien-ffrench actually
blushed when he said, "With the ladies."

Top-level business meetings were more
interesting than I had been led to believe.
It was impossible to tell if I was being
chastised or elevated to partner.

It was neither. Lancy got up and came
around to me. "Ian, I'd like you to come
down to Hampshire for the weekend. Very
informal. A bit of shooting, a chance to
talk. No dressing for dinner. Just a few
friends."

He shook my hand. Sir Edward was too intrigued with his cuticles to bid me good-bye. Mr. O'Brien-ffrench looked up and nodded to me, his face a roseate hue. Three proper Victorians in the presence of a great libertine. I found the whole thing amusing.

CHAPTER 18

ave you decided, Dr. Greenberg?"

Amy looked up. The first round of movies was over. The flight attendant was looking at her expectantly, clipboard at the ready. "Your entrée?"

"I'm sorry, I haven't—"

"Boneless breast of chicken à la Galway, boeuf tenderloin, or our vegetarian selection, which today . . ." Siobhan Farrell—here in business, the plastic nametags were a nice gold color—was a tall black woman with a full-blown Irish accent. There must have been a look on Amy's face as she tried to match the way the woman looked with the way the woman sounded, because the attendant said, "Yes, I'm Irish. Black Irish." And then she smiled. "It's a joke. I get that look all the time." And then she turned her attention back to the clipboard. Amy watched her flip pages with extraordinarily long fingers. "Our vegetarian choice today is pasta primavera. County Cork vegetables in a—"

"Thanks. I'll take it."

Ms. Farrell seemed pleased that her clipboard work had hit pay dirt. "We'll be coming around with lunch shortly." She turned to the big man sitting next to Amy. "And for you, Mr. . . ."

Again, pages were flipped. And flipped back. He took mercy on her. "Kaltenbrunner."

Amy must have gasped or something, because they both looked at her. She covered the moment with a cough. Ms. Farrell was writing. "2B . . . Kaltenbrunner. Forgive me. You ordered the vegetarian meal as well?"

Amy looked at the man. Could you get that big just by eating your vegetables?

Kaltenbrunner, if that really was his name, glanced at Amy before replying. "No, that was my colleague. He gave up his seat to me at the last moment. I'm a meat and potatoes man all the way. Give me the beef."

Siobhan Farrell made a notation and turned to the people across the aisle. On cue, Amy's seatmate turned to her. "Is Doctor really your first name?"

She laughed despite herself. "It's Amy. Is Kaltenbrunner really your last name?"

He extended a huge paw. "Harvey. Harvey Kaltenbrunner."

It was like shaking hands with a bear. "You're the second Kaltenbrunner I've met this morning." What are the odds of that? she thought.

He read her mind. "It's a ten-million-to-one shot. Of course, in Germany it's like Williams or Brown."

Brown. Scott Brown. Her *fiancé* Scott Brown. She'd forgotten to see if he'd sent her his daily e-mail. Amy undid her seatbelt and reached down for her ThinkPad. It was under the shopping bag with the scarf she'd bought for Scott in a last-minute, Brian Devlin–inspired guilt trip to the duty-free shop.

There comes a point in a transatlantic relationship when you either break it off or you're committed to four more hours of small talk. Harvey Kaltenbrunner took the hint and put on his headphones. Looking over, Amy could see he was scrolling through the audio choices. While she booted up, Amy wondered if she could send e-mails from the plane. She didn't see one of those places to plug in on the console. At least she'd be able to read anything she'd received before she'd checked out of the hotel.

Her home page showed she had mail from Scott. It said, "Miss you. Hurry home. From New Haven with Love, Scott." He'd fallen harder for Ian Fleming than she had. A second message was from friends@lycos.com. A dating service? She clicked on it.

You're in danger. Don't get on the plane. They know. Page 3 of tomorrow's Irish Independent. *Your hotel phone is bugged. Wait for us at the airport.*

We'll explain. Whatever you do, don't get on the plane.

Amy shut her ThinkPad without waiting to turn it off. The message had been sent at 10:36 last night. For twelve hours, it had just been sitting there. Who were "they"? And what did they know? And what could it have to do with her? She didn't know anything. If it was about her having the manuscript, what was the danger? Robbery? On an airplane?

Kaltenbrunner. A last-minute passenger . . . He must be one of them. "They." Was he waiting for her to doze off? Maybe when the second movie was on and the cabin was dark. With those huge hands around her neck, she'd have no chance. Got to move. Don't let on.

She stuffed the manuscript and her laptop into the duty-free shopping bag. "Excuse me, Mr. Kalten-brunner. Harvey." He still had the headphones on. A look of something like annoyance crossed his face. Then he heaved himself out of his seat and stood in the aisle.

Amy said her "Thank you" without making eye contact. The sign on the forward lavatory said Vacant. But she wanted to put as much distance between them as she could, so she headed toward the one in the back of the business section. A man was waiting next to the Occupied sign, reading

Newsweek. She stood next to him and gazed back at her fellow passengers. People were reading or sleeping or listening to music. Siobhan Farrell was four feet away in the galley, preparing lunch. She could easily get her attention, but what would she say? That someone she didn't know had sent her an e-mail warning her of danger from other people she didn't know?

A very literal shiver started up her spine from the small of her back and ran up to her neck and right on out through her hair. The fact that fear could become an actual physical sensation was terrifying all by itself. Amy grabbed hold of the nearest partition. She thought she might pass out standing up.

When she didn't, she opened her eyes and saw she was holding on to one of the built-in racks where they kept the reading material. The magazines were at eye level, the newspapers farther down. She knelt to look at them. The *Financial Times*, *Barron's*, the *Times* of London, and the *Guardian*. No *Irish Independent*. Then she got a break. The couple in 5C and 5D had dozed off, and they had dropped a couple of newspapers on the floor. The *Daily Express* and, under it, the *Independent*. Amy helped herself to their paper and, realizing the bathroom had become vacant, locked herself in.

CHAPTER 19

Two die in fiery crash on the Rathmines Road."
The headline ran the full width of page 3. The
picture, four columns wide, showed the charred
wreckage of a car that had slammed into the back
of a truck in a Dublin suburb around nine the night
before. Witnesses told different stories. A teenager
insisted that two men on a noisy motorcycle
had passed a small foreign car on the left, just before
there was a flash of blue-white light. He had particularly noticed that the man on the back of
the motorcycle had on bulky goggles. An older
woman who had been standing at a stoplight said
the crash was caused by a lorry that backed out of
a side street at high speed, directly into the path of
the car.

The third paragraph caught Amy's eye. "Police
pulled two bodies, a man and a woman, from the
1997 Fiat 124, which is registered to a Mrs. Colleen
O'Beirne of Dunsmere." An inset photo showed Mrs.
O'Beirne from the bank, smiling in happier days.

It was a good thing Amy was in the bathroom, because now she had to throw up. She lifted the toilet seat and let the sick feeling take over. Then she ran the water in the sink and soaked a paper towel. At least they hadn't yet served lunch.

The cold water felt good on her face. She looked in the mirror. A scared, serious-looking woman looked back at her. How had she gotten here? And into so much danger? Hadn't she, just a minute ago, been the little dark-haired girl playing hide-and-seek with her grandfather? They'd play in the Yale rare book library after closing hours. Her favorite place to hide was out in the open on the upper floor, behind the pedestal that held the Gutenberg Bible in its glass case. He'd always find her in the closets and storage areas but never under the Bible, right there in plain sight.

There was mouthwash next to the sink, and paper cups. She used them and sat down on the seat. Her hands were trembling. The next wave hit her so hard, it was all she could do to keep the bile from coming up past her throat. She'd never known fear before. Everything—the Space Mountain ride at Disney World, her dissertation orals in front of the faculty— were things she knew would have a beginning, a middle, and an end. She could tell herself, "In ten minutes or two hours, for better or worse, this will be over," and mentally project herself on the far side of them. But a death threat, or whatever this was . . . There might not be a far side.

"Don't get on the plane." Too late for that. She looked down at the manuscript. What could be so dangerous about a handful of pages that somebody—Kaltenbrunner?—would kill people for them? And if the O'Beirne woman was killed in a car crash yesterday, how could she have upgraded Amy's ticket this morning? And if not her, who? She had to find out.

Someone tried the bathroom handle. Amy knew she'd call attention to herself if she stayed here. She flushed the toilet to buy a couple more seconds, then ran some water in the sink. She had to find a place where she could read the Fleming story and know what he had wanted her to know. And then maybe she'd know what to do about it.

When she finally opened the door, three people glared at her. Sorry. She looked toward the front of the plane and saw the big form of Kaltenbrunner blocking her return to her seat. So she turned in the other direction and walked briskly into coach.

Row 39, the last three seats in the tail of the plane, was empty. Amy sat down next to the window. Now no one could come up behind her, and any passenger who meant her harm would have to show his face coming down the aisle. With fingers trembling a little, she opened the manuscript and started in again.

CHAPTER 20

R. BRUCE LOCKHART

March 2, 1935

Spoke at length with the Prince of Wales at Emerald Cunard's. He returned to his familiar theme – the rise of Adolf Hitler and the German economic miracle. He said two things that alarmed me greatly. First: "I hope and believe we should never fight a war again, but, if so, we must be on the winning side, and that will be the German, not the French." And, a little later, that "England and France are slip-shod democracies. Dictators are very popular these days, and we may want one in England before long".

And this in front of Ribbentrop!

<u>PROVENANCE</u>

Looking back, that moment in late February
1935 when Lancy Smith ushered me across the
threshold of Mottisfont Abbey, lately
transformed into a rustic country home, was
the moment Alice climbed through the
looking glass. Only, I was Alice. Famous
faces I had seen in the newspapers or the
newsreels were smiling at me, talking with
me. Bankers, journalists, ministers (both
church and government), and assorted
personages confided important (and, I would
have thought, confidential) things. All to
further my education in Wonderland.

There was a magnificent Gothic saloon
painted from top to bottom by Rex Whistler
in the trompe l'oeil manner to suggest
trophies on the walls, Roman urns, and a
coat of arms bearing the motto *Che sarà,
sarà.* On a long refectory table was a
paperboard box that read, "World's Largest
Jigsaw Puzzle. 10,000 Pieces." The box bore
a picture of the Coronation of King George
V, taken from the official photograph of
the event and then hand-coloured. Puzzle
pieces nearly covered the mahogany. Every

little while over the next two days, ad hoc
groups of weekend guests, either going out
or coming back from shooting, would
congregate around the table, working on the
puzzle as well as international politics. I
was expected to sit there and absorb—
neither of which are favourite activities
of mine.

Saturday night's entertainment, after
the roast squab had been reduced to bones,
was to be provided by an after-dinner
speaker the Lancy Smiths had laid on. A
backbencher in Parliament, considered a
has-been by most of the country and almost
all of his own party, his was an entrance
Barrymore would have envied.

"Young Mr. Fleming! Have you a light?"
Winston Churchill produced an Upmann
Presidente from within his absurd black cape
and spent his first few moments lighting the
thing. He was even rounder and pinker than I
had remembered. Someone put a glass of the
Cockburn '24 in his hand, and he imbibed.
Then he ceremoniously seated himself in the
wing chair positioned comfortably near the
fire. Only then did he say, without looking
up, "The story up till now?"

Robert Vansittart said, "We've been waiting for you, Winston."

My godfather fixed me with a look that was all bulldog at the mouth and twinkle in the eye. He was enjoying himself immensely. "Ian, we've asked you to come by to see if you will do us another little service. Am I right in thinking you've made the acquaintance of Mrs. Simpson?"

The penny dropped. "Yes, sir, I have. Skiing in Kitzbühel."

He seemed amused. "I've heard it called many things, but never skiing in Kitzbühel."

So I was there to be a laughingstock. I must have been good at it: the laughing went on for a while. The amused to my left included the severe-looking Geoffrey Dawson, editor of the *Times*; Canon Alan Don of Westminster, believed to speak for the Archbishop of Canterbury; and Alan Lascelles, formerly the Prince's private secretary. Over on the right by the mantle was Conrad O'Brien-etcetera; the banker Sir Edward; a tall American I had met that morning, George Messersmith; and an older man wearing a Royal Flying Corps pin in his

lapel. Several others were seated behind
me, wandering in and out to refill their
glasses or relight their cigars.

"My boy," Winston finally resumed, "our
friends who have been good enough to join
us tonight agree on very little
politically. That our form of government is
a salubrious one, certainly. That the
Empire must be preserved, absolutely."
Everything he says always sounds like it's
meant to go down in history or else is a
direct quote from the Oracle of Delphi.
"And moreover, that I would have no
standing here—as in fact I have none in the
country—were I not entrusted with the moral
guidance of Valentine Fleming's
son . . . positively."

There were demurrals of "No, Winston" and
"Bosh!" He ignored them. The moment of
humility, if that's what it was, had passed.
"In everything else, we are as chalk and
cheese. So when I tell you we are of one mind
tonight, you will understand the importance
of the thing. And when I tell you no one else
in the Government is with us on this, you
will understand its secrecy."

I literally gulped.

"We are faced tonight with two threats
that will only grow more vexing with time.
Beyond our borders, Mr. Hitler means to
undo the peace of 1919 and—"

"Winston, really." It was Edward Peacock.
"We agreed not to go into that."

"All right, then. *Some* of us here, namely
me, believe Mr. Hitler means to extend
Germany from the Black Sea to the Atlantic.
Others of us have not yet read *Mein Kampf*.
But we all agree the French are paralyzed,
and the decision has been taken that we
ourselves can do nothing until we rearm. Or
at least, think of rearming. But that is
partly an economic problem, and it need not
concern us tonight.

"Within our borders, though, the threat
is constitutional. And more immediate. We
have it on good authority—good medical
authority—that the King may not last the
year. And the future king—well, we believe
he intends to take a personal hand in
running the country. Or more exactly, he
seeks to lay both hands upon it and give it
to Messrs. Mussolini and Hitler.

"So, Ian, here's what we propose to do.
You will sit there and our friends will

produce the evidence that convinces us the
coronation of the present Prince of Wales
must never be allowed to occur."

Amy flipped ahead through the rest of the papers she was holding. There was a lot left to go, at least a hundred pages. One old document even looked like someone's dental records. Where was all this going? And what did it have to do with her?

And then the faintest of smiles crossed her lips. Ian Fleming was one unbelievably lucky man. His indictment, or whatever this was, had found its way across time and geography into the hands of a woman who had willingly, happily, counted the 180 delicate tracings that made up a 1,200-year-old Celtic letter W. A woman who could tell the difference between old ink and original ink. You got a tricky, involved case to make, Mr. Fleming? Bring it on.

CHAPTER 21

MARCONIGRAM

WIRELESS COMMUNICATION WITH U.S.A. CENT. & S. AMERICA, ABYSSINIA, AUSTRIA, AZORES,
BULGARIA, CANARY IS., CAPE VERDE IS., DUTCH E. INDIES, EGYPT,
FOREIGN W. INDIES, FRANCE, GREECE, HEDJAZ, IRAQ, ITALY,
SOMALILAND, JAPAN, MADEIRA, PALESTINE, PHILIPPINE IS.,
PORTUGAL, PORTUGUESE E. & W. AFRICA, RUSSIA, SPAIN,
SWITZERLAND, SYRIA, TRANSJORDANIA, TURKEY, YUGOSLAVIA, ETC.

OFFICE STAMP

Please quote this number in any enquiry regarding this message   No

Received   *"Via Marconi"*   at   m.

FROM WALLIS SIMPSON
TO   BESSIE MERRYMAN
C/O   THE SHOREHAM HOTEL, WASHINGTON,
2/11/35
AUNTIE, I'VE BEEN LAUGHING SO HARD
ON THE INSIDE I JUST HAD TO

PROVENANCE

The man with the lapel pin got up and stood
next to Churchill. I found out later that
Squadron Leader Frederick W. Winterbotham
was head of Air Intelligence for what is
now called MI6. A decorated pilot in the
Great War, Winterbotham's pin showed that
he was a member of the Brotherhood of the
Air. After the war, while the foot soldiers

of each country formed themselves into the British Legion, the German Legion, the American Legion, and so on, the various flying aces whose sorties had known no national boundaries created an international fraternity of their own.

Through his opposite number in Germany, Freddy Winterbotham had been granted a private interview with Herr Hitler just a fortnight before. Now he withdrew a small black notebook from his breast pocket. "I asked the Chancellor, in several different ways, to describe for me his vision of the future of Europe. He said, 'There should be only three major powers in the world: the British Empire, the Americas, and the German Empire of the future, which will include the rest of Europe and the lands to the east. England, with one or two exceptions, will continue her role in Africa and India while Germany will take Russia. And together we can decide the policy for China and the Far East.' "

Winterbotham paused for effect before looking back at his pad. "And I quote, 'All we ask is that Britain should be content to look after her Empire and not to interfere

with Germany's plans for expansion. I place
great faith in your next generation of
leaders.' "

Then he put his notebook away and looked
right at me. "The Chancellor showed me a
letter from the Prince of Wales, written
less than a month ago. 'If the Great War has
shown us anything, it is that the Hun
peoples of England and Germany must never
again be divided by national differences.'"

"Thank you, Freddy. George." Sir Thomas
Beecham never conducted at Covent Garden
any more imperiously than did Winston now.
"George" was the lanky Texan, George
Messersmith, Roosevelt's Ambassador to
Austria and later his Coordinator of
Intelligence. Earlier that afternoon I'd
been terribly impressed when he completed
the entire area of the puzzle around George
V and the throne in about twenty minutes.
It seemed he had a talent for taking bits of
information and making connections.

He walked over to Winston and stood in
the precise spot where Winterbotham had
been. The prosecution was well rehearsed.
"Mr. Fleming, two days after your, um,
encounter with Mrs. Simpson in Kitzbühel,

I happened to attend a dinner party in Vienna at the Brazilian Embassy. The Prince and Mrs. Simpson were the guests of honor. Coffee had just been served when we had an unexpected visitor, the secretary to Chancellor von Schussnigg. He handed me a message stating that a train bound for Italy from Germany had derailed in Austrian territory. Rescue workers had just discovered hundreds of German naval shells meant for Mussolini's fleet in the southern Mediterranean. Naturally, proof that Hitler is helping rearm Il Duce is of great interest not only to the Austrians and Americans but to Great Britain as well.

"When I returned to the table, Prince Edward pressed me pointedly as to why von Schussnigg had sent his man round. As it happens, a few people in your country and mine had been looking for an opportunity of just this sort."

"An opportunity?"

"For some time, we've been having trouble with leaks. Secrets that have turned up in other hands. So I told the Prince about the naval shells, swearing him to secrecy.

Later, over brandy, I noticed him speaking with the number three man in the Italian Embassy, who immediately left the dinner party. The next day, my military attaché gave me this."

He took a paper from his breast pocket and unfolded it before laying it in front of me. It was a decoded transcript of a message sent the night before by the Italian Ambassador, Preziosi, to his Foreign Office in Rome. It quoted the Prince as saying, "The cat is out of the bag as far as the naval shells are concerned."

I found it quite unbelievable. My future King in league with Fascists and Nazis? Had I not seen the message with my own eyes . . .

Messersmith took the paper back, refolded it, and put it away. From the same breast pocket he withdrew a sealed envelope. It was addressed "To Mr. Ian Fleming, to be delivered by hand." The assembled guests watched me open the letter. All except Winston, who rose and walked over to the window, puffing loudly on his cigar.

I looked first at the signature: "F. D. Roosevelt." The letter read, "My dear Mr.

Fleming, The former naval person informs
me you are a young man of trustworthy
character. He has asked me to commit to
paper, for your eyes only, my personal
backing for your upcoming endeavor. And
to assure you that you have friends on
this side of the Atlantic who are
prepared to assist you and your godfather
in any way possible. Regards, F. D.
Roosevelt."

I looked up from the letter. "What
endeavour?" Instead of answering,
Messersmith simply walked over and took the
letter from me. Without a word, he dropped
it in the fire.

"A wholly honourable one." Winston took
another cigar from his pocket and offered
it to me. They were such favourites of his,
the company renamed them Sir Winstons after
his knighthood. I declined. He gave me a
you-don't-know-what-you're-missing look
and put it away again.

All this stage business was too much for
O'Brien-ffrench. "We want you to continue
your acquaintanceship with Mrs. Simpson."

I was trying to make sense of the thing
when Canon Don spoke up from my left. "Mr.

Fleming, do you know the origin of the word *acquaint*?"

Before I could answer, Geoffrey Dawson of the *Times* put in, "Is this one of your Latin brainteasers, Canon?"

The clergyman seemed a little put out. "It's Old English, actually."

They didn't do much Old English in the little time I spent at Sandhurst. Winston rescued me. "Then, my boy, you shall have the pleasure of looking it up. But I'll give you a clue: it's part of a woman's body."

There were snickers from the educated regions of the room. What the hell had I gotten myself into? Initiation night at the Oxbridge Old Boys' Club?

Winston leaned forward and pulled on my elbow, making me look him in the eyes. "The thing is this: most people believe that in Wales' solar system, he is the Sun and Mrs. Simpson is, let us say, an asteroid, caught in his gravitational field and destined to burn up to cinders when she gets too close. We know it to be precisely otherwise. The Prince is in her thrall and will gladly go round and round to receive a flicker of illumination from her. We need someone to be to her what she is to Edward. Someone whose magnetic force can bring her round to us."

I don't think my eyes could get any wider. "And that's me?"

"I." Canon Don was the kind of teacher who made grammar a living hell.

"But sir—*sirs*—I just met the woman the one time. What makes you think—"

Winston was not to be dissuaded. "She is what Clemmie would call a man-eater. And Ian, you're the biggest hunk of meat we could come by."

Finally, the dawn. "You're asking me to be a . . . a gigolo?"

Winston clapped his hands together. "You see, gentlemen, I told you he was sharp!" And then back to me. "You've caught the spirit of the thing exactly."

"*S'il vous plaît*, Winston, proffer to him the rapier." Claude Dansey's right-hand man, Stephane Lefevre, was the only Frenchman in the room. I would work with Claude and his people years later during the war. In 1935, he ran something called the Z Organisation, recruiting anti-Fascist

businessmen to keep their eyes and ears
open for Winston.

"I don't know if I'd call it a rapier,
Stephane. Ammunition, rather. Ian, when
President Roosevelt referred to friends who
were ready to assist you . . . well, some of
them are, shall we say, well-placed at the
Western Union company. They have been good
enough to keep an eye out for any
correspondence coming from or going to Mrs.
Simpson. I happen to have one such to
hand . . ." Here he rummaged around in his
pockets before extracting the case for his
reading glasses. A telegram was neatly
folded inside.

"As you can see, Mrs. Simpson sent it a
week ago to her aunt, a Mrs. Bessie
Merryman." He handed it over to me. I read
it. "Auntie, I've been laughing so hard on
the inside I just had to share it with
someone. The P of W is absolutely bonkers
for me. He follows me around like a puppy
dog. Were I in love, it would be magical,
instead of merely comical. He's invited you
over to cruise with us . . . NEXT WEEK! I
need your reply urgently. Say yes . . . it's
such a big boat. W."

"They're on that cruise now." Robert
Bruce Lockhart got up and Messersmith sat
down in the perfect synchronicity of one of
those German town clocks with the moving
figures. "They embarked from Trieste
yesterday, bound for the Greek Islands and
Istanbul. The Prince gave the Fascist
salute to the crowd as the boat pulled
away."

"So, Ian." Here it comes, Winston the
salesman asking for the order. "We want you
to meet the royal party on the island of
Rhodes. Bruce and Conrad have prepared a
little narrative for you—"

Lockhart appeared to be the logistics
officer of the enterprise. "We'll go over
it together later. You're an English
businessman on holiday, whose
transportation has been commandeered by the
Caliph of—"

"You did say later, Bruce, did you not?"
Winston can be so bossy. "All we need, Ian,
is the nod from you. You must insinuate
yourself into Mrs. Simpson's affections and
await further instructions. Will you do
it . . . for England?"

What did they say to the virgin on her

wedding night? "But my job at the bank—"

Lancy Smith put a hand on my shoulder. "For the time being, this *is* your job. We've passed the hat to cover any extra expenses."

"Well then, gentlemen—" My actual acceptance was drowned out by the *hear, hears* and a raggedly heartfelt chorus of "For He's a Jolly Good Fellow." All in all, I was being sent off to consort with a married woman like a battleship being christened. They even had the champagne.

CHAPTER 22

The pages in her hand were shaking so much, Amy thought they'd hit a pocket of turbulence. And then she realized, *she* was the turbulence.

She had a bad case of the shakes. They'd been coming on for a while. Whatever the big secret was—and whoever wanted it kept a secret—what chance did one 120-pound assistant professor of art history have? A thinker of thoughts. An observer of things. She was no heroine. She'd never had to take any real action in her whole life. Look at Katie, holed up halfway around the world on Ayres Rock for weeks at a time and loving it. Amy had always stayed on the sidelines, following the path of least resistance—living in the same place where she grew up; doing the same thing her grandfather did. No, that wasn't quite true. Chief had been in the war. Chief had become "Chief" in the war, thanks to the men in his unit. He'd carried a gun. He'd shot people, or at least he'd shot *at* them.

Amy hadn't felt this alone since the day he'd died. Mima and Chief had always been, well, *there* for her. After Mima died, he became her whole family. Now he was gone and Scott was thousands of miles away and she was on her own. If it were a battle of wits, that would be one thing, but—

Amy looked up. She could see that two flight attendants were working a food trolley down the aisle, about eight rows away. Behind them, momentarily blocked, appeared the hulking form of Harvey Kaltenbrunner.

He was methodically scanning the rows of passengers left and right. And then his eyes locked onto hers. All of a sudden, sitting in the back of the plane seemed like a really stupid idea. She could see him coming, all right. But she was trapped back here in row 39. Once the trolley rolled to the next row, there was an empty aisle seat where he'd be able to get by.

All Amy could think of was to pull the call button over her seat. A pinging sound started and a light went on. The two attendants stopped serving and turned toward the sound. But before Amy could say anything, Kaltenbrunner used the moment to step on the arm of a seat and jump around the trolley and its two attendants.

The woman working on Amy's side of the cart

was holding a plate of chicken. "We'll be right there, miss."

Now Kaltenbrunner was between them and Amy. "That's okay. My wife just wanted to get my attention."

Amy blurted out, "I'm not his wife!" Several nearby passengers turned in their seats to see what was going on.

Kaltenbrunner had reached her row. He jammed himself into the middle seat, locking Amy in. He looked at her as he spoke, but his words were meant for the people watching this little domestic tableau. "You're right, honey. Two days to go. Prewedding jitters, I guess." The heads slowly turned back to what they'd been doing, leaving the nice couple behind them to work things out.

Amy gripped her ThinkPad tightly with both hands. If he turned away for a second, she'd crash it down on his head. He put out one meaty arm and laid it over both of hers, preempting her strike.

"Listen, lady—Dr. Greenberg—why'd you pull a stunt like that?"

Amy was still holding the computer so tightly her knuckles were white. "Like what?"

"Like leaving your seat and making me go looking for you."

"You know perfectly well why." Amy could hear the fear in her voice. And the defiance. "You're one of them."

"No." He took his arm off hers. "I'm one of us."

Amy noticed he was breathing hard. From climbing over the seats, or out of anxiety, she couldn't tell.

He lowered his voice a little. "*I* sent you that e-mail." He was smoothing his hair, trying to make himself look more presentable. "So why'd you get on the damn plane?"

Amy tried to keep her voice low like his, but it came out like a croak. "Because I only read it after I got on. Am I really in danger?"

Instead of looking at her, he was looking forward, scanning the heads of the other passengers. "Yes. Really."

"Who are you, anyway?"

He reached into his jacket pocket and palmed a plastic ID card. He showed it to her. It said "James Sheridan" under his picture. At the top was an official seal of some sort and the words "United States of America."

"Are you FBI?"

Sheridan pulled a face. "Nah. We're the other guys."

"So who is Kaltenbrunner?"

"The man they sent to kill you. The German from your hotel."

This time the cold shock wave ran down Amy's body in the reverse direction, from her hair to her feet. "Kill me?"

"That's why they upgraded you. To put you two together."

"And he gave you his ticket?"

"I sort of took it. He's still in the airport men's room."

"Is he—"

"Dead? You think I'm an amateur? No, he's not dead. But he'll have to wear a neck brace."

He was still facing forward, so she did too, trying to look for whatever he was looking for. "But why would anyone want to kill me?"

"That book you're reading. Those papers. They want it."

"But why? And who's *they*?"

Kaltenbrunner/Sheridan turned and looked at her, so she did the same. His face, like his body, was big and tough, but his eyes were kind. "You really don't know?"

"No, I honestly don't."

The next thing he said was "If you want classical music, they have opera favorites on channel nine."

Amy looked at him, bemused. And then she saw

Siobhan Farrell, the flight attendant from the front cabin, coming down the aisle toward them. She had two lunch trays. "Pasta primavera and boeuf tenderloin. We don't like our business class customers to go hungry."

Amy was not in the least bit hungry, but she dutifully pulled down her tray table. Ms. Farrell put a linen cloth down and then Amy's meal and her utensils, saying, "We don't usually lose customers to the back of the plane." She did the same with Sheridan's steak. It was crazy being served this way in coach. The people nearby stared openly. Before returning to the front of the plane, Ms. Farrell smiled and said, "Enjoy your meals."

Sheridan cut his meat into pieces and then did the same with his vegetables, green beans mixed with chopped nuts of some kind. Not almonds. Peanuts, maybe. He alternated eating the meat and the green beans without coming up for air. Amy couldn't understand how he could have an appetite. She couldn't touch her food. "Why are people after me? What's the big secret?"

Sheridan seemed to realize he had more green beans than steak. So he stabbed several beans with his fork and added them to the mouthful he was already working on. He caught her disapproving look. "Hey, I didn't have breakfast." He made a big show of daintily patting his mouth with his napkin. If he'd chewed before swallowing, Amy had missed it. "I don't know who they are. This is the Brits' operation. They call us in like this when a plane's gonna land in the States. All my bosses told me is not to let you get killed today. And I don't know what's in the book. You're the one who's reading it. You tell me."

"It's some kind of memoir from the nineteen thirties. Who'd get so worked up over something that happened seventy years ago?"

He'd almost brought the last forkful of meat and beans to his mouth. He held it there as he said, "I don't know. But people still get worked up over stuff that went on two thousand years ago, don't they?"

He started in on the new potatoes. Pop, pop, pop into his mouth, one after another. Amy couldn't stand his being so calm. "So what am I supposed to do now?"

"We've got three more hours before we land in New York. Why don't you just sit there and read and then let me in on it. I'm going with those opera favorites." He took the headphones out of their plastic bag, plugged in, and hit a few buttons on the remote. Then he leaned back in his seat. Conversation over.

Now that it was Sheridan and not Kaltenbrunner next to her, the shakes were gone. Okay, Amy decided, back to Mr. Fleming.

CHAPTER 23

M̲ HRH THE PRINCE OF WALES   Dated DEC. 9, 1935

In account with

VAN CLEEF & ARPELS

World Famous French Jewelers

LONDON

VC◆A

quant.		description	amount	
ONE	1	DIAMOND HAIR CLIP		
TWO	2	JEWELLED BRACELETS,		
	3	ENGRAVE ONE: God bless WE		
	4			
	5			
	6			
	7			
	8			
	9			
	10			

Note: *house account*

<u>PROVENANCE</u>

The plan went well at first. I was
airlifted to the Aegean Islands and dropped
down on Rhodes the morning of the Prince's
arrival like some deus ex machina. Unlike
the Greek gods', my machine was Lord
Hawksley's private aircraft, and I shared
the flight with a thousand pounds of
provisions intended for Hawksley's villa.

In the afternoon, feeling every bit like
a sack of potatoes—or, more to the point, a
side of beef—I played my little stranded
tourist scene for Wallis's aunt, Mrs.
Merryman, on the rocky plage in front of
the Excelsior. She in turn reproduced my
story for Wallis and the Prince,
importuning him to take pity on one of his
subjects. I affected a forlorn expression
while Wallis stood slightly behind the
Prince, hands on hips and smiling at me
conspiratorially. His rented yacht, the
Nahlin, slept thirty, and as there were
only a dozen or so in their party, he was
gracious enough to take me in. And give me
my own cabin in the bargain.

The next morning I awoke early and

wandered about the boat. I discovered the
books in the library had been replaced with
crates of golf balls. Later, while the Prince
and the Earl of Sefton practised their drives
into the Mediterranean, Wallis found me and
informed me she would be developing a
"headache" that would keep her from joining
Edward and his party on an archaeological
tour of the island. I was to have previously
established that I had business papers I
needed to go over in my cabin.

I heard the launch putter away from the
yacht, followed at a decent interval by a
soft knock on the door. The first thing
Wallis said was "Can you be discreet?"

I said, "Madame, I am the soul of
discretion," which, since you're reading
this, I obviously am not.

She made a business of closing the little
curtains over the portholes and sat down on
the edge of the bed. "So what's the real
story?"

I took the plunge. "I wanted to see you
again."

She laughed. "Okay, you've seen me."

In for a penny, in for a pound. "I wanted
to have you again."

She put her hand on me, drawing me down beside her. "I knew I liked you."

Nothing I had done before had prepared me for premeditated sex with Wallis Simpson. In 1935, I was twenty-six years old, in my prime, so to speak. I had been intimate (such an Edwardian phrase) with thirty to forty women. Girls, mostly. Usually I had been—or had been given the illusion of being—in charge. Wallis was in her fortieth year, and she was most definitely in charge. Hardly a beauty, she was flat and slim, with nothing to hold on to. But she was as sure of her sexual attractiveness as any Garbo or Lamarr.

I was then, and still am now, in awe of her vaginal muscles. She had what you might call fine motor skills and could work her various muscle groups the way Toscanini could work an orchestra. For another thing, she was as agile as an eel and had no fear of appearing unladylike in one of her two-person "arrangements." She never turned the lights down or closed her eyes. She was always terrifyingly *there*.

Over the next few days, we had two more rendezvous before I was obliged to take my

leave to return to my "business." But I had
laid the groundwork, so to speak, for a
continuing relationship when Mrs. Simpson
returned to Bryanston Court.

And what of *Mr*. Simpson in all this? By
1935, Ernest was no longer included when
his wife was invited to the Prince's place
at Fort Belvedere. And certainly not on
their Mediterranean cruise. At first, he
had been honoured that the future King had
taken an interest in his wife. Then, when
friendship had turned to passion, he had
become jealous. And now, he seemed resigned
to losing her.

In a way, her dalliance with the Prince
made my time spent with Wallis easier to
account for. Ernest was already accustomed
to turning a blind eye to his wife's
comings and goings. It was really the
Prince and the Special Branch security
detail assigned to him that I had to dodge.
So I was given an extra ace up my sleeve.
O'Brien-ffrench had enlisted a sympathetic
London motor car dealer, one Guy Marcus
Trundle, to provide me with a safe house
five minutes away from Bryanston Court. All
I had to do after "visiting" with Wallis

was to affix my hat on my head, turn up my
coat collar, and stroll over to Trundle's
home. I'd unlock his door with the spare
latchkey I'd been given, saunter through
the place (waving to him if he was home),
and leave through the back door and the
gate at the end of the garden. If anyone was
watching—and several pairs of eyes were—
they'd think I was Trundle. I thought I had
the thing knocked.

CHAPTER 24

IN THE   **IPSWICH**   **COUNTY COURT**
No. of matter 85D511

Between   Wallis Warfield Simpson   Petitioner
and   Ernest Aldrich Simpson   Respondent
and   Co-Respondent

Referring to the decree made in this cause on the
27th   day of   October 1936,
whereby it was decreed that the marriage solemnized on the
21st   day of   July 1928,

at   Chelsea Registry Office, London
between

       Wallis Warfield Simpson   the Petitioner

and

       Ernest Aldrich Simpson   the Respondent

be dissolved unless sufficient cause be shown to the Court within six weeks from the making thereof why the said decree should not be made absolute, and no such cause having been shown, it is hereby certified that the said decree was on the   3rd   day of   May 1937,   made final and absolute and that the said marriage was thereby dissolved.
       Dated   3 May 1937

<u>Note: Divorce effects inheritance under a will.</u> Where a will has already been made by either party to the marriage then, by virtue of section 18A of the Wills Act 1837, from the date on which the decree was made absolute: —

(a) any appointment of the former spouse as executor or trustee is treated as if omitted and;

(b) any gift in the will to the former spouses lapses; unless a contrary intention appears in the will.

Address all communications to the Chief Clerk AND QUOTE THE ABOVE CASE NUMBER

THE COURT OFFICE AT
is open from 10 a.m. till 4 p.m. on
Mondays to Fridays only

Certificate making decree Nisi Absolute (Divorce)

MATRIMONIAL CAUSES RULES
Rule 67(2)

            ALEXANDRA HOUSE,
            NEW STREET, IPSWICH
            SUFFOLK.

<u>PROVENANCE</u>

The death of George V changed everything.
As 1935 became 1936, Britain's Depression
deepened. Men were in the streets: a
million unemployed had marched in December.
Sir Oswald Mosley's British Union of
Fascists were in the streets now, urging
the new king to back Mussolini's invasion
of Abyssinia. (Of course, Mosley was on Il
Duce's payroll.) In March, the Germans
would walk into the Rhineland, breaking the
Locarno Pact and the Treaty of Versailles
once and for all. France, with a quarter
million men under arms, waited for British
support, which never came. The new King
echoed Lord Lothian's summing-up of the
Wehrmacht's march into Köln: "The Germans
are just going into their own back garden."

The caterpillar that had been David, the
Prince of Wales, had spread its wings and
become King Edward VIII. But was he a
monarch butterfly or a moth? Six months
into his reign, Edward seemed ready to give
the whole shop away to Hitler. Turning a
blind eye to the geared-up war machine that
sent Stuka bombers over Valencia, he again

praised Nazi economic progress as a
"miracle"—this time at the annual reunion
of the British Legion—and he even sent a
congratulatory note to both dictators on
the formation of the Rome-Berlin "Axis."
Just before the old King's death, I was
personally close enough to overhear George
V speak the famous line about his son to the
new PM, Stanley Baldwin. "After I am dead,
the boy will ruin himself within twelve
months." Edward managed it in ten.

And what about Wallis? Notwithstanding
his mother's pledge to never accept or even
speak to Mrs. Simpson—"the woman is
unsuitable as a friend, disreputable as a
mistress, and unthinkable as the Queen of
England"—the King made Wallis his constant
companion. Dinner parties at the homes of
the ladies Colefax and Cunard; skiing (of
both the snow and water sort) and cruising
the Mediterranean. I happened to attend a
"musicale" one evening at Emerald Cunard's
place at 7 Grosvenor Square. This was one
of the last evenings when Ernest would be
invited to attend along with his wife. We
were having coffees when the King decided
it was time to leave. He bade good-bye to

his hostess and, at the door, stood staring
at Wallis as his car was brought round. She
unceremoniously got up and left with the
King. It fell to me to bundle her teary-
eyed husband into a cab alone. By the
summer, Ernest had decamped from Bryanston
Court to his club, and in October, Wallis
filed for divorce.

Even so, the situation could still be
retrieved. Edward's investiture and
coronation, the ceremony at which the
thousand-year-old crown first worn by
Edward the Confessor was to be placed upon
his head at Westminster Abbey, by tradition
was not scheduled to happen until after
Saint George's Day, in May of 1937. Until
then he was *"un roi sans couronne."* The
trap, if there were a trap, had to be
sprung now.

Winston, a fervent supporter of the
monarchy and the Empire, supported the King
publicly at every turn. But privately he
sent Bruce Lockhart and O'Brien-ffrench
round to my flat with a carrot and a stick.
I was to tell Wallis that if she managed the
King's departure before the crown was
placed upon his head, she would receive an

income for life equal to what she would
have been given as Queen, to be raised
equally by Churchill's friends in England
and members of the Room, Roosevelt's
patrician circle in New York. And this sum
was to be settled on her whether she
eventually married Edward or not.

The stick actually was to be wielded by
the PM, Stanley Baldwin, who had been
brought into the plan by his Foreign
Secretary and Winston's good friend,
Anthony Eden. It seems Winston had
manoeuvred the King into allowing Baldwin
to poll the major Dominion countries—India,
Canada, South Africa, Australia—on their
willingness to accept a Queen Wallis the
First. My godfather's thinking was that the
smart set in London might countenance a
divorced woman as Queen. But he was
counting on Ottawa and Canberra to vote a
resounding no.

The stick had an extra little barb:
Baldwin had in his possession the China
dossier compiled by Scotland Yard's Special
Branch, describing in vivid detail Wallis's
escapades abroad in the 1920s. I was to
present both the carrot and the stick to

Mrs. Simpson as if I were bringing her a
confidence from "friends of friends." And
to let her know the dossier would be given
to the King, and if need be, the press,
should she not prove complaisant.

It was two days before she was to be
granted her preliminary decree nisi from
Ernest. I had let myself in the servants'
entrance and we were sitting in the back
parlour when I described the situation
and made her the offer. When I had
finished, she simply withdrew her hand
from mine and looked at me for a long
moment. More like three long moments. Her
look was the one Caesar probably gave to
Brutus. And then she said no so quickly, I
spilled my sherry on the Axminster. It
could have been worse; it could have been
the amontillado.

"But Wallis, why? The Dominions are
against you, there's the dossier . . . and
think of all that money." Was any barrister
ever more succinct in his summing-up?

She shook her head so vociferously, I
could see the diamond hairclip in her bun
with every defiant shake. "Because then
she'll be Queen."

"Who, Mary?" I thought she meant the dowager Queen.

Wallis lit one of her American cigarettes. "Of course not. I mean Cookie. The Dowdy Duchess."

Came the dawn. Cookie, née Elizabeth Bowes-Lyon, was married to Edward's brother, Albert, the Duke of York. She was the woman Wallis loved to hate. She had also been the woman Wallis loved to imitate, until the Duchess had caught her at it one Sunday morning at Fort Belvedere. "If Edward isn't King, it's Bertie and Cookie." Wallis always called him by the old King's pet name. "Makes a girl want to fwow up just thinking about it. No, I simply can't."

That's how things stood for a fortnight, until I received assistance from an unexpected source. On November 1, the Sunday before the American election, Wallis's Aunt Bessie was invited out of the clear blue by Vincent Astor to join him for a day of sailing around the Chesapeake on his steam yacht, the *Nourmahal*. In itself, this would have been most unusual, as the

Astors were Hudson River and not Chesapeake
gentry. More unusual still was the identity
of the yacht's third passenger that
afternoon. Aunt Bessie realized later that
she should have guessed it the moment she
saw a wicker wheelchair coming aboard with
the baggage. In the varnished wood and
white saloon, Astor introduced her to
Franklin D. Roosevelt.

I have it on good authority the
negotiations were as cutthroat as any FDR
had had with John L. Lewis of the United
Mine Workers. Aunt Bessie had raised
Wallis, had unfailingly reminded her that
"I sacrificed my own welfare" for her (as
she so melodramatically—and untruthfully—
put it now to the President), and was bound
and determined to cash in. Roosevelt
appealed to Mrs. Merryman's patriotism.
Mrs. Merryman appealed to Mr. Roosevelt's
wallet. In the end, Aunt Bessie was cut in
for a third on top of whatever Wallis would
get. All she had to do was convince her
niece to exert her own immense
gravitational pull on the King. The aunt
could console herself with the thought that

the object wasn't to remove Wallis from the
King. It was to remove the King from the
throne.

From now on, Aunt Bessie would be
Wallis's "American controller," a title FDR
invented for her on the spot. And until the
old woman's death after the war, the deal
included Wallis's reporting back everything
she saw or heard Edward do. Would the Woman
Who Would Be Queen go for it?

Rather than just hope for the best, we
English decided to help things along.
Beginning the day after Aunt Bessie's
excursion, Wallis received a delivery of
seventeen red roses from the best florist
in Mayfair. The card was signed "Always"
in English, but in an obviously German
hand. These deliveries, always seventeen
roses and always "Always" but no signature,
continued for the next several weeks. One
time, the standing order for the roses was
"mistakenly" included in the delivery. It
suggested the secret admirer's initials
were JvR. Naturally the servants removed
the florist's paperwork from the
arrangement when it was given to Wallis,
but they had seen it as they were meant to.

Their story, when it got around, was that
Mrs. Simpson must have had a fling with
Joachim von Ribbentrop, an affair to
remember. Always. The story was denied, of
course, by Ribbentrop. But it supported the
malign rumour that Wallis was privy to the
secret papers the King left lying around
Fort Belvedere, and that she was ready,
willing, and able to pass such sensitive
information on to her friends the Germans.
It would make the prospect of a Queen
Wallis I that much more distasteful.

The straw that would break the
dromedary's back came from Wallis's own
hand. On 6 December, Sir Oswald Mosley and
Diana Mitford were secretly married at the
home of Dr. Joseph Goebbels in Berlin—a
ceremony that featured Adolf Hitler as
guest of honour. Our good friends at the
telegraph office were kind enough to
intercept a congratulatory telegram written
to the newlyweds by Wallis Simpson and
reroute it to us at Whitehall. The next
step was simplicity itself: insinuating to
the King that he might some morning open
the *Daily Express* to discover Lord
Beaverbrook had printed not just

photographs of the wedding but the contents
of Wallis's cable. For the British public
to discover, after a two-year press embargo
on the King's affair (engineered in large
part by the same Lord Beaverbrook), that
his inamorata was enamoured of Fascists
and Nazis would damn her in the eyes of the
British public and make it impossible for
Edward to marry her and keep his throne.
Wallis, who could see the handwriting
on the wall better than most, naturally
chose discretion and a lot of money over
valour.

So on the night of 11 December, the
British Broadcasting Company's senior
producer found himself counting down from
ten on his fingers in the Augusta Tower at
Windsor Castle. At five, BBC Director-
General Sir John Reith had planned to
intone, "This is Windsor Castle. And now,
Mr. Edward Windsor," which everyone agreed
was unnecessarily common. So he changed it
to "His Royal Highness, Prince Edward,"
attesting to the fact that "the Little Man"
was the only Englishman in history to be a
prince for a day after being a king. Even as
the strangely wavering voice read the

abdication speech in his Americanised London-Cockney accent, no one could have known he would play a far greater role in determining the fate of Britain as the Duke of Windsor than he ever could have done as King Edward VIII.

CHAPTER 25

Amy looked up from the pages and glanced out through the thick glass of the plane at the clouds building up below her. She had once learned what the different kinds were called. There were stratus clouds and cirrus . . . the ones like cotton candy. She thought the storm clouds out there now were something-cumulus. Either nimbocumulus or cumulonimbus, she couldn't remember which.

This is what you get when you're an only child raised by old people. Fun games at the dinner table like "name that cloud." Pop quizzes about the presidents or state capitals. The other kids in high school were having "study dates": light on the study, heavy on the date. Mima and Chief had decided that schoolwork was something you accomplished on your own, with the radio off and both feet on the floor. If she hadn't met the Girls in college . . .

Her mind wandered, as it often did, to Scott. How much had his mother, Maggie, gotten on him about his schoolwork? She probably didn't have to. Scott's brain never stopped. Maybe he could figure out what was so threatening in what Fleming had written. Hadn't he figured out what Caravaggio was saying about sixteenth-century Florence just from the positioning of the figures in his paintings? Which character in each group represented those in power; whether that character was foolish or wise, weak or strong? She could use Scott's brain right now. And maybe her friend Blanche's too. Three heads were better than one, right?

Rather than asking herself more questions, Amy picked up the manuscript again, hoping for a few answers.

ONDON GAZETTE ❦ MAY 29, 1937

The King has been pleased by letters patent under the great seal of the realm, bearing the date of the 27th of May, 1937, to declare that the Duke of Windsor shall be entitled to hold and enjoy for himself only the title, style, or attribute of Royal Highness so however that his wife and descendants, if any, shall not hold said title, style or attribute.

PROVENANCE

What turns a man against his country?
Especially a country that has given him as
much as it has given any of its sons? What
makes a man a Pétain, a Quisling, an
Arnold? More likely than not, he has
developed the aggrieved feeling that the
country has turned against *him.* The thing
that turned Edward, now the Duke of
Windsor, had nothing to do with matters of
power and state. And everything to do with
a curtsy.

When the last of the champagne had been
downed on East Sixty-second Street in New
York and the last Ming figurine sacrificed
to Wallis's petulance at the Villa Lou Viei,
it remained for the famous lovers to
actually marry. It had been assumed all
around that the woman who married His Royal
Highness the Duke of Windsor would become
Her Royal Highness the Duchess. Leaving
nothing to chance, Edward telephoned his
brother Bertie—now officially King George
VI—every day. In part, the calls were full
of brotherly advice, a genuine attempt to
assist the new King in playing a role for

which he had never been trained. In part, they were the former King's way of lording it over his younger brother. But, *au fond*, they were about one thing and one thing only. Would George VI grant Wallis Simpson the title of Her Royal Highness or not? Would visitors be required to bow and curtsy in the presence of the Duchess or not? Every call—and at trunk rates from the Continent, the telephone bills ran into the hundreds of pounds—began or ended with the same query.

The settled rule had always been "The wife takes the status of the husband." The most recent precedent on point had been Elizabeth herself, the new King's wife. Although she was the daughter of an earl, she had been a commoner before marrying Bertie. Now, believing the party responsible for the abdication, Wallis, should be punished and not rewarded, she took her case directly to the lawyer for the Crown, the Home Secretary Sir John Simon. Using an especially tortured line of reasoning, she got Sir John to argue that the title HRH should be borne only by members of the royal family in the line of succession, from which Edward's abdication had removed the Windsors and any descendants. Edward's own HRH appellation could be viewed as a gesture of generosity on the part of his brother, who as Fount of Honour was uniquely in a position to confer such a title.

"Is she a fit and proper person to become a Royal Highness after what she has done in the country; and would the country understand if she became one automatically on marriage?" was the mostly rhetorical question the new King put to Stanley Baldwin. Baldwin's own final act as PM was to pass on the question to his Cabinet and the Dominion Prime Ministers, whose negative response was comfortably predictable.

Edward and Wallis had to wait until 3 June 1937, after his brother's coronation, to say their vows at the Château de Candé near Tours, the Renaissance castle they'd been lent for the wedding. I had previously made it my business to travel to the Riviera on the pretext that I was "breaking it off" with Wallis before her marriage. She was good enough (and devious enough) to let me join a luncheon party given in their

honour. So I was right there when the
Duke's closest friend and associate, Walter
Monckton, having travelled from Britain to
France by plane, handed Edward a letter
from his brother George VI. It informed him
that an announcement would be published on
the eve of the marriage denying the royal
title to Wallis. It was the only wedding
gift the Duke of Windsor really esteemed
for his wife. Edward read the letter
standing up and was transfixed, as if
poleaxed. Then an oath burst from him:
"Damn them. Damn them all. I'll make them
pay for this." And he broke down in tears.
That night, the Duke called his brother one
last time to announce "my complete
estrangement from all of you."

Later that summer, when his youngest
brother, the Duke of Kent, sent the
Windsors a Fabergé box as a belated wedding
present, the Duke sent it back with a note.
"The only boxes I am collecting at present
are those that can be delivered on the
ears." The Duke was heard to say he would
one day "get back at all those swine, and
make them realise how disgustingly and
unsportingly they have behaved."

All along, Wallis had been more realistic. To a friend, she had written that the title would produce "a little extra chic." She had no illusions, though, about her standing with Queen Cookie. And the Duke made all their visitors plié to her anyway.

Not a single member of the royal family attended "the wedding of the century." The King's argument was that, as head of the Anglican Church, it would be hypocritical of him to attend the wedding of a divorced woman, a marriage that could never be countenanced by the Church. As for the Windsors' London friends, it was made clear to them that they had to choose: friendship with the former King or the current one. The wedding party, then, came down to Aunt Bessie; Monckton; Herman and Katherine Rogers, Wallis's American benefactors in Peking and, more recently, at the Villa Lou Viei; a couple of the lesser Rothschilds; Andrew, a deposed Greek prince who lived in Paris, with his wife and gawky fifteen-year-old son, Philip; and Charles and Fern Bedaux, owners of the Château de Candé.

An uninvited thought made Amy pause. She had so much to get done before her own "wedding of the century." First off, she had to come up with a maid of honor. How could she possibly choose among the Girls? Or a matron of honor . . . maybe Scott's mother. And she wouldn't mind having a few more wedding guests, maybe a couple of the lesser Rothschilds. Or, more likely, the Friday night pizza regulars from the history of art department. That meant invitations. And there'd have to be shoes to go with the dress and—

Suddenly, the whole ritual seemed ridiculous. Even the abrupt way Scott had asked her. What was it with men, anyway? They act totally uninterested in getting married for years and years, and then out of a clear blue sky . . .

She looked out her window again. The sky was anything but clear blue. If they had bad weather, it would probably be worse here in the tail of the plane. She decided to concentrate on the pages in front of her. Where had she left off? Oh, the wedding guests.

A little about the château's owner, this Charles Eugene Bedaux. He was a naturalised American millionaire of French origin, a well-built man with dark, brilliantined hair and prominent ears who habitually wore double-breasted jackets of the best cut, trousers with knife-sharp creases, and two-toned brogues. He was one of those men who had the ability to charm his way in or out of any situation, and his reputation as the kindly philanthropist friend of the Windsors had been very carefully stage-managed.

Known as the "Speed-Up King," he was the inventor of the Bedaux system, a management efficiency plan so ruthlessly successful it came to be lampooned by Charlie Chaplin in *Modern Times*. A factory owner would hire Bedaux to examine his production line and study the routine of his workers. Bedaux would then set new work rates for the staff according to a "formula" that rewarded workers who reached their quotas with small bonuses, penalizing or firing those who came up short. Production increased at minimal cost, and the factory bosses were delighted, even if the "time and motion" studies set the goals so high it was nearly impossible for the workers to achieve them. It was unexciting stuff, but it did present advantages for a man engaged in espionage for Germany.

By the very nature of Bedaux's business, he had access to a client's entire production scheme. He would use a camera with a specialized Bausch and Lomb Tessar $8\frac{1}{4}$ inch lens to photograph the factories where he was consulting and then reduce the photos to postcard size. His first postcards were of Belgian factories before World War I. After he resettled in the American Midwest, he did the same with plants that produced warplanes and munitions and with docks, airfields, Muskegon Naval Harbour, and an armoured car factory.

Fluent in English, French, and German, Bedaux set up efficiency companies throughout the Americas and Europe after the War. By far his most successful company was Deutsche Bedaux-Gesellschaft, thanks to his connections with Dr. Hjalmar Schacht, Director of the German Reichsbank, and Dr. Robert Ley, head of the German Labour Front (men who would one day sit side by side in the dock at Nuremberg). The way it worked by 1936 was that Schacht would impose the Bedaux system on a select group of industrialists, and Ley would make sure that labour in the plants concerned would not be allowed to dissent.

His contracts with Ford, General Motors, Du Pont, ITT, Standard Oil, and I. G. Farben meant Bedaux could keep luxurious apartments in New York's Chrysler Building and 1120 Fifth Avenue, at the Ritz in Paris and the Hotel Adlon in Berlin. At the top of a graceful sweep of marble stairs, the Adlon's room 106 directly overlooked the Brandenburg Gate and was across the road from the German Foreign Ministry and Hitler's brand-new Reich Chancellery. But it was only after the Duke's wedding that Charles Bedaux really began to endear himself to the Führer.

CHAPTER 26

PROVENANCE

Wallis and Edward (the shorthand *WE* had
been inscribed onto Wallis's wedding band)
returned to Paris after the honeymoon,
installing themselves in a suite of rooms
at the Hotel Meurice. Meanwhile, British

Intelligence had been tipped off that the
movie star Errol Flynn had sailed for
Europe on the *Queen Mary* carrying a bank
draft of $1.5 million, raised by Communist
and Loyalist sympathizers in Hollywood to
aid the Spanish government in Valencia
against Franco's forces. MI5 believed Flynn
meant to divert the money to the Irish
Republican Army, while the FBI thought
Flynn meant to double-cross the Loyalists
and hand the money over to Franco's
Falangists.

So two MI5 men and two from the FBI were
staking out Flynn at the Hotel Plaza-
Athénée when he jumped in a cab for the Gare
du Nord and boarded a train for Berlin. Who
met him at the station? Charles Bedaux.
Together, they travelled to the Kaiserhof
Hotel. While Washington and London were
trying to deduce what it meant, Flynn left
the hotel accompanied by two well-dressed
Germans with suitcases, who turned out to
be the Deputy Führer of the Third Reich,
Rudolf Hess, and Adolf Hitler's private
secretary, Martin Bormann. The three then
boarded the overnight express back to
Paris.

The agents followed Flynn, Hess, and Bormann to the Hotel Meurice, where they were shocked to find two more MI5 agents standing in the foyer. To their utter disbelief, the man the last two agents had been sent to guard, an immaculately dressed man of slight stature, sauntered down the grand staircase, reached out to Hess, and firmly shook his hand. He then shook hands with Bormann and Flynn and led them back upstairs to his suite. After several hours, the three visitors left, *without their suitcases.*

It was only after the war that I read Hess's personal report to his Führer, which said, "The Duke is proud of his German blood and is keenly interested in the development of the Reich. . . . There is no need to lose a single German life in a future invasion of Britain. Edward and his clever wife will deliver the goods." So it appears the Hollywood money became a down payment on services to be rendered. And that it went neither to Ireland nor to Spain but rather into the wide-open pockets of the Duke of Windsor.

In October, Charles Bedaux arranged for

the Windsors to be received by Hitler and the Nazi hierarchy in a full-blown state visit. The takeover of Austria was still six months away. Even so, relations between London and Berlin had grown increasingly frosty, to the degree that Edward and Wallis were warned against making the trip by British officials who worried what kind of signal it would send. The Duke and Duchess, who had no such worries, arrived at Berlin's Friedrichstrasse Station on Monday, 11 October 1937. They were greeted by a glittering array of Germany's new elite, among them Schacht, Ley, and Germany's new Foreign Minister, the omnipresent Joachim von Ribbentrop. To the Duke's delight, several hundred citizens rhythmically chanted, "Heil Windsor!" and "Heil Edward!"

A few interesting bits I learned about their trip: While Wallis would stay at the hotel and rest or shop, Edward toured factories and workers' housing in the company of high German officials. At night, dinner parties included Ribbentrop, Himmler, Hess, and Goebbels, whom Wallis described as "a wispy gnome with an

enormous skull." At all times, Wallis was
scrupulously bowed to and addressed as
"Your Royal Highness."

One afternoon, the Goerings invited them
to tea at the Air Minister's famous hunting
lodge, Karinhall, in the pretty Schorfheide
countryside thirty miles north of Berlin.
Emmy Goering was very much taken with
Wallis, saying later, "This woman would
certainly have cut a good figure on the
throne of England." Meanwhile her husband,
"Fat Hermann" in his huge white uniform,
had taken the Duke to see his well-equipped
gymnasium, the massive dining room that
could accommodate a hundred guests, and the
attic "playroom" that housed his nephew's
magnificent train set.

The Commander-in-Chief of the Luftwaffe
probably gave his hand away when he showed
the Duke how to employ a model aeroplane to
cross the playroom on wires and scatter
wooden bombs on the trains below. In
Goering's study, the Windsors were treated
to a glimpse of the future. On the wall
behind Hermann's desk was a large marquetry
map, showing most of Europe and Russia as a
German possession, the Greater Germany and

Reich. With the Austrian *Anschluss* still in
the offing, Edward asked him, "Isn't that a
little impertinent? A little premature?"
"It is fated," Goering replied with a
shrug. "It must be." (In the plebiscite the
next year, the Austrians voted 99.75
percent to join Greater Germany.) After
the Windsors had left, Goering stared out
of the French doors to the estate's lake
and its brand-new boathouse and mused to
his wife, "The natural opposition between
British and German policy could easily
be set aside with such a man as the
Duke."

A few days later, the Windsors attended a
political rally in Düsseldorf, organised as
a folk and craft exhibition through the
Reich's Strength Through Joy program.
Wallis sent me a few snaps she took of the
event. They show Edward, flanked by an
SS guard of honour, wandering about looking
at the textile weaving and quaint floral
wreaths made to look like swastikas. In
one, he is clearly returning the Nazi
salute. Back in London, government alarm at
the Duke's behaviour was such that all
photographs and newsreels of the visit to

the exhibition were cut or doctored to take out any of the offending salutes.

I was in the cinema when they showed one such newsreel. The censor must have ordered a last-minute change because the film literally jumped out of its sprockets where an edit had been made, just as the Duke was about to greet a delegation of Hitler Youth. We had to wait an eternity for the projectionist to put things right.

By the time the Windsors' tour reached Leipzig, the former King was completely comfortable flinging out his right arm at dramatic moments. In returning the adulation of the four thousand Germans who greeted him at the train station, Edward said, "I have travelled the world, and my upbringing has made me familiar with the great achievements of mankind. But that which I have seen in Germany, I had hitherto believed to be impossible. It cannot be grasped, and is a miracle; one can only begin to understand it when one realizes that behind it all is one man and one will . . ."

On 22 October 1937, the Windsors arrived by train at Obersalzberg, where a car took

them on a visit to Lake Königsee. At 2:30
exactly they were driven up the
mountainside, followed by three carloads of
detectives and SS men. Hitler stood waiting
at the bottom of a flight of steps. He was
dressed in the brown jacket of a Nazi party
official, black pants, and patent leather
shoes. It took Wallis all of ten minutes to
take the measure of the man. Afterwards, in
a rather indiscreet letter I must admit was
opened and passed around to great delight
among the men of British Intelligence,
Wallis wrote to Aunt Bessie, "Mr. Hitler
does not care for women."

Dominating the entrance hall was a
portrait of Bismarck. Passing between a
double row of tall, muscular, fair-haired
guards, Edward and Wallis followed their
host down three marble steps to a huge
reception room that looked out on the
sloping green meadows and snowy peak of the
Untersberg. There was a great marble
fireplace, tapestries of soldiers on white
chargers from the period of Frederick the
Great, a cherry red carpet, and matching
red marble tabletops. As I heard it from
Wallis, the conversation began with the

Duke saying, "The German and the British races are one. They should *always* be one, as they are both of Hun origin." Wallis slyly told me, "I fear he was forgetting the Norman Conquest."

While tea was being prepared, Hitler showed off his house and gardens, pointing out Salzburg from one of the balconies. They spoke of the comparative working conditions of Welsh and German miners, boring Wallis to distraction. After tea, the men retired for a private forty-minute conversation while the Duchess was given a tour of the grounds. Wallis regretted that protocol had prevented Eva Braun from being invited to join them. She was sure they had a lot to talk about.

Five years later, over dinner with the American oilman J. Paul Getty, the Duke was asked if the Führer had been receptive to his ideas. "Yes, I think so. The way was open, ever so slightly, for further progress. Had there been any proper follow-through in London or Paris, millions of lives might have been saved." Getty took this to mean the Duke had proposed a permanent peace with Germany and the mass emigration of Jews, rather than their extermination. Wallis told me the Duke had also proposed things even a King would not have been in a position to deliver: to meet Germany's colonial needs, he suggested ceding the northern part of Australia to German settlement, thereby creating "a powerful shield for British interests against Japanese incursion."

CHAPTER 27

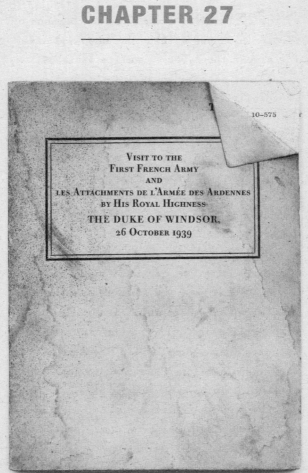

10–575

VISIT TO THE
FIRST FRENCH ARMY
AND
LES ATTACHMENTS DE L'ARMÉE DES ARDENNES
BY HIS ROYAL HIGHNESS
THE DUKE OF WINDSOR,
26 OCTOBER 1939

<u>PROVENANCE</u>

By the fall of 1939, the Duke and Duchess of Windsor had done nothing but shop and dine for almost three years. Wallis was a regular at several couturier salons, especially Mainbocher, and the couple maintained house accounts at, among other places, Cartier and Van Cleef & Arpels. At night, they held elaborate dinner parties at their new home at 24 Boulevard Suchet in the *seizième arrondissement* near the Bois de Boulogne—when they weren't the star couple at other peoples' parties or travelling to the Riviera.

Adolf Hitler, on the other hand, had been a busy little bee. The Condor Legion of the Luftwaffe had bombed Republican Spain throughout 1937, obliterating the town of Guernica in the process. In March of '38 Hitler had swallowed Austria, followed by Czechoslovakia twelve months later (Munich treaty or no Munich treaty). In late summer of 1939, he had Ribbentrop negotiate a nonaggression pact with Stalin, freeing him to mass his troops on the Polish border.

I have it straight from one of the

servants that on 3 September, Edward was
called from the swimming pool at their
rented Villa la Croe in Antibes for a
telephone call. "Great Britain has declared
war on Germany," he informed Wallis on his
return. "I'm afraid in the end this may
open the way for world Communism." With
that, the ex-King of England executed a
neat swan dive into the pool.

The next six months of military buildup—
after Poland had disappeared into the
Greater Reich—was called the Phony War by
the Americans and the Sitzkrieg by the
Germans. To Wallis it was the Bore War. The
draft had scooped up most of the young men
who drove the trucks that brought the
flowers and meat and fish to Paris, who cut
the fabric in the back rooms of the couture
houses and set the gems for the *joailliers*,
who laid the tables and opened the doors
for the privileged. The Windsors were not
accustomed to doing for themselves.

The Duke, formerly Commander-in-Chief of
His Majesty's Armed Forces and still a
commissioned officer in his brother's army,
was offered the job of Deputy Regional
Commissioner for Wales (you will recall he

had once been the Prince of Wales). So with
the cairn terriers Pookie, Prizzie, and
Detto, he motored with Wallis and Fruity
Metcalfe to Cherbourg, to be picked up by
HMS *Kelly* and deposited at Portsmouth.
Winston by now was First Lord of the
Admiralty and had managed to lay on a guard
of honour, in tin hats and gas masks, and a
Royal Marine band at the dock. But at the
end of the red carpet stood just two
figures, Walter Monckton and Fruity's wife,
Lady Alexandra. No royal escort or member
of the royal family; no message of welcome
from Bertie or even a royal car.

As Monckton drove them away from the
Portsmouth quayside that September night,
Edward exploded to Wallis, "The short
version, by God!"

"The short version of what?" Wallis
wanted to know.

" 'God Save the King.' The monarch gets
the full treatment, other royalty only the
first six bars. I'd become rather used to
the full treatment."

Meanwhile, the King had been made to
realise that, in Cardiff, his brother would
be within easy reach of London and the

still-substantial group of appeasers there.
So the Welsh offer was withdrawn, and
Edward was appointed Liaison Officer to the
British Military Mission to the French GHQ,
which meant an almost instant return to
France.

Over the next three months, the Duke was
given unparalleled access to the Maginot
Line, the much-vaunted defence system
designed to shield France from German
attack. By day, he would tour each sector,
starting with the First Army Group under
General Billotte, immediately to the right
of the British Field Forces around Lille,
and then each army in turn, ending in the
hook where the Maginot Line turned south.
In the evening, he and his aide would write
up detailed reports on the strengths and
weaknesses he found and have them posted to
London.

Had Chamberlain or the War Office
regarded Edward as anything other than a
nuisance they were glad to be rid of, they
never would have countenanced the kind of
comment an anonymous analyst scribbled on
the first one to arrive at headquarters:
"This report by HRH the Duke of

Windsor . . . you will not, I think, want to
read it." It did, though, make very
interesting reading in Berlin.

Two days after Christmas the Dutch
military attaché in Berlin happened to be
carrying a note from his ambassador to the
Reich Chancellery. He recognized Charles
Bedaux getting out of a Luftwaffe staff car
and, having met him before, approached with
the intention of speaking with him. Bedaux
had a gift-wrapped package under his arm
and waved the man away. Then he gave the
Nazi salute to someone in the car and
hurried up the steps into the Chancellery.
Strange behaviour for a neutral American,
even a naturalised one like Bedaux. The
next morning Paul Thummel, our Agent 54
inside the Abwehr, reported that fresh
information had been received the day
before "by courier" concerning the military
preparedness of the French army all along
the Maginot Line. He told us it was "inside
stuff, meticulous in detail and exhaustive
in scope."

Coincidentally, the Duke's various
reports to British GHQ in London had been
meticulous in detail and exhaustive in

scope, had anyone chosen to read them. Here
are a few excerpts of what Hitler received:

"The front line consists of a belt of
1500 to 2000 yards in depth, with a series
of blockhouses sloped toward the line of
attack. These block-houses have only
lateral fire with a very narrow
traverse. . . . There is a periscope for
observation, the top of which projects
through a movable steel cupola which
appeared vulnerable and was very
conspicuous. No anti-gas arrangements as
regards the loop-holes were visible. The
wire entanglement running through the woods
is held in place by stakes no better than
broomsticks."

I was slaving away at my job in room 39
for Naval Intelligence when the Duke's
report on the defences around Dunkerque
(Dunkirk, in English) crossed my desk. A
copy had been sent us because the sixty-
eighth Division of the BEF, responsible for
the coastal sector just north of the French
Seventh Army, was technically under
Admiralty command.

"The defence of the coast will require
low areas to be flooded, which will take a

minimum of six days and a maximum of
fifteen to fill to a depth of two feet. It
cannot be said that this front is ready to
withstand attack by armoured vehicles."

Edward concluded his report on the French
Ninth Army under General Corap, opposite
the Ardennes forest, by writing, "During
this tour of the front line sector, there
were very few troops to be seen, only one
company of infantry on the march being
passed. It is the strong belief of the
General Staff that the Ardennes will be
impassable to the German army."

Doubtless, the Duke of Windsor viewed his
actions in an honourable light. He was one
of many who believed that if Hitler gave
the British army "a bloody nose" at the
war's outset, Chamberlain's government
would fall and the ensuing armistice would
permit Germany to turn everything it had
against Bolshevik Russia—destroying the
greatest threat to world peace and saving
Western Europe from the horrors of modern
warfare.

However one chooses to view the ex-King's
actions, we British would soon lose our

toehold on the Continent. And the French
would lose Paris, with the rest of France
to follow. I was sure it was all due to the
Duke's treachery and was itching to give
him a bloody nose. But we couldn't prove a
thing. At least, not yet.

CHAPTER 28

This time the turbulence was all too real. The first jolt of weather made the bottom drop out of Amy's stomach. Each succeeding blast had the plane seesawing through the air. In row 39 it felt as if some enormous dog were shaking them like a chew toy.

In the row ahead, a young mother had been surreptitiously nursing her baby in the window seat. The airplane blanket fell to the floor with the first dip of the plane and now the baby was crying. Also crying, more from terror than hunger, was the woman's little girl sitting on the aisle.

Amy could see a corner of the blanket under the woman's seat next to her black computer bag. She unbuckled her seat belt and leaned down, snagging the blanket and pulling it toward her. Then she shook it out quickly and leaned between the seats in front of her. "Here. I think you're going to need this."

"Oh, thank you so much," the woman said. "You're too kind."

The moment she covered her baby with the blanket, his crying stopped. The daughter was a different story. She was eight or possibly nine and very frightened. As Amy leaned back into her own seat, she heard the mother say, "It'll be all right, Samantha. Think of this as something exciting to put in your diary."

Just then the plane bucked and reared another time. One of the overhead bins flew open and the man in the aisle seat across from Samantha half got up and made a nice one-handed catch of someone's carry-on before it hit anyone.

The word *diary* had started Amy thinking. Who had been talking about a diary recently? She herself had never kept— Scott. On the phone yesterday at her hotel, hadn't he said something like "take care of yourself and the diary"? Strange. Amy was pretty sure she had called *Provenance* an unpublished manuscript by Ian Fleming. Wouldn't anyone hearing that have thought it was a novel?

Amy leaned back in her seat and refastened her seat belt. Next to her, Sheridan was lying back, openmouthed in the seat next to her, his meaty arm hogging the armrest and his shoulder leaning into hers. A lot of good the CIA was in a crisis.

CHAPTER 29

Paris, December 23, 1939

Dear Aunt Bessie,

This man is going to be the death of me.

Mrs. Bessie Merryman
c/o The Sherry-Netherland Hotel
781 Fifth Avenue
New York, New York

PROVENANCE

Just before Christmas of 1939, Wallis wrote her Aunt Bessie a letter. Although our agreement with Mrs. Merryman was that she

would be Wallis's American controller, in
practice it took too long for information
to go from the Duchess to Aunt Bessie to the
FBI to British Intelligence. So we simply
diverted directly to MI6 any mail she
posted and read it before resealing the
envelope and sending it on its way.

Her letter read,

> This man is going to be the death
> of me. I have to tell you what he
> did all day yesterday. Instead of
> helping me wrap the servants'
> presents, he holed himself up in the
> library writing and muttering to
> himself—in German, no less!

> As you know, my brain is like
> that cluttered attic of yours,
> stuffed with all sorts of odd things
> I can't seem to get rid of, my high
> school German vocabulary among them—
> or at least the easy bits. The thing
> is, one of the phrases I heard Dukey
> repeat over and over was "der
> Seelöwe." Well, that's simply "see,"
> which in English is "sea," and
> "löwe," meaning "lion." (I always

thought it queer that the king of
beasts should have such a "lowly"
name.) But I do prattle on. Edward
was repeating the German word for
"sea lion." He seemed to be highly
wrought. I tried to change his mood
by assuring him no sea lions had
been sighted in Paris recently. And
if there were any, they knew better
than to show up on Christmas. No
smile, nothing. He just looked at me
queerly and kept on. We were
expected at the Bedauxs for dinner,
so I let it drop.

Well, we had a lovely dinner—
their man can poach a fish like no
one on the Right Bank, though I
thought the consommé would have been
"peppier" with the least sliver of
truffle—and decided to open our
Christmas presents early. Charles
and Fern gave us one of those new
gizmos for telephone numbers, where
you press a letter of the alphabet
and the lid springs open to the
right page. They had me press B, and
I found their names and number

already written in. Clever. Edward
gave them our gift from the little
leather hold-all he carries around:
a simple ballotin from La Maison du
Chocolat, done up in that gay red
and gold paper we found in that shop
on Madison Avenue. You remember.

Later, after the servants had
brought our coffees, the men
absented themselves an
unconscionable twenty minutes. Fern
and I used the time to put the
finishing touches on the big party
coming up at our house this weekend.
When they returned, Charles had what
looked to be another present under
his arm, the size and shape of a
Paris telephone book. And it was
wrapped in the same red and gold
paper as our gift! It was definitely
the same paper—I could see where the
creases had been. Even stranger,
Charles was folding a handwritten
letter again and again horizontally.
It made a seven-inch by one-inch
packet, which he put away in the
breast pocket of his sports jacket

(the loud one you detest). I knew it was the letter E. had been laboring over; it was on that cream paper I got for him last year. Anyway, I had the fleeting thought, absurd really, that the folded letter would fit exactly in the hatband of Charles's fedora. Re-used wrapping paper and a folded letter. You see the state I'm in?

Anyway, it was after eleven and we had to say our good-byes. Edward surprised me by standing up and draining the last of his cognac with the words, "To the British Lion!" That sort of cheap patriotism is so unlike him. Well, damned if Charles didn't repeat the gesture and add, "Yes, to the Sea Lion!" You see, all that time E. must have been helping Charles wrap presents and bending the poor man's ear about those sea creatures. So, never one to miss a chance for a remark, I raised my coffee cup and did my own toast: "To the British Christmas Seals!" From the silence, you'd have thought I'd

stepped on the Magna Carta or
something. At least Fern laughed.

I think Edward needs a hobby, I
really do. Between the German and
the 'pipes, I'm going mad. I write
this holding the ear clips he gave
me for my birthday, with the rubies
and diamonds. One day I shall write
a book on the restorative powers of
jewelry.

> Affectionately yours,
> Wallis.

At any other time I probably would have
consigned the above message to the circular
bin. But we had received a briefing just
days before from our Berlin agent, Paul
Thummel. He told us Hitler had that week
approved a code name for the projected
invasion of England. It was to be Operation
Seelöwe.

CHAPTER 30

Joie et paix, 1939

GRAND QUARTIER GÉNÉRAL
DES ARMÉES FRANÇAISES

Avec mes vœux très respectueux,

Colonel Petibon,

Noël 1939

<u>PROVENANCE</u>

In 1939 the Duke had put his military responsibilities on hold for the holiday season. His only official act was to request that his cook—drafted as an infantryman into the French army with the commencement of hostilities—be reassigned to "the Duke's mess" (i.e., back to his Paris kitchen). The request was denied. As for me, my French had got me assigned to our Paris Embassy as a member of the brand-spanking-new 30 Assault Unit. By day I trained the clerks there on how to dispose of sensitive documents in a moment's notice should the Germans invade. At night I was *absolument libre* and available to accept the Windsors' invitation to their Christmas Eve fête.

As I made my way across the *seizième arrondissement* to the Boulevard Suchet, the streetlights were just coming on all over Paris. Meanwhile, they were going out across the Continent. In just ninety days, Poland had gone the way of Austria and Czechoslovakia and completely disappeared—the western half into the Greater German

Reich while the eastern Poles were given over to their historic enemies, the Russians. Franco was triumphant in Spain and Mussolini equally so in Africa and the Balkans. In the East, the Japanese warlords were moving from one success to another in their ambition to create a "Greater East Asia Co-Prosperity Sphere." And it would be another two years before Franklin Roosevelt, who would win a third term in office with the slogan "He Kept Us Out of War," could swing America to the Allies.

In the spring, the Germans would overrun the Low Countries and then wheel through the "impassable" Ardennes forest to kill two birds with one enormous sledgehammer: threaten Paris by breaking through the Maginot Line in the very sector Edward had so obligingly pinpointed in his reports, and trap the 350,000-man British Expeditionary Forces between the advancing Wehrmacht and the sea at Dunkirk.

But tonight, the Windsors' party would be a grand affair. With every light ablaze, the house glittered like a Christmas tree. There was the tinkling of

a piano, the groaning of bagpipes (Edward
loved nothing better than to put on his
ceremonial kilt and parade through a party
blowing into his "pipes" and wreaking
havoc), and the laughter of thirty very
select guests. Wallis had somehow put her
hands on hundreds of orchids, lilies, and
white chrysanthemums and several pounds of
foie gras. Noël Coward was called on to
sing his ever-popular "Mad Dogs and
Englishmen" and, later in the evening, to
sing it again, this time accompanied by
Maurice Chevalier. I could have done
without the off-key caterwauling of the
vaguely familiar-looking and very tipsy
young man in a British Navy uniform who
made it a trio. Or the tiresome English
ritual of wearing silly-looking party
hats. Mine was a particularly loud shade
of pink.

Despite the war, everyone agreed, the
party was a great success. Charles Bedaux
and his wife had joined the merrymakers.
He now carried an American passport but
gave everyone to understand he had been a
French soldier wounded in the Great War.
At one point I saw him off in a corner in

ardent conversation with General Sikorski
of the Free Polish Forces, headquartered
at Fort Vaux. Later I was pulled aside by
our number two man, Sir Richard Howard-
Vyse.

"Ian, have you been watching that Bedaux
fellow? He just asked Sikorski what he
thought of Fort Vaux. Apparently he served
there in the Great War and thought it had
been too badly damaged to be used again."
Howard-Vyse was in rather a state. "No one
is supposed to know the Poles are at Vaux.
Surely the point is, the Duke must have
told him."

I thought over what he said, but I
suppose I didn't look agitated enough to
suit him because he went right on. "This
begs the serious question, is HRH's value
to us outweighed by his inability to keep a
confidence? I'll have to inform Command
that we've come across this American. Or
shall I leave you to do it?"

Putting a calming hand on his shoulder, I
said, "Let me handle it."

I watched Bedaux like a hawk for the rest
of the evening, but he was very good at
acting Mr. Hail-Fellow-Well-Met (although

the experience taught me that evil people still look evil in Christmas party hats). His exit had its comical moments. When the servant was slow to retrieve Bedaux's snap-brim fedora, he announced he would find it for himself. When he reemerged from the walk-in closet, he had two hats: his own and a Navy officer's cap. *"J'ai ton chapeau, Philip,"* he said, and the tall young naval officer who had so badly harmonized with Coward and Chevalier stepped forward. As a jest, Bedaux gave "Philip" his own fedora and put the young man's headgear on himself. In English he announced, "These party hats never fit," before swapping them back.

As I said, it was a very successful party, especially as Bedaux's *Vaux pas* led us to finally put a tail on him. Had we not, we would never have known about the scrap of paper Blunt and I had to grab from the Hesse family at the end of the war.

CHAPTER 31

Paris, den 25. Dezember 1939

reicher Reise zurück, die mich nach

gelang es mir, einige interessante

zeitlich habe ich mit die Freiheit

Bekannten, Herrn B., meinen

kaum in der Lage die strategische

tionen genügend zu betonen, weshalb

gemeinsamen Freund alles im Detail zu

begrüsse ich Ihre Pläne für die Zukunft und

zur Verfügung stehen, die Führung

men, nachdem die Feind

Seelöwe Erfolg gegönnt war.

wie bisher, zur Seite stehen.

<u>PROVENANCE</u>

It's one thing, in peacetime, to disagree with the foreign policy of one's own government. It's quite another to give "aid and comfort" to the enemy in time of war. Any ordinary Englishman who did so would expect to be hanged. Or, if the courts were feeling especially lenient, shot. Edward, HRH the Duke of Windsor, clearly expected to be crowned.

To accuse a member of the British royal family of treason, one needs what Conan Doyle called "the smoking pistol." We wouldn't get such a pistol for another sixteen months. And then it would literally fall out of the sky.

On Saturday night, 10 May 1941, the Deputy Führer of the Nazi Party of Germany, Rudolf Hess, bailed out of his specially fitted-out Messerschmitt Me-110 into a field at Floors Farm, Eaglesham, Scotland. The flames from the crash of his plane were visible eight miles away at Dungavel, the ancestral home of the Duke of Hamilton. The Duke was conveniently not receiving visitors (being held in temporary custody nearby), but we were. By "we" I mean myself and a handful of officers from the various intelligence services, a detachment of the Argyll and Sutherland Highlanders Home Guard, and RAF officers from Turnhouse and Abbotsinch, near Glasgow.

The Hess flight was the first great sting operation of the war. We had discovered that Adolf Hitler planned to attack the Soviet Union in June of 1941. Winston personally gave Uncle Joe the nod, but Stalin rightly distrusted us as much as he did the Germans, and nothing came of the information. But Hitler's plan required a cessation of hostilities with Britain so he could throw the full weight of his armies against Russia. The "bloody nose" hadn't worked in 1940; now he tried to get through diplomacy what he couldn't take with arms. (And it must have seemed a delicious irony that he might arrange a nonaggression pact with us to use against his then-current partner in nonaggression.) So Rudolf Hess, with Hitler's approval, started a correspondence with the fourteenth Duke of Hamilton, Scotland's preeminent peer.

As the Marquess of Clydesdale, Hamilton

had been one of the British pilots who first flew over Everest in 1933. Hess, a Great War "Knight of the Air" himself, one who had been shot down in 1918 and had survived a Rumanian soldier's bullet to the chest, had caused Clydesdale's *The Pilot's Book of Everest* to be translated into German and made mandatory reading in Germany's aviation schools. Now, believing he was in contact with "a fellow internationalist and peace lover," Hess wrote Hamilton suggesting a meeting in neutral Lisbon to discuss a "comprehensive peace plan"—the condition being that a member of the royal family, possibly Edward's youngest brother, the Duke of Kent, attend as a proof of English good faith.

Sadly, good faith was in short supply in 1941. We discovered that Hess would suggest a twenty-five-year mutual nonaggression treaty with us, if only Winston Churchill were removed from office and the "warmaking" George VI ceded the throne back to his older brother. The carrot they dangled was that, in return, the Junkers in the officer corps would

guarantee the removal of Hitler as
Chancellor of Germany.

You can imagine what Winston made of
such an offer, especially when Agent 54,
shortly before he was captured by the
Germans, told us Hitler had signed off
personally on every detail of the plan.
Deception can be a two-way street, and it
was in this case. We had taken over the
correspondence from Hamilton weeks before
Hess suggested the Lisbon meeting. With
the pretext that the Duke of Kent could not
risk leaving the British Isles, we lured
Hess into a solo flight to Scotland,
ostensibly to parley with Kent, Hamilton,
and other pro-German aristocrats at
Dungavel. We'd even stand down the usual
RAF coastal defences to make the flight
easier. Hess fell for it lock, stock, and
barrel.

It was after eleven when an airplane
approached from the east and circled
directly over my head as I stood in the
West of Scotland Signals HQ. Then it
headed off towards the west coast before
returning and circling twice more. On the
second pass the engine cut out and the

pilot parachuted to safety into a farmer's field. We jumped into a car and drove towards the fireball that showed us where the plane had crashed.

The usual accounts of the next two hours have assorted locals and ragtag members of the Royal Observer Corps, drawn by the flaming wreckage, dropping by, chatting up the Deputy Führer, and offering him tea. Not quite. As the designated German-speaking debriefer, I had half an hour with the man in the tiny bedroom of the ploughman's cottage before any locals got a word in edgewise.

Hess sat down in a chair by the fire and spoke to me in a slightly accented German that I later learned was as a result of his growing up in the German colony of Alexandria, Egypt. His first words were "My name is Hauptmann Alfred Horn. I am on a special mission (*der Sonderauftrag*). Please tell the Duke of Hamilton I have arrived."

In the interest of honesty, I told him he was not Alfred Horn but Walter Richard Rudolf Hess, deputy party leader and the third-ranking government official in Nazi Germany. And then, in the interest of dishonesty, I told him I was the Duke of Hamilton's personal representative. It was as easy as that. He handed me two letters. Or rather, one and a half letters. The first was addressed to Hamilton with a suggested agenda for the "peace conference" he was still expecting to attend. The other was the fragment of a handwritten note that I have included above. It was torn down the left side and bore neither the name of the addressee nor the writer's signature.

Hess explained. "When you hand this half of a letter to your master, please say that the person to whom it was originally written retains the other half. At the successful conclusion of this peace conference, and the formation of the new British government that is to follow, the left side of the letter will be returned as well."

As that son of Scotland Robert Burns once put it, "The best-laid schemes o' mice and men / Gang aft a-gley; And leave us naught but grief and pain / For promised joy." I took the torn, crème-coloured note carefully from Hess and placed it in my satchel. Then I just as carefully handed

Hess over to the Home Guards. I'm afraid he never did attend that "peace conference."

In translation, the fragment of the letter I took from Hess reads:

from an eventful trip to the
I managed to hear some interesting
since taken the liberty
acquaintance Mr. B. my
cannot stress enough the strategic
our common friend in such great detail in
find your ideas for the future welcome
available, the interrupted stewardship
upon the end of hostilities
and the success of Sea Lion.
Mr. B. acts for me

Garbled? Of course. But the handwriting is the Duke of Windsor's, he was obviously passing some information to a German reader, and it's clear he knew about "Seelowe" when no one else but the enemy did.

The next day I personally put that torn bit of paper into Winston Churchill's hands. I was impertinent enough to ask what he intended to do with it. He said straight out, "We'll let the King decide. It's his brother."

Why not just scoop up the Duke and sweat the truth out of him? Unfortunately, by 1941 the Duke and Duchess had already been scooped up (ahead of the advancing enemy) and deposited thousands of miles away in the Bahamas as the new Governor-General and wife. Winston had given the order and Bertie had signed it because neither man had wanted the couple to pop up in Berlin, flapping their gums. And neither man now wanted to explain to anyone—not even the Bahamians—precisely what kind of man was living in Nassau's Government House. So I presumed that Winston gave the King the incriminating missive we'd taken from Hess and that no more would be said about it.

The exiled Windsors' war would be a comfortable one of whitewashed villas and golden sands, punctuated by clothing drive luncheons and lavish dinner parties in "the St. Helena of the Caribbean," as Wallis put it. By summer's end of 1945 they would be back in Paris at Boulevard Suchet, their home miraculously untouched by five long years of German occupation.

CHAPTER 32

The *ping* Amy heard was the signal it was time to fasten her seat belt for landing. They had left the bad weather behind them over the Atlantic, and she had been engrossed in Ian Fleming's tale for more than two hours. There were several chapters to go, and the flight attendants were collecting the glasses and trays.

She'd have been done by now if her mind hadn't kept wandering to the flaming wreck of a car on a Dublin street. Who'd want to get their hands on *Provenance* enough to kill for it? If Fleming was to be believed, there was the royal family, for starters. In the eyes of his people, Edward's treason might be the straw that would break the present-day Windsors' backs. Especially with Princess Diana gone and Charles remarried to his own divorcée. Or did it have something to do with Churchill? He'd dismissed a peace mission out of hand, hadn't he? And that was well before North Africa and the Italian campaign and D-Day had cost so many lives.

And what about the other side, people who'd kill

to make sure the story got out? You could start with neo-Nazis, bent on reworking Hitler into a classic German politician—one who was ahead of his time in trying to defeat "the evil empire" before Reagan gave it the name. Well, you couldn't be named Greenberg and think *that* idea was gonna fly. Or maybe the surviving members of Rudolf Hess's family. He'd made a dangerous flight across the channel on a mission of peace (even if it was to be a dictated one), and it had all been a ruse by British intelligence. They'd have plenty of reasons to get Fleming's story out. Or even, how about some leftover Communists who might want the world to know how elements of the English nobility had secretly worked to help Germany defeat the Russians?

The little girl, Samantha, in row 38 was kneeling on her seat, trying to get Amy's attention. "I have a journal. Wanna see?"

Relieved to be taken out of her thoughts for the moment, Amy leaned forward to look at the girl's diary. Samantha tried to hand it back to her but dropped it instead at Amy's feet. Picking it up, Amy could see there were crayon drawings on some of the pages. She was just about to tell Samantha about her own day planner and its drawings when she realized she couldn't sit back in her seat again. Something big and bulky was digging into her back.

It was Sheridan. When she had leaned forward, the big man slid all the way to his left, so his torso was actually behind Amy. Time for his wake-up call. In frustration, she half turned in her seat.

In death, his skin was gray and his lips were blue. Sheridan's mouth had fallen open, and a white spittle was coming out of it. It was wetting Amy's back, right in the middle. Of course she screamed.

CHAPTER 33

The last call from Delta flight 106 before its final approach to New York's JFK Airport reached a one-time-use cell phone on the ground in New York.

"We have a problem." Siobhan Farrell's Irish-accented voice on the phone was lowered, as if she were speaking where others could hear.

The mobile phone's owner felt his temper rise. Lord save us from the amateurs. "Don't say 'we,' " he told her. "Say, 'There is a problem.' "

"Okay, there is a problem . . . that we have."

He tried to keep the anger out of his voice. "I know that, or you wouldn't be calling. Damage?"

"Just one."

What did they teach them at flight attendant school—stupidity? "Which one?"

"Him. Permanent damage."

"And her?"

"No damage."

It didn't make sense. Airline food, what there was

of it, was bad. But who doesn't take a single bite? "And the material?"

There were loud voices behind her on the phone. He distinctly heard a loud male voice say, "Row thirty-nine."

She finally answered. "She still has it."

"Well, can you get it?"

"I'll have to improvise."

What he wanted was to tell her to improvise a way to jump out of the plane and kill herself, so he could save himself the trouble of going out to her pathetic apartment near the airport and doing it there. What he said was "You're still landing on schedule?"

"We're dropping wheels now. Luckily the guy's in the back row, so we'll be able to exit the passengers—"

"And the bracelet?" he asked impatiently. This woman really got his Irish up.

"First thing I did. We're in the clear."

There was that "we" again. He tried counting to ten.

After a few seconds, she said, "You still there?" Her voice had its own irritation now. "Look, I have to go. What do you want me to do?"

"Get the package. And leave the rest to me."

He clicked off. No one in the terminal saw the man drop his cell phone in the trash.

CHAPTER 34

The chaos had begun with Amy's scream. Within seconds, all the people sitting around her had pressed their flight attendant call buttons, and the din of the resultant *ping*ing just added to the confusion. A dentist two rows ahead of her had been the first medical professional to prod and poke James Sheridan. An Irish gynecologist pulled rank on him and then, when the furor had reached the front of the plane, a New York cardiologist strode back from business class. Siobhan Farrell accompanied him all the way to row 39, ineffectually suggesting he return to his seat.

For several minutes, no one paid any attention to Amy, trapped next to the window, her hysteria building. Finally, the black flight attendant clasped both hands around the dead man's wrist and pulled his bulk off Amy. A tall man with a blond brush cut finally identified himself as a federal sky marshal and persuaded most of the passengers to return to their seats.

Right then, Amy pretty much stopped thinking. Like one of those motorized toys that runs into a wall, grinding its gears and getting nowhere, Amy's mind kept insisting to herself that Scott, the original before-all-the-doubts Scott, was going to walk onto the plane any minute now and rescue her from this nightmare. That they were still several hundred feet over Long Island on the glide path to JFK didn't make any difference: she needed him to be here, take her into his arms, and make everything else just go away.

The pilot came on the intercom. "Folks, as many of you know, we've had a medical emergency in the second cabin. Air traffic control has cleared us for an immediate landing. Flight attendants, please prepare for landing and cross-check."

Amy heard it, but the only thing that registered was "cross-check." What was cross-check? Her brain had shifted from Blank into Numb. If she just thought stupid thoughts and kept looking out the window as the ground came up toward them, it might be possible to block out the fact that she was sitting next to a large, gray, drooling dead man. A man who was supposed to have been protecting her.

Hands reached in and fastened her seat belt for her. Hands shoved her carry-on things under the seat in front of her and took her still uncleared-away lunch tray along with Sheridan's. Hands with long graceful fingers; a black woman's hands.

Almost immediately the plane bumped down a couple of times on the tarmac and the air brakes came on. Despite another announcement from the cockpit about keeping their seats, panicked passengers were already in the aisle, grabbing their bags as Delta flight 106 taxied to the gate.

When the plane finally rolled to a halt, Amy could see the Jetway swinging out to meet them. Now it was a woman's voice on the intercom, with a broad midwestern accent. "Deplaning passengers are requested to follow the instructions of Airport Security upon leaving the Jetway. Due to our"—she paused for just a moment—"to our medical emergency, authorities have requested that you be detained for a short period of time. We apologize in advance for any inconvenience." This last sentence was all but drowned out by the groans from the passengers, which only grew louder as the woman went on to say, "Delta Airlines recognizes that you had a choice of air carriers today. And we appreciate your choosing Delta. Oh, and welcome to New York."

It took an agonizingly long time for the line of passengers to shamble toward the exit. When the aisle had cleared enough for her to get out, Amy climbed over the dead man's body without looking at him. It was too awful. His lifeless legs were splayed under the row of seats ahead and she didn't dare step on him. Now to get her stuff. Leaning back across Sheridan's body and keeping her eyes toward the front of the plane, she reached under the seat and gathered up her things.

Just ahead of her, Siobhan Farrell, blocked by the bottleneck of coach passengers, was waiting impatiently for the aisle to clear so she could make her way up to the galley with the two stacked lunch trays she was holding. Amy followed her up the aisle.

You're *supposed* to miss a lot when your mind's on Numb. Amy missed the detective getting on the plane. She became aware of his presence when he stopped the tall black hostess just before she reached the galley. "Sorry, ma'am, but what's with the trays?"

She looked a little flustered to Amy. "Just clearing up."

The look on the man's face said a black person with an Irish brogue didn't compute. "Sorry. Nobody clears anything until the ME gets here."

The flight attendant tried to push past him. "I have a job to do."

"Me too. Sorry." Lt. Gerard Pinsky of the New York Police Department/JFK Division—according to the badge clipped to his suit jacket pocket—was the kind of short, stocky man who would have looked at home behind a deli counter. So far he was three for three on sentences with the word "Sorry." That might have been all Amy would know about him if he hadn't put his two hands on the food trays and wrested them away from the determined Ms. Farrell. As he did so, he loosened her grip and inadvertently tilted the trays just enough so the thing that had been wedged between them dropped onto the bulkhead seat.

It was Amy's manuscript.

"What's this?" Detective Pinsky was looking at Siobhan Farrell, who was already saying, "One of the passengers must have forgotten—" when Amy interrupted her.

"It's mine." Amy shifted a little toward the other woman. "You saw me reading it. Twice. Once in business and once back there."

"I'm sorry, Dr. Greenberg. I served a lot of people today. In the confusion . . ." She really was an awful liar.

Pinsky shifted his focus to Amy. His eyes were two different shades of brown. "And you—you're a medical doctor?"

"Ph.D. Dr. Amy Greenberg." Her voice sounded like a croak. There was no air in the plane.

"Show me some ID." While Amy fished her passport out of her purse, Pinsky turned the manuscript over to the cover page. He asked Amy, "If this is yours, what's it called?"

"*Provenance*. By I. Fleming."

Satisfied, the detective seemed about to hand it over when he said, "That's in the South of France, am I right?"

Amy stifled the urge to correct him, which was the second urge she was stifling at that moment. The other was to whack Siobhan Farrell as hard as she could and run outside where she could breathe. Instead she made herself say, "Look, Detective, I have to talk to you about this thing."

He gave her the thick sheaf of papers. "A passenger died. I think that comes ahead of someone mistakenly taking your stuff. Don't you?"

He had already lost interest in the manuscript. Amy put it in her computer bag. She had to get off the plane.

CHAPTER 35

She hadn't taken her cell phone on the trip, so Amy had to wait in the cordoned-off departure lounge where they had been gathered until all the other technophobes had used the one pay phone to call their loved ones and describe in lurid detail the reason for their lateness. When she finally reached Scott's cell, the group of passengers was already being herded to an employee lounge that had been cleared for them in the bowels of the terminal. She got his greeting, which was her own voice saying, "This is Scott Brown's mother. He can't come out and play. Please leave a message." At the time, she'd thought it was hilarious. Now it seemed sad in a much-too-Freudian way. Why the hell wasn't he picking up? At the beep, she yelled, "Scott! The man sitting next to me on the plane . . . died! We're being held at JFK. Are you still in New Haven? Can you come down to the city? I don't want to make the trip alone! I'll call again when I get a chance. Love you. Bye."

She started to make a second call, to Susan at work, when a stubby male finger pressed the hook on the pay phone, disconnecting her. His exact words were, "One call, lady."

The mechanics' rest area had uncomfortable chairs, an out-of-order coffeemaker, illegal cigarettes piled up in illegal ashtrays, and a ladies' room unfit for ladies. All of it added to Amy's growing agitation. She didn't want to read Fleming's manuscript in front of the other passengers, so she contented herself with sketching their faces in her day planner.

Finally it was her turn. Pinsky and a colleague, a gray-haired cop named something unpronounceably Polish, had been taking statements from most of the passengers who'd been sitting in the coach section of the plane. Now they double-teamed her. Amy was ready for them.

"Look, Officers, someone's trying to kill me."

Pinsky seemed to be half listening. "And they got your fiancé instead? Is that your story?"

"My fiancé?"

Polish Cop butted in. "The deceased. Mr. Sheridan." He read something from a leatherette flip pad. "You and your fiancé bought separate tickets. You made separate reservations. How come?"

"He's not my fiancé. I met him on the plane."

This statement made leatherette flip pads fly back

and forth in both pairs of hands. Pinsky said, "At least a dozen witnesses heard the deceased call you his wife-to-be."

His sidekick said, "His exact words were, 'Two days to go. Prewedding jitters, I guess.' "

Amy waited for them to look up, but they kept flipping their pages of notes. She started in anyway. "My fiancé's name is Scott Brown. I met Mr. Sheridan for the first time today sitting next to me on the plane. When I moved to the back row, he followed me. The wife thing—that was just his idea of a joke."

Pinsky looked at her then. "Oh, unwanted advances. I see."

Polish Cop was still on the previous idea. "A lovers' quarrel?"

Amy stood up. "Look, it wasn't love. And it wasn't a quarrel. The guy wanted to talk to me."

Pinsky was solicitous. "Please sit down, Doctor. No need to get huffy. Okay, he was just some guy on the plane who wanted to talk to you. What about?"

Was this the time to get into the whole story? Ian Fleming and the Duke of Windsor? Rudolf Hess and von Ribbentrop? That some people she still knew only as "them" wanted her stack of now dog-eared papers enough to kill a CIA agent for it? "Look, Detective, Mr. Sheridan thought I was in danger. I *am* in danger. I have something somebody wants. And I guess he was killed trying to protect me."

Amy wanted Columbo. What she got was the Keystone Kops. "Now that's more like it." Polish Cop actually licked his lips. He looked at Pinsky. "Mystery and intrigue at JFK!" He flipped to a new page in his pad and asked Amy, "This mystery and intrigue. Is it drug-related?"

"No, it's not about drugs. I—"

"No? 'Cause we get a lot of drug stuff here." Polish Something was like one of those oil tankers. Hard to turn around.

Amy would have said more, but a pimply guy arrived in the room with a report of some kind. He handed it to Pinsky. As the detective scanned it, Polish Cop tried to read over his shoulder. Pinsky saved him the trouble. "From the ME."

Something in Detective Pinsky's attitude had changed. "Dr. Greenberg, did you happen to notice what Mr. Sheridan had for lunch?"

Amy could see his fork pop-pop-popping as if it were still happening. "He had the beef."

"And the vegetables?"

Were interrogations always this weird? "Potatoes. New potatoes. And green beans with some kind of nuts mixed in."

"Peanuts?"

"Could have been. Look, I really need you to—"

Pinsky gave his wrist a little flick, closing his pad. The other detective did the same. Obviously, the interview was over.

Amy stammered, "What?"

Detective Pinsky got to his feet. "The medical examiner says Sheridan wore a MedicAlert bracelet. Allergic to peanuts. He probably died of that prophy-lactic shock."

He held out his hand to Amy as he told Polish Cop, "No mystery. No bad guys. No murder."

As far as Pinsky was concerned, Amy had ceased to exist. He turned and spoke more loudly to the other passengers in the lounge. "Thanks, folks. You're free to go. Sorry to have held you up."

Ten minutes later, as Amy stood in line for customs, she thought Gerard Pinsky was one sorry detective.

CHAPTER 36

Through a special arrangement with the U.S. Immigration Service, international passengers departing from Irish airports clear passport control before boarding their flights. So Amy and her fellow passengers were ushered directly into the customs hall at JFK. The line of people doubled back on itself, and the wait gave Amy time to dial down her anxiety and gather her wits. If Sheridan had really died from anaphylactic shock, then maybe this whole thing had been a crazy concoction of his. All she really knew about any danger was the e-mail he had sent her, and his alleged triumph in the Dublin men's room over the German Kaltenbrunner. Maybe the champagne and the upgrade had been on the level; maybe the only plot was in Sheridan's fevered brain.

Amy tried to talk herself into it. But the death of Mrs. O'Beirne in the paper—that had been real. And what kind of fool wears a MedicAlert bracelet and then wolfs down a meal obviously sprinkled with the very thing that can kill him?

As she inched closer to the customs lanes, Amy moved on to a more immediate problem. Should she declare the manuscript or not? In the panic on the plane, she'd forgotten to fill out the little white card declaring the value of items acquired abroad. What was *Provenance* worth? Seemingly quite a lot, to somebody. Should she declare it at all? Why risk anyone's knowing what she had in her computer carrying case?

Don't trust anyone.

She had reached the point where the line made its final serpentine turn toward the customs agents when she saw a face she recognized. It took a moment to register: it was that Englishman from the Dublin lounge, Brian Devlin. He was standing behind a Plexiglas barricade off to the left, waiting with the families of passengers and the limo drivers with their handwritten signs. And he was looking right at her.

How had he done that? He certainly hadn't been on the plane. Don't trust anyone. Amy hurriedly filled out her declarations card—including the scarf for Scott, which was duty-free anyway, but not the manuscript—and walked toward customs lane 21. It was only about thirty feet from the Plexiglas, but Amy never looked over there. She opened her computer bag for the inspector, who ignored the thick sheaf of papers and asked her to turn on her

ThinkPad. When the man heard it buzz as it came to life, he took her form, stamped something, and was on to the next customer. So far, so good.

To get to the exit, arriving passengers have to pass through the Plexiglas partition. Amy looked up and saw on the back wall of the customs area what looked like a temporary sign that had been put up during some long-ago construction and never replaced. It had arrows pointing in opposite directions, one to the left marked "Terminal Exit" and the other for "International Transfers." In smaller block letters underneath the arrow to the right were the words "Airline Business Lounges." Not wanting to face anyone but Scott, Amy wondered if her business class ticket would allow her into the Delta lounge, even though her flight was over. Well, nothing ventured, nothing gained. And she really had to pee.

CHAPTER 37

It was the first piece of good news for Amy in hours. An escalator took her to the Delta Crown Room, where the woman behind the desk told her that her upgraded ticket—never mind the fact that she had spent most of the flight in coach—gave her twenty-four hours of access. She was delighted to find that the ladies' room was habitable and that next to the business center with its computers and copiers was a row of telephone cubicles, mostly empty.

Drinks at the bar were free. Amy got a Bloody Mary—for energy, she told herself—and parked herself in one of the cubicles. From where she sat, Amy watched a well-dressed businesswoman feed a little stack of papers into a copier. The machine spit them out and collated them faster than the woman had put them in. For a business traveler, the Delta Crown Room was nirvana.

This time Scott picked up on the first ring with "Sweetie, are you okay?"

Relief cascaded down her body. "Physically, yes. Mentally I'm a wreck. Where *are* you?"

"I'm coming down to get you." Six wonderful words. "The Delta website showed you were delayed on the ground, so I did the terrifically gallant thing and jumped on the train. Must have been in a tunnel when you called before. This train is making every stop between New Haven and Grand Central. We're just coming in to One Hundred Twenty-fifth Street."

Help was on the way. The thought of it was better than Zoloft. She let Sheridan and Devlin and Pinsky recede a little into the background. She said, "No more trains. We need to buy a car. A nice car." One, she thought, with locks on all the doors.

"*We* can't afford a nice car. But maybe Mr. Bond can."

Amy gave the little laugh that told Scott he was impossible. Wonderful but impossible.

Scott went on. "I'm sure someone will pay a packet if the story's true . . . truly written by Ian Fleming. Look, grab a cab into the city and I'll meet you at the Yale Club."

"I'll get there as soon as I can. Bye."

In ten minutes, Amy was cooler, calmer, and definitely more collected as she headed for the exit, wheeling the overnight bag with her overstuffed computer case strapped to it. As plans go, hers wasn't much. But it might be enough.

What were the odds there'd be a cab?

CHAPTER 38

It had been more than two hours since he'd ditched the mobile phone. Twenty minutes had been taken up with moving the car from one short-term parking place in the limo holding area to another, and the rest of it had been spent shifting from one foot to the other right here, watching Delta flight 106 on the Arrivals board go from On Time to Landing to Delayed to off the board entirely. And still no Amy Greenberg. The unexpected wait was killing him. He suddenly regretted not getting one of the New York people to do this, conveniently forgetting for a moment that he was doing this himself because there had already been too many loose ends. It was hot in this daft wig and mustache. You'd think an organization as well furnished with Irish-American cash as theirs could do better than a third-rate off-Broadway wardrobe mistress. The spirit gum on the mustache had been so globbed up, he'd had to scrape it off with his penknife and start again.

He checked himself for the umpteenth time in the

mirrored reflection of the Altitunes music kiosk. The fool looking back at him resembled one of those pictures in the barbershop you were supposed to point to when you wanted a generic haircut. "Give me the Playboy. I want to look like a horse's arse."

Something else was wrong. Something about his limo driver kit was wrong. He looked again at the sign in his hand, black marker on white paperboard. It said, "Dr. Greenburg." They'd spelled her name wrong!

Get hold of yourself, man. Just a misspelling. She must get that a lot. And since when do real limo drivers know how to spell? Still, if he'd have used a local . . . Or even better, one of the Dublin boys. Drive a car full of bombs without breaking a sweat, they could. Siobhan Farrell's dad was one. One of the best, before the Constabulary had ambushed him. He could have waited for the target all day on one foot if he had to.

He knew the "compliments of the bank" ruse wasn't going to keep working on this side of the Atlantic. But that didn't particularly trouble him. He had always placed great faith in his improvisational ability, and the Greenberg woman's delayed flight had given him another excuse to get her into the car. As long as she didn't have someone meeting her, he was home and dry.

CHAPTER 39

The first thing Amy saw when she passed the Plex-iglas barrier was her name spelled wrong. A limo guy in an ill-fitting suit jacket was holding a card with "Dr. Greenburg" printed on it. The second thing she saw was that Brian Devlin was no longer in the waiting area. She experienced the same little pang she'd felt that morning in the Dublin airport. Weird.

The limo guy approached her. "Dr. Greenberg?"

"Yes?"

"The car is right outside." He started to reach for her rolling bag with the computer case.

Amy clutched it tighter. "I didn't call for a car."

He gestured vaguely beyond the exit doors. "It's the gray Town Car."

"But I didn't call a car."

"I'm sorry, Dr. Greenberg, I should have explained." His speech had an Irish lilt to it. "You were delayed on the ground for more than ninety minutes, so Delta provides this service for all the business passengers who were thus inconvenienced."

Thus inconvenienced? Amy looked at him. He wore a pretty bad rug. The giveaway was that his mustache was a slightly different color. Don't trust anyone. "A limo for every passenger? C'mon."

Maybe he mistook her skeptical "c'mon" for "let's go." He put out his hand again, this time gently taking her elbow as if to lead her toward the door. "No, ma'am, a van took the other passengers about ten minutes ago. We didn't want to hold them up waiting for you, so I brought my car around."

Why was she being coddled by another son of the Auld Sod? Her antenna was up. "Okay, how did you know I was Dr. Greenberg? I didn't tell you my name."

The man smiled. Was there something else that was familiar about him? "You didn't have to. The tag on your suitcase says flight 106, priority handling. That means business class. So you're it."

Amy looked down at the tag and snapped it off her bag.

The man gave a gentle tug on her suitcase handle, just below the point where she was holding it. "If we didn't make an effort with our best customers, they wouldn't still be *our* customers."

Against her better judgment, Amy let the creepy man take her bag and lead her to the row of doors.

Immediately outside was the taxi line. Leaning against the stanchion at the back of the line, smoking, was Brian Devlin. If she turned down this ride, she'd have to share a cab with him. But there was just something about the attractive Englishman popping up this way that didn't feel—

The bus to Grand Central chose that moment to wheel around the car rental vans and hotel shuttles, pulling to a stop outside the row of glass doors. Amy followed the limo driver through the automatic door and then grasped the handle of her American Tourister before he could step into the crosswalk. She could see the Lincoln parked on the other side of the pedestrian island. A card in the front passenger window said City Cars/Dr. Greenburg. She broke the news. "Thanks but no thanks, Mr.—"

The man turned and looked at her in surprise. He didn't offer his name or let go of her suitcase.

"I've decided to take the bus. Have a nice day."

The man noticed the two military guys before Amy did. They were part of the beefed-up security at the airports these days, and they had guns. The man let go of her bag.

She rolled her suitcase over to where the bus driver was starting to collect tickets and cash from the small knot of people who were getting on. Amy jammed the extendable handle down into her bag so she'd be able to lift it up the steep steps by the strap. "How much?"

The driver didn't look up. "Thirteen."

Amy juggled a few things so she could get at her wallet. She found a ten and three ones. At the same time, the driver had produced a ticket perforated near the bottom. He snapped off the stub and gave it to her, never once making eye contact or thanking her. Welcome to New York.

Amy managed to get her luggage onto the bus and took the empty seat by the partition behind the driver. She wasn't going to make the same mistake she'd made on the plane. Amy reached into her case and fished out Fleming's pages. The ride would take up to an hour, knowing the Van Wyck. Maybe she could finish the thing.

She was watching the people who were boarding the bus, so she missed the gray Town Car with the misspelled name pulling out at high speed around them to the left and racing on ahead.

What she did see was the commotion outside at the taxi stand. Two older people with big suitcases were practically bowled over by someone jumping the line and grabbing their cab. A man with slicked-back hair and a deep tan: Devlin. Good thing she was safely here on the bus.

CHAPTER 40

DENTAL TREATMENT CARD.   Army Form I 3033.

Date of First Examination 30.1.41   Place ....   Dental Officer J. M. Barrie

| Order Number | Rank | Name | Date of Enlistment | UNIT | Age | Period of Enlistment | Period of Engagement |

JONATHAN

R ← L

BRIDGE →
→ M.O.D. Inlay
NOTATION
8765432 | 12345678
8765432 | 12345678
← CROWN
BRIDGES →

R ← L

REMARKS.
Oral Hygiene — GOOD

Decay Caused	Reference Number	Date	TREATMENT	Initials of Dental Officer
		30/1/41	Inspection	J.M.B.
		3/2/41	61 Crown. Stoned to	
			prevent wear to	
			occlusal surface of 61	
			13 porcelain crown	
			has chipped lingually.	
			Stoned off sharp edge	
			and reduced height	
			of 13 to ease pressure	
			Scaled and polished	
			all teeth	J.M.B.
			(over)	

NOTE THIS CARD MUST NOT BE FOLDED.

DENTAL TREATMENT CARD   Army Form I 3033

Name 'J'
Army No. and Rank   P.O.W.
Unit
Signature of Officer
Age   45
Date of Enlistment
Period of Engagement

Signature of Dental Officer W.B. Purcell, Lieut
Date and Place of Examination 21 April 43 - Lunindieff Camp P.

R ← L

NOTATION
8765432 | 12345678
8765432 | 12345678

L ← R

Remarks. Oral Hygiene —
Good
SLIGHT SUPERIOR PROTRUSION

NOTE — THIS CARD MUST NOT BE FOLDED.

<u>PROVENANCE</u>

By the end of the war, I knew of only six people for certain who had ever seen the complete text of the Duke of Windsor's letter of Christmas 1939: the Duke himself, Charles Bedaux, Adolf Hitler, Rudolf Hess, King George VI, and your humble correspondent. Once I had seen both halves of it, I was in no doubt of the ex-King's treachery: he was ready and more than willing to assume the throne—and quite possibly liquidate his brother and sister-in-law—the moment Hitler and the Germans won. Nor did I doubt why his brother then, and his descendants to this day, believe suppressing the letter to be a matter of life and death for the Crown. In my painstaking way, I hope to have you convinced as well when I have finished.

That May Day of 1945 when we drove to the Friedrichshof with your grandfather, two of the six witnesses were already dead by their own hand: Adolf Hitler had killed himself less than twenty-four hours before, and Charles Bedaux too was a suicide,

though in very different circumstances.
When Paris fell, Bedaux revealed his true
Nazi colours and was given the task of
liquidating all Jewish businesses in
Occupied France. Installed in a set of
offices on the Champs Élysées with a
hundred German clerks, it took him two
years to finish the job. Then it was on to
his next project for the Germans:
overseeing the building of an oil pipeline
across the Sahara from Ouagadougou to
Algeria.

On Saturday night, 7 November 1942, he
went to bed in a hotel in Vichy-controlled
Algiers. But he awoke on Sunday morning to
find himself in Free French North Africa,
liberated overnight by the Allies. He also
found himself in the custody of the
Military Security section of the Deuxième
Bureau, who held him for a year despite his
protest that he was a naturalised American
citizen. His claim was finally upheld in
December 1943, and he was shipped to Miami
for interrogation by the FBI. It was there,
confronted with undeniable proof that he
had aided the enemy in time of war, that he
took his life by swallowing Luminal, a

concentrated form of phenobarbital, on 18 February 1944.

So that left the two royal brothers, a naval commander (me) bound by the Official Secrets Act, and the man Winston Churchill had clapped in irons for most of the war, the Deputy Führer of the Nazi Party: Rudolf Hess.

Twenty years later, I'm beginning to understand why Rudolf Hess had to die. An unreconstructed Nazi who would have given the game away if allowed to speak freely, Hess certainly would have used his abortive "peace" mission as a defence against the charge of war crimes. That he was murdered on Winston's orders—while the war was still on—I have no doubt. Nor do I doubt that the man who stood trial at Nuremberg was an impostor.

These days it's a badly kept secret that MI5 and MI6 did a rousing business in doubles (in German, *Doppelgängers*) of both British and Nazi leaders. Our cover was blown in 1943 when our Churchill look-alike did such a good job of looking like Churchill that he fooled the Luftwaffe into blowing him out of the sky over Gibraltar, a flight that also cost the life of the actor Leslie Howard.

At the behest of a couple of us in room 39, the Empire had been scoured for people who looked like Hitler, Goebbels, Goering, and the rest. Pickings were especially good in prisons, mental wards, and the armed forces, where those chosen for the dubious honour of acting like Nazis couldn't say no. It was our bright idea to undermine German morale by creating tableaux vivants of these men in sexually compromising positions, photographing them, and reproducing the photos by the thousands, dropping them over German cities and countryside during our nighttime air raids. I know for a fact that we had at least two Hesses so employed by the middle of 1941.

Late last year, a well-placed acquaintance gave me (and my Minox camera) twenty minutes alone with Rudolf Hess's complete medical file. The man we tried for war crimes was supposed to have been shot through the chest in the Great War. Miraculously, the scar from that wound no longer existed. The dental records were even more definitive: the gold tooth of the

man we captured in 1941 had come back to
life by '43!

Hess knew too much. He had seen the
entire letter. He knew the King's brother,
the ex-King, was a traitor. What would
happen to British morale if word got out?
Could Winston take the chance?

Of course, I knew none of this when the
war crimes trials opened in late November
1945. I was back in London, having wangled
the managing editor job with the *Sunday
Times*. Assigning myself to the trial, I
drove to Nuremberg to experience at first
hand Rudolf Hess's testimony. The place was
nothing like the beautiful old European
city it had been, or the Nazi showplace it
became in the 1930s, when those huge
exercises in fanaticism and mass hysteria—
organised by the same Rudolf Hess—brought
Germans by the millions. There was no
water, no electricity, no telephone or
postal service, and nearly no architecture:
ninety percent of the buildings had been
pounded into rubble by the eleven major air
raids during the war. But there was a
brand-new Palace of Justice and its
adjacent lockup with cells for 1,200

prisoners, built on the site of the
windowless, fire-blackened shell that had
been the old central court of Bavaria.

There was no jury either, only an eight-
judge tribunal—two each from Britain,
France, America, and the Soviet Union. When
it came time for the twenty-one prisoners
to enter pleas, twenty chose "Not guilty"
and one, Hess, simply said, "Nein."
It was to be the only official word he spoke
for months. Behind the scenes, the talk was
more revealing. The other prisoners agreed
that Hess had radically changed. When
Ribbentrop was told Hess was denying all
knowledge of certain events crucial to the
defence, he asked, "Which Hess? You mean
our Hess? Or the Hess we have here?"

Before sentencing, the defendants were
permitted twenty minutes to make a
statement. On the morning Hess was to make
his, Goering taunted him during a break in
the proceedings. "By the way, Hess, when
are you going to let us in on your great
secret? I make a motion Hess tell us his big
secret. How about it, Hess?"

As it turned out, Hess did reveal a
secret. Not in what he said but in the way

he said it. While using his time to praise
Adolf Hitler and dispute the right of the
Allies to have put him on trial, Hess
betrayed none of the Egyptian-inflected
German I had heard so clearly that night in
Scotland. The other prisoners, certainly
Goering, must have known it too. But before
Fat Hermann could make his statement, he
was found dead in his cell of cyanide
poisoning. Suicide, they said.

CHAPTER 41

Daily Mirror ⑪⑯
Tuesday SEPT. 11 1951
FORWARD WITH THE PEOPLE
* *
CAMBRIDGE PAIR FLEE BEHIND CURTAIN

PROVENANCE

And so we reach the present. Or nearly so.
Following the war, I took that job editing
the *Sunday Times*, took a wife (the
beautiful Ann), and took a vacation from
the job with the wife in Jamaica, which I
think of as a small part of paradise.

I began writing fiction, or what I call
"faction" (as I like to use the actual
places and procedures and brand names of
guns and cars and liqueurs an agent like

Bond would know) in the islands. By a
stroke of good fortune, the Cambridge
spies—Guy Burgess and Donald Maclean—had
just flown the coop for Moscow. So the
world of secret agents was on everyone's
lips just as I stuck my toe in the water
with *Casino Royale*. But it was John F.
Kennedy who made my career.

In 1961, *Life* magazine asked the new
American President to list his ten
favourite books, and JFK put *From Russia
with Love* at number nine, just ahead of
Stendhal's *The Red and the Black*. Joy.
Rapture. Sales. Suddenly, all my books were
best sellers in the States, and the orders
for reprints and new translations were
flooding in to my publishers from all over.
Even one from the Workers' Paradise itself.

I am proud to say I agreed to let a
Russian-language version of *From Russia* be
smuggled into the Soviet Union. It was then
photocopied again and again: they call it
samizdat, or self-publishing. One copy made
it into the hands of Oleg Penkovskiy, a
senior official on Khrushchev's General
Staff in the Scientific Section who just
happened to be our A-Number One double

agent, and the CIA's as well. (How good was he? He was the one who told the Americans that the Soviets had missiles in Cuba.)

I'd set my book partly in Istanbul, and it seems Penkovskiy had worked there for Soviet intelligence in the 1950s. Before that, we had similar wartime jobs: reviewing material from whatever source and distributing it to the various comrades in charge.

I suppose he developed an unspoken bond (pun intended) with me, his parallel officer working the other side of the street, or should I say Curtain. (And, of course, my book has Tatiana Romanova developing feelings for 007 across the same Curtain.) At any rate, during one of his debriefing sessions with Greville Wynne, his MI6 cutout, he passed on a message for me. I still remember it word for word. "Tell Fleming that if he wants a really big secret to write about, he shouldn't waste his time on decoding machines. He should write about the Nazi traitor in the royal family. I've seen the proof. In writing."

Penkovskiy's message had a galvanizing effect on me. Ever since that last

assignment up the hill with your
grandfather, I'd tried to keep what I knew
(what *you* know now, as well) in a mental
folder stored in the pigeonhole in my brain
called Despicable Things That Happen in
Wartime and Are Best Forgotten. There are
so many, though, that my pigeonhole is
crammed to the limit with folders: The
Promises We Made to Poland but Didn't Keep,
Deliberately Blowing a French Resistance
Network Because They Were Communists and De
Gaulle Wouldn't Have It, Well-Placed
Friends of the Government Who Bought Their
Way Out of National Service and Lied about
It, How We Could Have Used the Pope to Save
At Least Some of the Jews but Didn't.

But if the Russians knew about the Duke,
maybe it wasn't best forgotten. Maybe
they'd already done something with the
knowledge. They've put up a wall in Berlin.
Did we hesitate to act because Khrushchev
has something to hold over us, some dirty
secret that would undermine the monarchy?
Free nations have gone missing behind the
Curtain; there was a revolution in Hungary
that went on without us. We occupied Suez
along with the French in '56 and then

folded our cards. Nasser was a Russian
client. Was the Windsor card played then?

I may be many things, Amy. A dilettante,
an entertainer, possibly even a snob. A
serial philanderer too, even though I
wholeheartedly love my wife. But here's the
bedrock me, the thing I put right out in the
open with every 007 book I write: I'm a
patriot. Of the most disgustingly true-blue
sort. In the balance scale, I owe much more
to my country than my country owes to me.

It's why I so willingly did all those
chores for Winston, why I joined the
Service. And it's why I'm telling you all
this. To root out a single evil. To right a
single, continuing wrong. Like a maths
proof, I've had to take you through all my
thinking. So when we arrive at my
conclusion, I'll be able to say, *"Quod erat
demonstrandum."* I'll have proved my case.
And you'll know what to do.

That's why, for the past eighteen months,
I've been telling people I'm researching a
new 007 book when what I've really been
doing is running to ground every
possibility, every individual who could
have told the Soviets about the letter (as

I can think of no other proof of the Duke's
betrayal), both on our side and the German.
(One person I can no longer go to for
information is Penkovskiy himself. The
Soviets caught him with state papers, held
a quick show trial in Moscow, and shot him a
few months ago.)

Thanks in no little part to the few
friends I still have in the Service, I've
read the files and interviewed everyone who
had even the slightest opportunity to see
or hear about one half of the letter or the
other, and they've all come up Persil, save
Anthony Blunt. The third chap in that jeep
with Chief and me.

The rumour about Blunt, which I think he
put about, was that he was the illegitimate
son of King George V and a woman in Queen
Mary's circle. Personally, I've never
believed it. The only thing holding the
improbable story together is the strong
facial resemblance of Blunt and the Dukes
Windsor and Kent. Of course, if it were
true, the story would go a long way to
explaining the otherwise inexplicable
preference Bertie showed to Blunt
throughout his life. Chalk it up to

brotherly love. Or half-brotherly guilt.
But George VI bestowed favour after favour,
honour after honour upon this withdrawn,
rather chilly man. The knighthood came
after the King's death, but I'm sure the
list was drawn up while George was still
above ground.

So what led me to Blunt? For starters, he
knew Guy Burgess at Cambridge. Knew him in
the carnal way that many people knew
Burgess. What we choose in England to call
a "confirmed bachelor," Blunt was a young
don at Trinity who seemed to have the run of
Burgess's rooms. And vice versa. Then, in
1934, he made what I think was a voyage of
political discovery to the Soviet Union.
Either he turned Burgess or Burgess turned
him. But turn he did.

Think of it as a connect-the-dots
picture. Burgess, Maclean, and the third
Cambridge spy, Kim Philby (we'll call them
the Marx Brothers) are three of the dots
among a dozen more. Draw a line in a certain
way, and you've drawn a portrait of the
Fourth Man, Anthony Blunt.

In the crime business, they say it's all
a matter of motive and opportunity. As a

faithful follower of Marx and Engels, Blunt would have been looking for proofs that the decadent ruling classes of Britain had sided with the Fascists against the interests of the common people. I know from speaking with him that Blunt believed Edward's interest in the plight of the miners and other workers in Britain to be a sham. To have been presented with the ex-King's disloyalty to his country on a plate would have justified Blunt's entire double life. So put a big red tick next to motive. As for opportunity, well, Chief was there to see me hand the torn bit of paper to Blunt.

Falling back on my training, I set about to work through the puzzle: the Duke had written Hitler a letter. It had been torn in half. I had taken the right half from Rudolf Hess in a farmer's field and given it to my godfather, Winston Churchill. Then Blunt and I had "liberated" the left half from a German castle at the end of the war. All right, if Anthony Blunt communicated the text of the left half of the Duke's message to his supposed masters in Moscow, how did he do it? I thought of three ways:

One, he could have memorized it or shown it to his KGB controller before handing it over to the King. Two, he could have made a copy, which he would have "posted" in one of the many drops the Soviets maintain in London. Either way he was home free. But I thought Blunt would have been more enterprising than that. I thought he did the third thing: make an exact copy and give the *copy* to the King, passing the original left half of the Hitler note on to Moscow. This third option would have the advantage of denying the British Crown possession of the damning article, burying it for safekeeping in the vaults under Lubyanka. It's what I would have done.

If I were right, Blunt would have needed something more than opportunity. Time, for one thing. It would take at least forty-eight hours to somehow conjure up an exact replica of the fragment so it would appear to "marry" with the half I had so obligingly given to the authorities four years before. And he would need a facility nearby to manufacture such an item. There was no way of confirming or denying any communications Blunt might have had, short

of torturing it out of him. But there was an
easier way of telling whether we had the
authentic left half or a clever copy. It
ought to be covered with fingerprints—the
Duke's, the Führer's, Bedaux's, and who
knows how many more. All I had to do was
locate it and fingerprint it.

This line of reasoning supposes that
Blunt really did have at least a couple of
days after our arrival back in London on 2
May 1945, before he had to hand the
fragment to the King. I did a quick check at
my local library of the Court Circular—at
one time a broadsheet of limited
circulation that described events at Court
and in later centuries a daily record of
royal lives, published in the *Times*, the
Daily Telegraph, and the *Scotsman*—for the
weeks before and after 2 May. Beginning 30
April, the King was at Caernarvon Castle in
Wales, marking the tenth anniversary of his
father's last visit there during his Silver
Jubilee of 1935, and did not return to
Buckingham Palace until the evening of the
fifth. So there was enough time for Blunt
to pull off the presumed switch.

But wouldn't King George have simply

destroyed the offending letter as soon as
he had it in his possession? I didn't think
so. Knowing what I know of their sibling
rivalry, and the likelihood that Bertie and
his family would not have survived a German
occupation with Edward back on the throne,
I thought the King would have kept the
letter to hold over his older brother.
Their mother, Mary, was still alive after
the war, and I think the Duke would have
done anything so that his mother (former
German princess though she may have been)
would never learn of his treason.

While I couldn't be sure at the time what
had happened to the Hess half of the Führer
letter I had come up with four years
earlier, I was working on the assumption
that the King had the Blunt half and hadn't
destroyed it. I made it my business to get
my hands on it and authenticate it.

CHAPTER 42

The bus lurched away from the American terminal, its last stop at JFK, even as a young couple struggled to hoist their duffel bag into the overhead rack. She sat next to Amy and her boyfriend took the one across the aisle. It looked like they'd be engrossed in each other for the rest of the trip. Good. No small talk.

Behind the accelerating bus, two limos from City Cars pulled away from the curb. Amy was starting to notice these things. In the oversized side-view mirror of the bus, she watched three tanned children in shorts get into one of the black cars along with their equally underdressed parents, back from a Florida vacation. Funny thing about the second limo. No one had gotten in, but it started anyway. Amy kept looking, but there was too much glare to make out the driver's features.

And another strange thing. Amy's subconscious mind must have been putting in overtime, because now she remembered that stilted phrase of Scott's on the phone, that "if the story's true . . . truly written by Ian Fleming" thing. He doesn't talk like that.

Amy caught herself. She was seeing, and hearing, things. An empty car. A turn of phrase. Get a grip, Amy Greenberg. She twirled Scott's ring around her finger, praying for the restorative powers of jewelry to kick in.

BBC Home • June 12, 1962

"I'm never without my box of keepsakes."

PROVENANCE

How do you "case the joint" when the joint you want to burgle is a palace? The only thing I could think to do was to be invited there. As you know, I was playing a long shot: that King George VI had kept the damning evidence we had retrieved from that German castle. So I went back to my connect-the-dots thinking. The King has been dead since 1952. Who would have his most personal effects? That was easy: Elizabeth, the Queen Mother. If the King had wanted something to hold over his brother, his wife would have wanted it twice as much, if only to throttle Wallis with.

All right, it's 1963. The Queen Mum has long since moved out of Buckingham Palace and gone across the street to Clarence House, a three-storey town house made over for William IV in 1830 and the home of some royal or other ever since. Here's where my 30 Assault Unit training comes in again, that art of getting documents from people who have no intention of letting them go. I equipped myself with plans for the upper storeys of Clarence House—the first floor being all public spaces—and I did some reading in the back numbers of

women's magazines, home and garden
stuff. And lo, after an hour or so, I
found a picture of the Queen Mother in
her third-floor sitting room. Beneath it
she says, "I'm never without my box of
keepsakes." Another photo shows her
holding a polished walnut box given to
the King on his visit to Bechuanaland
in 1938. While the article is all about
the Regency furnishings in the room, the
caption quotes her as saying, "I keep
the King's ring, a lock of his hair and
other cherished mementos from that happier time in this room. I'm quite fond
of sitting here and going through them."

I managed to have an acquaintance of
mine with a locksmithing background—
gained mostly by a lot of late-night
work on other people's locks—study an
enlargement of the photograph. He told
me that the box, though handmade in
Africa, looked to have an imported
English lock. And that Swindon & Cowles
were still making similar ones. For a
small fortune, he gave me three
different keys for Swindon & Cowles
prewar locks and told me my odds were

sixty percent of opening the box with one of them. (I knew my odds of finding something besides rings and locks of hair were far lower.)

Access to the house would be easier to obtain. The Queen Mother Elizabeth has for years been holding gatherings at Clarence House, garden parties in the summer months, dinner parties the rest of the year. The guests are always a mix of the famous and the talented. After writing eight best sellers, I've made it into the former group, if not the latter. So it was merely a matter of bruiting it about, in the English way, that I was available to attend one of the Queen Mother's evenings, and I was duly invited for the soiree to be given on a Friday evening November last.

I arrived for the cocktail hour promptly at seven, fully prepared to bide my time and wait for a chance to excuse myself (a trip to the gents', perhaps) so I could explore upstairs. But events overtook me. A half hour earlier in Dallas, Texas, President Kennedy had been shot. He had been taken to hospital by the time I walked in the door, and all the anticipated formalities had gone by the boards. The Queen Mother and her guests, including the actor Peter Sellers and the pianist Vladimir Horowitz, were crowded around two television sets on the first floor—one of which had been brought in from the servants' quarters. I'm a little ashamed to say that I did not greet my hostess or observe any of the usual niceties. Instead, as soon as I was over the initial shock of the news, I made my way up the back stairs to the third floor, passing two liveried gentlemen on their way down with a large colour television set.

The sitting room looked as it had in the magazine, and I immediately recognised the walnut box, about twelve inches by ten inches, sitting on a long-legged marble-topped table near the window. The second key I tried opened the lid. To make what is already a very long story a little shorter, under some other articles that included an ornate man's ring and a lock of grey hair in a folded-over piece of paper, I discovered an acetate envelope on the bottom of the box. Inside the acetate I could see a sheet of notepaper with handwriting on it. My anxious brain thought I detected the sound of the servants coming back, and I used my handkerchief to take the acetate envelope from the box and put it inside my dinner jacket, in the widened pocket I'd rigged up for the occasion. I closed the box and made my way back down the stairs without anyone's stopping me (I still had my alibi of "looking for the gents' " if anyone had done).

It was strange watching the news of the President's death alongside Peter Sellers without having spoken a word to him or the other guests or even my hostess. It was stranger to do it with what I hoped might be a purloined artefact of great historical importance in my pocket. I had no way of knowing that I had scooped up not half the letter but all of it. Two torn half sheets of notepaper—the Hess half and the Blunt half—had lain one on top of the other in the clear envelope since the war.

In any event, less than an hour after I had arrived, Elizabeth asked us to take a moment to pray for Mrs. Kennedy and the new American President, Mr. Johnson. And then she graciously, regretfully, suggested it was not an appropriate evening for the merriment she had planned and asked us to take what you Americans call a "rain check." And so I made my escape through the front door of Clarence House with the others.

CHAPTER 43

Lieber Herr Hitler,

vor Kurzem kam ich von einer erlebnis
Norden zurücke. Innerhalb einer Woche
Meinungen zu vernehmen. Zwischen
genommen, meinem Freund und Ihrem
Urlaub detailliert zu schildern. Ich bin
Bedeutung und Nichtigkeit der Informa
ich mir die Mühe machte, unserem
erklären. Wie ich bereits betonte,
teile sie. Ich werde auf alle Fälle sofort
meines Volkes erneut zu übernehr
seligkeiten beigelegt worden und
Unser gemeinsamer Freund, Herr B, wird mir,
und behilflich sein.

Edward P.

<u>PROVENANCE</u>

Q lives. The real-life counterpart of the
quartermaster in the Bond books is alive
and well and counting the days to
retirement in the basement of Whitehall.
The forensic laboratory there rivals what
anyone other than the Americans has built.
It is easily the latest, most up-to-date
government facility in the United Kingdom.
I lifted it in toto—adding only a few small
touches—and gave it to my fictional Q. The
factual Q (who shall remain nameless) heads
a team of highly competent technicians who
can equip an operative for the field,
eavesdrop on a bedroom in Karachi, or, more
to my purpose, tell you who handled any
object over the past thousand years.

While I no longer have any formal
standing in the game, I have from time to
time rung up a couple of the chaps left over
from the war and bombarded them with
queries for use in my "factions." Effective
killing zones of firearms, the half-life of
secret inks, that sort of thing. And they
have become used to my bringing all sort of
invented matter to them for "probability"

vetting: could such a thing be put to such a use and, in all probability, work?

I was reasonably sure Q would view my request to analyse a torn piece of notepaper as another one of my put-up jobs. But just to be sure nobody but me saw the complete text of the letter, I only gave him the left-hand fragment of my lucky find. I gave the right-hand side to another of the forensics boys. All right, the results, right side first: In the presence of certain chemicals and viewed under a particular kind of light, the side I got from Rudolf Hess revealed the fingerprints of many individuals. Facsimiles of the prints were fed into the massive UNIVAC computer full of government files that sits in its own temperature-controlled glass room. The names of the owners of the matching prints were spit out on a long white computer tape, and among them were Charles Bedaux, Adolf Hitler, and the former King Edward VIII. The right half also bore the thumb and index fingerprints of Winston Churchill, near the upper right corner, and my own fingerprints, put there when I had taken the fragment from Hess.

(Strikingly, no prints were found which matched those of Rudolf Hess—at least according to the official British records. Hmmm.) While I trust the man who did the testing not to discuss my request, I thought it best to be rather generous in "reimbursing" him for his time and trouble before swearing him to secrecy "until the book comes out."

The left half of the note yielded no such treasure trove. Only two men had ever handled it: Anthony Blunt and the then King of England, George VI. Not the Führer and certainly not the Duke of Windsor. The results of Q's tests couldn't be denied. The right side was authentic and the left side was not. And the culprit, Sir Anthony, had been caught red-handed, or red-fingered, if you prefer. But definitely Red.

I recently read an article reprinted from an American business journal that described what they're calling "decision trees." If, to reach a decision, one has to make choices among a number of competing possibilities (or branches)—and if following any branch leads to more branches

and more choices—one can literally plot on
a piece of paper a tree with all its
attendant branches for any decision one
must make.

My current decision tree would look like
this: If the wrong people know about the
Führer note, how do they know? Blunt. Of
Blunt's options, which did he take?
Stealing the original and substituting a
copy. Next branch: How did he do it? Before
I edged out onto a branch that wouldn't
hold my weight, I asked myself how one
could make a lightning-fast facsimile of
something one had only just obtained.

The results of my cogitation: the King
must have shown him the Hess half of the
letter before the mission ever left
England. Otherwise, how would he have known
what we were looking for? If that were the
case, Blunt might have been able to
research the Duke's notepaper of the period
(or have someone do it for him) and find the
proper pen and ink for his forgery.

The actual reproduction of the letter
would have been right up Blunt's street.
Before the war he had been tipped to head
the Courtauld Institute of Art and had been

given the flat on the top floor of the
Institute at 20 Portman Square, the best
Adam house in London. All the pictures had
been evacuated to the country for the
duration, and Blunt had the run of the
place. Though it manifests the discreet,
well-mannered air of a London club, the
Courtauld is one of the world's preeminent
centres for the study of art history,
sending its experts hither and thither to
appraise and authenticate all manner of
objets d'art. Right from its start in the
early 1930s, the Courtauld established a
technological department for the scientific
examination and restoration of artworks.
Indeed, Anthony Blunt had told me on the
plane back to London from Germany that he
saw himself as an archaeologist of
paintings.

I have managed to ingratiate myself with
the Courtauld's technology director,
Stephen Hyde-Jones, and his assistant,
Maggie Brown, who were good enough to give
me a tour when the Director happened to be
on the Continent. Back in its place of
honour is the Van Gogh self-portrait with a
bandage covering his severed ear, just

inside the door to the palatial study adjoining Blunt's top-floor rooms. And though I didn't see it myself, as his bedroom is kept locked while he's away, I'm told the late fifteenth-century masterwork Botticelli's *Holy Trinity* hangs on the wall over Sir Anthony's bed.

One floor down is a laboratory that houses dozens of samples of paints, canvas, inks, and paper used through the centuries. I think Blunt had merely to come downstairs from his flat and use this facility to create his forgery. Then, possibly on the same night the King returned to London, he would have handed the fragment over. Blunt would have had little fear of the sovereign's independently authenticating the paper. The King wanted as few people to know of its existence as possible and, after all, he had just received it from the man he would have chosen to authenticate it!

CHAPTER 44

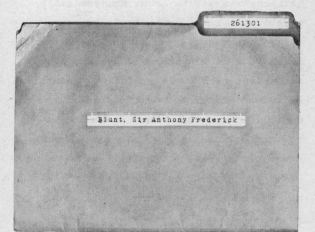

261301

Blunt, Sir Anthony Frederick

<u>PROVENANCE</u>

Nothing in this narrative so far explains
how I have been able to obtain for this time
capsule one of the most valuable scraps of
paper—save a Magna Carta or two—I have ever
laid eyes upon. The actual, honest-to-God
half of the Führer letter that I have
included at the end of this dossier should

have been tucked safely away in a vault on
Dzerzhinsky Street ever since V-E Day. And
it would have been there, had Anthony Blunt
been a heterosexual.

In the 1940s and 1950s, the practice
of homosexuality in Great Britain was a
crime, punishable by an extended gaol
term. Though gentlemen of influence and/or
means were usually able to avoid prison,
the threat of a public trial was enough to
drive the practice, and the practitioners,
underground. I mean that literally, as
the men's rooms in the Underground and
the subway passages that take pedestrians
under our traffic circuses became the
most frequented rendezvous points for
pickups.

There is a dossier at New Scotland Yard,
maintained by Special Branch, called the
Pink File. Unlike the ordinary police files
kept in each English borough and shire, the
Pink File details the indiscretions of men
whose position or title would leave them
vulnerable to blackmail—and, by extension,
would leave their Government vulnerable as
well. More secrets have, after all, been
betrayed by sexual blackmail of adulterous

husbands and homosexual lovers than have
ever been obtained by "spies."

The maintenance of the Pink Files is not
a hit-or-miss affair. Should an individual
come to be regarded as "notorious," defined
by Special Branch as someone with at least
three arrests for the euphemistically named
loitering or cohabitation, his mail and
telephone can be "entailed." Entailment
means intercepting (without opening) the
pieces of mail he receives, recording the
return addresses and post offices of
origin, and logging in the telephone
numbers of calls placed to him. This
furnishes the basis of further inquiries
into the lives of his correspondents. It's
a filthy business.

Anthony Blunt appeared prominently in
the Pink File. His name is mentioned on
at least five occasions, the last in
1952 when he was discovered with a
motorman's assistant in a bar in
Cheapside that was raided by the local
police. The irony is that Blunt really
couldn't be blackmailed. His preferences
were already so well known, there would
be no advantage an evildoer might gain

in threatening to disclose them. But eighteen months away from his beloved, rent-free Courtauld and his pictures . . . that was something he certainly *could* be influenced with.

In any event, Blunt's five arrests were all dismissed for a variety of reasons that add up to "insufficient evidence." This despite the fact that being caught in a "queer bar" was, at the time, all the evidence necessary to prosecute. Did Blunt have a Get Out of Gaol Free card? And was it torn on one side?

The Pink File revealed something else about Anthony Blunt, something I didn't expect. The last entry noted, "Married, 2 September 1963." I was baffled. Anthony Blunt is the least likely man I know, including Noël Coward, to marry.

In my perplexity, I decided to ignore the facts and return to the problem. What could have happened to the original left side of the Duke of Windsor's treasonous note to Adolf Hitler? Conan Doyle has Sherlock Holmes say something to the effect that, once you've eliminated every other possibility, what you're left with must be

the truth. The Fleming Corollary: if
there's no way of knowing a thing, forget
it and work on a thing you *can* know.
Penkovskiy's message made it clear Moscow
had at least a copy of the Führer letter.
Blunt's charmed life since the war
suggested that he had "an ace in the hole."
Was it really true that he was the King's
brother from the other side of the blanket?
I saw a more straightforward explanation.
He had to have made *two* copies, one for the
King and one for the commissars. And if he
had, the original would be tucked away
safely somewhere right here in London. The
trick was to make Sir Anthony lead me to it.

CHAPTER 45

It was approaching four in the afternoon, and the bus had just turned onto the Long Island Expressway, headed for the Queens-Midtown Tunnel. Amy looked out at the springtime sky over New York, grateful to see the Manhattan skyline stretched out to the left and right ahead of them like a big banner reading Welcome Home. Twenty more minutes and she'd be with Scott.

New York was Amy's second home. Though she'd grown up on the enclosed quadrangles of a small city's college campus, her grandparents had taken Amy to the plays, concerts, and museums they themselves had loved. Chief had had some kind of faculty membership in the Yale Club of New York on Vanderbilt Avenue and Forty-fourth Street. For a special treat, the three of them would stay there overnight after a particularly late dinner or show, and then return to New Haven in the morning. Most of the time, Amy was the only child in the place, like the fictional Eloise at the Plaza Hotel, and the staff became used to her racing up and down the corridors, squirreling herself away somewhere with a pencil and sketchpad, or pressing the staff into elaborate games of hide-and-seek.

The bus picked up speed as it merged onto the expressway. Maybe thirty pages to go.

PROVENANCE

The fact that Anthony Blunt had been declared notorious suited my research down to the ground. I had merely to avail myself of his microfiched files, starting with the most recent years (in exchange for a prewar Cheval Blanc I was loath to part with) to discover that he received an annual missive from Coutts Bank. As Sir Anthony regularly banks elsewhere, the once-a-year entreaty from Coutts could have been the bill for a rented safety deposit box.

Safety deposit boxes have a worldwide reputation they do not deserve. The iron bars, the hardened steel, the dual keys all lend an intended air of invulnerability. It's no surprise banks seek to reassure their clients by

publishing photos of their vault areas.
They really ought not to.

Another thing: the Swiss make a very nice
business of preventing themselves (and,
thus, anyone else) from knowing the
identities of their clients. By way of
contrast, British banks are mercifully free
of scruples about divulging clients' names.
Without boring you with the details, I
wangled the location of Sir Anthony's box
out of a comely miss in the records section
at the Coutts head office at number 440 the
Strand.

Depending on their size, banks may have
as many as six rows of boxes stacked bottom
to top, or as few as three. I was hoping the
target box would either be in the top row or
along the bottom, so I could use water. An
inside location would have necessitated
fire, which is much trickier. I had between
a one-in-three and a two-in-three chance
of a favourable position, et voilà: Blunt's
box was a top.

The fire sprinkler system was invented in
the United Kingdom by a Major Harrison a
century ago. But like so many of our
inventions, it was improved upon by an

American, Henry Parmelee, who wanted to protect his piano factory. To set off a typical automatic sprinkler system today takes a flame no hotter than that produced by the average cigarette lighter (about 68°C), held just below one of the nozzles in the ceiling. The heat causes a solder link to melt or the liquid in a glass bulb to expand and shatter the bulb, activating the sprinkler and sending a controlled amount of water over a deflector plate, which diffuses it in a wide pattern to put out the fire.

One fine Tuesday I entered Coutts and asked to rent a particular safety deposit box. When I had done so, a guard escorted me to the vault and helped me open my newly rented box, which "happened" to be close to Blunt's and, more to the point, was located directly under one of the older sort of video security cameras that sweeps the room in a fixed pattern.

I removed my empty box to one of the two confidential viewing rooms nearby. While these booths are also equipped with sprinklers, privacy requires that no surveillance equipment may be installed in the rooms themselves. Thus, with the door closed, I was able to place one of the upholstered chairs atop the sturdy wooden table in the centre of the room. Then I opened the attaché case I had brought with me. James Bond would have been disappointed: when turned, the locks emitted no deadly gases, and the lining concealed no gold sovereigns. In fact, all the case held were some adhesive and three fire sprinkler heads identical to the ones in the ceiling of the viewing rooms and vault. Or rather, *similar* to the ones in the ceiling, as each of mine had a tiny radio-controlled Minox camera where the glass bulb should have been.

By climbing onto the table and then onto the chair—and extending my lanky frame and arm to their fullest—I was able to affix one of the counterfeit nozzles with adhesive to the ceiling overhead. Then I climbed down and replaced the chair in its customary spot and picked up my attaché before taking the still-empty box back to the guard, a nice Mr. Turley.

He was just about to lock my box back in place with my key and his when I had a second thought. Had I left my wallet in the box by mistake? Mr. Turley took pity on me. "First time for everything, sir."

Overacting terribly, I carried my box back to the viewing rooms, only this time I entered the other one. Once inside, I went through precisely the same procedure: chair on table, faux nozzle on ceiling, and then everything back where it was. I called for the guard again, grinning what I hoped was an upper-class-twit-to-end-all-twits grin. "Can't drive without one's driving licence, what?"

Mr. Turley was more than accommodating. "That's what we're here for, sir." He took my key again and this time locked the box in place with our two keys. Of course, two keys require two keyholes. And that's where the boxes are vulnerable.

I have to hand as I write this a souvenir: one of the three "funny cigarettes" Q had furnished me with. Not the kind they sell on the beach at Ocho Rios, but a cigarette-shaped compound of rubberised plastic with a double core: an outer layer that conducts heat and, when that burns off, an epoxy inner layer that

melts and eventually hardens into a new
shape. A kind of wick extends out a quarter
inch from where a real cigarette's tobacco
would be.

On my second trip to Coutts, I
ostentatiously jingled something in my
pocket—what? coins?—that seemed to require
urgent storage. Mr. Turley recognised me
and, believing I now knew what I was about,
sauntered off after inserting the keys.
When he was out of view, I waited for the
video camera on the wall to sweep past
before I opened my cigarette case and
fished among the real smokes for two of Q's
"cigarettes." Stepping over to Anthony
Blunt's box, I slid the first one into the
upper keyhole, the one the bank guard uses
for his key. Then I did the same for the
lower, client keyhole. I took out the
Dunhill lighter I'd inherited from my
father and set fire to both wicks. While
each cigarette was melting into the shape
of its keyhole and then beginning to
stiffen in that shape, I opened my trusty
attaché and extracted the remaining
counterfeit sprinkler head. Then I stepped
into my own empty box and used it like the

rung of a ladder to stick the nozzle
directly over the spot where Blunt's box
would be if it were open. Finally I took out
my Dunhill again and reached for the
nearest working nozzle, all the while
keeping clear of the camera. The downpour
ruined a perfectly good Club tie.

CHAPTER 46

PROVENANCE

The really wonderful thing about the
British Isles is the miniature scale of the
place. A century ago, the sun never set on
the Empire. Today, a single time zone suits
us nicely. You could plop the whole
business, including Northern Ireland, down

inside one of those anonymous American
states like Oregon.

As small as it is, the UK is broken up
further into counties, cities, shires, and
boroughs, all with their ministers,
departments, mayors, Lord Mayors,
councilmen, et al. What power there is is
sliced and diced into tiny spheres of
influence the size of your pinky finger. Is
it any wonder then that peacetime Britain
resembles nothing so much as wartime
France? It's always just after D-Day here.
No one knows who's in charge. Lines of
command are blurred and chaos would be the
order of the day—if orders weren't
regularly countermanded. So the mischief
maker with a little attitude has the run of
the place.

It's amazing what you can get a Briton to
give you by acting superior. I mean, I
flooded a rather large bank and was asked,
in future, not to smoke. Naturally I was
sternly rebuked by the Assistant Manager
for smoking in a prohibited area and
setting off the fire system. But as I
hadn't actually deposited anything in the
only open box in the place (except my

foot), nothing seemed to have been damaged
in the indoor rainstorm. And as I had
withdrawn my manufactured keys from Blunt's
box during the downpour—with no one the
wiser—I was allowed to leave on condition
it wouldn't happen again. (Though, looking
back, I saw the withering look Mr. Turley
gave me for my idiocy.) All because I was
determined-looking or wearing the right tie
or something.

It must have been dismaying for Sir
Anthony to read the letter from the
Assistant Manager of Coutts Bank. Mandated
by the Borough of Westminster's Fire and
Safety Code, it is sent to all clients
whenever there is an "irregular discharge"
of the sprinkler system. The wording tried
to make light of the inadvertent soaking
all the top row of Coutts boxes had
received, even as clients were urged to
inspect the contents for water damage. From
my stakeout in a teashop on Gloucester
Place, I watched Blunt leave for the bank
immediately after the postman had arrived.

Now it's time to give my dear Ann the
credit in this narrative that she deserves.
While our domestic bliss has not been

unadulterated (and I choose my words carefully), our professional association has been a complete go. To help things along, Ann had agreed to loiter inside the bank the day Blunt received the flood letter. She followed him down to the vault before retiring to the call box near the elevators. After a minute or so she started our cameras going with the little radio device I had given her. With thirty-six shots to be taken five seconds apart, we had a window of about three minutes to capture whatever Blunt did. (As I had no way of knowing which viewing room he would use, we were photographing them both.)

Bright and early the next morning, I introduced Ann to Mr. Turley. As this was my third visit to the bank in a week—and having decided *I* was the family nitwit—he chose to curry Ann's favour. So while she chatted animatedly with him under the video camera near my box, I was able to remove the pseudo nozzles with the cameras from the two viewing rooms. And when she idly wandered over to the rooms to inquire about the maker and quality of the chairs and their upholstery, I could snatch the third sprinkler head and camera just before they ambled back. The adhesive left a slight mark, but Ann made sure Mr. Turley was looking at her.

As the former wife of the publisher Lord Rothermere, Ann Fleming knows her way around a newspaper's city desk, printing plant, and photographic darkrooms. *The Sunday Times* keep quite a nice darkroom actually, where Ann developed the negatives from my three cameras and then the three series of pictures from them.

All thirty-six photographs of viewing room 1 produced the same still life I choose to call *Wooden Table with Chair*. So it was a great relief to see that the twenty-fifth snapshot of viewing room 2 revealed an open safety deposit box on the table, with a single envelope inside the box. Picture number 26 captured a good likeness of Anthony Blunt picking up the envelope, on which his own name was discreetly embossed. Number 27, a little alarmingly, showed him using his handkerchief to dab at the envelope (the boxes *are* water-resistant, aren't they?), and my blood pressure shot up almost as high as Blunt's. By picture 29, he had extracted the torn piece of notepaper I'd hoped for, holding it at a very good angle for my purposes. Picture 31 had the satisfied art historian returning the envelope to the box, and the thirty-fourth shot showed him leaving the viewing room with the box under his arm. Finally, the camera in the vault area caught him handing his key to the indefatigable Mr. Turley, who then locked the box in place and gave Sir Anthony back his key. If you're going to blackmail someone, the pictures you use should be crisp and clear. I don't honestly know if they would have come out any better had Blunt posed for them.

The next day, Ann made a show of depositing a quite nice pearl necklace in what must have been the most frequently visited storage box in London. When poor Mr. Turley was forced to tear himself away to attend a client in another part of the vault, that "nice Mrs. Fleming with the awful husband" waited for the video camera to swing away and then quickly put the two now hardened keys into Blunt's box. I was apprehensive they might snap off in the locks when turned, but Ann said they worked like a charm. She pinched the small white envelope with its prize inside, getting away scot-free (a very good thing when you're married to a Scot named Fleming).

CHAPTER 47

Paris, den 23. Dezember 1939

Lieber Herr Hitler,

vor Kurzem kam ich von einer erlebnis reichen Reise zurück, die mich nach Norden führte. Innerhalb einer Woche gelang es mir, einige interessante Meinungen zu vernehmen. Zwischen zeitlich habe ich mir die Freiheit genommen, meinen Freund und Ihrem Bekannten, Herrn B., meinem Urlaub detailliert zu schildern. Ich bin kaum in der Lage die strategische Bedeutung und Nützlichkeit der Informa tionen genügend zu betonen, weshalb ich mir die Mühe machte, unserem gemeinsamen Freund alles im Detail zu erklären. Wie ich bereits betonte, begrüße ich Ihre Pläne für die Zukunft und teile sie. Ich werde auf alle Fälle sofort zur Verfügung stehen, die Führung meines Volkes erneut zu übernehm men, nachdem die Feind seligkeiten beigelegt worden und Seelöwe Erfolg gekrönt war. Unser gemeinsamer Freund, Herr B., wird mir wie bisher zur Seite stehen. und behilflich sein.

Edward P.

PROVENANCE

And now, my dear Amy, this is the part where the magician reaches into the top hat. If there's a rabbit in there, it's made quite a journey. A scrap of paper penned by the former King of England and signed Edward P (for Prince—even the Duke felt "Windsor" wasn't grand enough) to Der Führer that made its way to Winston Churchill and King George VI, not to mention the Queen Mum, the Surveyor of the King's Pictures, a Hesse, and a Hess. Oh, and Yours Truly.

I hereby bequeath it to you, the granddaughter of Dr. Raymond Greenberg of New Haven, Connecticut. His, as you know, was a cameo role. Small, but extremely well played. While my job was to get us to the document and Blunt's to put it safely in the hands of George VI, your grandfather's was to drive the bus and know nothing more about it.

To make amends for all the secrecy, I'm enclosing the article in question and an English translation.

Paris, 25 December 1939

My Dear Herr Hitler,

I have recently returned from an eventful trip to the North and over

a week's time I have managed to hear
some interesting opinions. I have
since taken the liberty to describe
my holiday in great detail to my
friend and your acquaintance Mr. B.
I cannot stress enough the strategic
significance and importance of the
information, which is why I have
taken pains to go into such great
detail in explaining all of it to
our friend. As I have stressed
already, I find your ideas for the
future welcome and I am of the same
opinion. I will make myself
available to resume on a moment's
notice the interrupted stewardship
of my people upon the end of
hostilities and the success of Sea
Lion. As always, our mutual friend
Mr. B. acts for me in this matter.

                              Edward P.

Such a small piece of paper for such large
consequences.

CHAPTER 48

The New York cab with the Englishman in the back seat slipped in behind the bus as it slowed a quarter mile from the automated tollbooths guarding the tunnel. Ahead of them, the limo from City Cars was already through the tunnel and a couple of blocks from Grand Central. The mobile phone rang, and the man in the vehicle briefly fumbled with it before answering. "Yes?" It was half question, half bark.

A strangely unemotional male voice, given the context, overenunciated in a clipped Oxonian accent. "This is a priority call. It will be terminated in exactly forty-five seconds."

A woman came on the line. "Do you recognize my voice?"

The cars and trucks outside created a low rumble that made it difficult but not impossible to recognize her. "Yes, ma'am."

"You have indicated that the material is not yet in our possession. Is that still the case?"

"Yes, ma'am."

"Then I hereby authorize you now to do whatever is required to retrieve the material. Is that clear?"

"Yes, ma'am."

"*Whatever* is required."

"Yes, ma'am."

The military network operator was as good as his upper-class word. At the forty-six-second mark, the connection was gone.

CHAPTER 49

PROVENANCE

I ambushed Anthony Blunt after a lecture he
gave at the Victoria and Albert Museum. His
subject was "From Humanism to Mannerism"
(as if Bolsheviks give a fig for either
humans or manners). I needed to get him in a
public place where he couldn't easily turn
me down, and the V&A is as public as you can
get in London, short of Wembley.

The crowd of acolytes had thinned a
little when I stepped forward and
threatened to give the white-haired ascetic

an Old Boy hug. "Anthony!" (By the way, one pronounces the *th* sound as in *Antony and Cleopatra*.) He must have retreated a good foot and a half before he recognised me, and then kept me at arm's length by sticking out his hand as far as it would go. "Ian Fleming. Didn't know you liked the Italian Renaissance."

"Of all the Renaissances it's my clear favourite. I'm simply gaga for it." The students and academicians around us gave us a surprised sort of titter. The Sun God of Art History and the Antichrist of Popular Culture. Now to set the hook.

"Look, a couple of us from the old days are having a low-key drinks thing at my club, and I've been deputised to drag you along."

"Tonight? I couldn't possibly—"

I was indignant. "What kind of untutored clod do you take me for? Thursday, eight-thirty, at Boodle's."

The look on his face showed me how much he wanted to reminisce about the war. I had to stay on the offensive. "Actually, you're the guest of honour. Twenty Years of Royal Pictures, or some such rot." I dropped my voice. "It's to be a sort of surprise, but we're all friends here, right?" Chuckles and a couple of genuine guffaws. The idea of Blunt having chums was laugh-out-loud funny.

I turned to go. "Eight-thirty Thursday. Cheers!" And I was out before he could say another word.

White's, Brooks's, and Boodle's, the trio of crusty establishments that form the backbone of Clubland in upmarket St James's, sit within steps of each other— White's having been there first. (A quarter of a millennium ago in *The Rake's Progress*, Hogarth drew a man who'd just lost his fortune in the gaming room at White's.) But Blunt is a fellow member there, and I wanted the home field advantage. Besides, Boodle's is a much more leisurely environment, better suited to the kind of shakedown I had in mind.

Set back several feet from its neighbours, Boodle's is distinguished by its oversized Palladian windows. The façade says Georgian England so perfectly, an exact copy of the place has just been erected by a homesick Brit in Hong Kong.

One passes through the swing doors and is greeted by the rich background smell of cigar smoke wafting down the wide staircase from the club rooms. The member who seeks the bar must cross the worn black and white marble floor and go down a flight of stairs lined with your usual genre paintings: nineteenth-century racehorses and long-gone members in muttonchops. (For a more complete description, may I direct you to M's club, Blade's, in *Moonraker*.)

The bar, though, is a bit public for my purposes, as is the saloon directly behind those grand windows. So I set up shop in the idiosyncratically named Undress Dining Room, where members may sup in casual clothes. I sat and opened my black gunmetal cigarette box, extracting one of the cigarettes of Macedonian blend with the three gold rings round the butt that Morlands of Grosvenor Square make for me. The new Undress man, Michael, brought me my I. W. Harper's American whisky and I waited. N.B.: I really think Pratt's have the right idea. They call all the waiters George. So much simpler.

I almost felt sorry for the old thing

when I saw him cross the threshold that evening with a wary grin and a boutonniere in his lapel. In all other respects he wore the uniform of St James's Street: grey suit and starched white collar, though his bowtie was perhaps a bit artsy—dark blue with white spots, loosely tied around the neck. The man who loves pictures and hates people had decided to make the best of a loathsome evening with drunken louts.

It wasn't until Michael had served him his Pimm's (Pimm's in winter!) that I let him know the "drinks party" was a con. He raised one eyebrow, which you have to practise if you're going to do well.

I started in. "Anthony, there's a picture I want you to look at."

"So that's what this is about." He seemed relieved. Then he turned into Mr. Business. "My fee for an appraisal is five hundred pounds."

"It's not that kind of picture. And *you* pay *me* the fee." I took out a copy of one of my holiday snaps—number 29 from viewing room 2—and pushed it across the table towards him. "That's you with the Duke of Windsor's letter, isn't it?"

He studied himself with the sangfroid with which he might have viewed Saint Jerome and the Lion. "There are secrecy laws. This is obviously a bank's client room. I shall have to take—"

"Legal action? I think you'll find employing extralegal measures to recover misappropriated goods is extra *extra* legal these days. And that's before we even utter the magic words 'national security.' "

He could try calling my bluff. And he did, dropping his voice impressively for greatest effect. "You know perfectly well the people who sent you can't afford for this to be made public."

"Well, that's where it's advantage Fleming. Because there are no People Who Sent Me. Just *moi* telling *vous*—sorry, Anthony, I can't bring myself to tutoyer a Knight of the Realm—that withholding the Crown's property during wartime doesn't go down well in these parts. Especially when it's He for Whom Provenance Is Everything doing the withholding." I took a swig of my bourbon firewater. It had a sweet thickness behind the alcohol. "Do you really want to

be defrocked over this? Moscow can be so
severe in winter."

He pushed the offending image back across
the table. "I don't know what you're
playing at, but I admit nothing. The
picture's no good without the actual
letter."

I picked up my glass and clinked his,
still untouched, with it. "I second the
motion."

I suppose my gesture didn't register
because, emboldened, he went on. "So. You
found out where it is. What's to keep me
from going down to Coutts first thing
tomorrow? I'll put my laundry list in there
and the letter some other place you don't
know about."

"Anthony, I have the letter."

He looked over the rim of his glass. "Impossible."

There's an adrenaline rush when you
finally have the other man where you want
him. It's why the Draxes and Goldfingers
like to stretch out the torture. I was
starting to empathise with those adrenaline
junkies of mine when I reminded myself we
had business to conduct. "What's impossible

is coming up with a torn piece of high-rag-content, silk-weave, crème-coloured notepaper and making two precise copies of it in forty-eight hours. One for us and one for Moscow Centre." I let him see the initials *AB* on the envelope I took from my pocket before putting it back. "Compared to that, what's a little old-fashioned Thirty Assault Unit undertaking against the combined defences of a single video camera and the redoubtable Mr. Turley?"

Blunt dropped his head slightly. I had taken him at the crest, and he had fallen. Crestfallen is such a delicious word.

"So then, what do you want with me?"

Lately I've been getting these burning pains in my gut and I find the bourbon is much kinder to my innards than Scotch whisky. I took a wee dram and wondered what Blunt's innards were doing at the moment. "Let's start with what I don't want. One, a full confession of your role as a Soviet agent. The whole Fourth Man thing: your relationship with Burgess, Maclean, and Philby, your Russian contacts, everything. Don't want it."

He had been stirring his drink as I was

speaking, overvigourously, and now he
spilled a little. "What did you say?"

"Two, an acknowledgement in writing of
your forgeries of the letter in question.
Don't want that either."

He stopped the stirring. "Then what in
blazes is it that you *do* want?"

"I want you out of the spy business, I
want the damage you've done . . . undone. But
the thing that I *need* is a certificate of
provenance from you for the real letter.
How we got it, where you kept it, how you
know it's the genuine article. A couple of
pages at the most."

Michael freshened our drinks without my
asking him to. It's one of the nice things
about clubs.

Blunt looked at me as if I were mad. "And
that's the lot?"

I made that gesture children make about
sealing one's lips and throwing away the
key. "Look, all I want is to stick a pin in
Windsor and his friends—pith him like a
moth on a bit of cotton. I'm going to add
what you give me to a rather large file I
already have and tie it up with a ribbon.
For posterity. The Government aren't in any

position to do it. And I won't be either, if
you don't help me."

It was a different look in his eyes when
he spoke next. "Kim Philby came to me
eighteen months ago, scared out of his wits
by someone poking around in the old days—"
His eyes widened. "That was you, wasn't it,
old boy? Anyway, he led Special Branch
right to my doorstep. I'm afraid I turned
him out into the cold. It's not that I've
gone soft. I was always soft. Just a
terribly bourgeois Bolshevik, I suppose.
There's my flat, my pictures. The letter
was my"—he looked like he was searching for
a particular word—"inoculation against
everything. But my protection died with the
King. So you see, if I stuck out my neck to
help Kim . . ."

Just at that moment I was helping myself
to my Kentucky elixir. Blunt assumed he
still had the floor and went on.
"Obviously, Bertie knew *I* knew about his
disgusting brother, the Duke. But I've had
no way of finding out if our quick little
tour of the American Zone, and the reason
for it, was ever communicated to the
present Queen. So I retired from the game.

Discontinued my foraging for young men.
Kept to the straight and narrow ever since.
Or, at least, the narrow."

I lit another cigarette and offered him
the case. He shook his head and lowered his
voice a bit. "People will say I'm no more
orthodox as a homosexual."

I thought it was time I said something.
"You mean your wife?"

"My quite pregnant wife."

I've been told that, for a fairly
handsome face, mine gets a very comical
look when I'm puzzled. Blunt took pity on
me. "Oh, Ian, don't take on so. One adapts.
If you know I've a wife, you've obviously
read my files. Under the new laws, one more
transgression and it's Borstal for me. The
Philby thing . . ." He had another little sip
of his drink. "It threatened to scatter all
the dust I'd so carefully swept under the
carpet." Now he looked at me. "I have it on
good legal authority that marriage—and even
better, paternity—is considered a
sufficient defence against the sort of
charges that used to arise against me. So
when my assistant found herself in the
family way and thinking of ending the

pregnancy, we were in a position to help each other. You've met her, you know."

"Who?"

"Maggie."

I recalled her then, showing me around the Courtauld with Hyde-Jones. Very easy on the eyes. "And you're telling me this because . . ."

My hand happened to be resting on the tablecloth, and he covered it with his own. For emphasis, I suppose. "I want to trust you, Ian. To be honest, I've always found your pursuits, your interests to be, well . . . vulgar. And yet. All I really have is my position and what remains of my good name. And now that I'm a raving heterosexual like yourself, a good name is something I intend to pass on."

Lord knows what the elderly Tory at the next table made of two members holding hands. I extricated mine to lift my glass to my lips. I suppose I could have used the other hand, but I wanted to let Sir Anthony know, indirectly, that he still had a lot to learn about being a raving heterosexual.

The waiter, Michael, must have been hovering nearby because he chose that

moment to inject himself into the
conversation. "Gentlemen, I was wondering
if the two of you might possibly feel like a
bit of a fool."

Blunt and I stared at each other.
Michael stepped aside slightly to reveal a
rolling cart on which sat a large cut-glass
serving bowl heaped with a sweet, sticky
confection that is the specialty of the
house: Boodle's orange fool.

Michael had two silver serving spoons in
his hands and two bowls at the ready. He
must have seen himself as comic relief. "I
realise, gentlemen, that you have not yet
had dinner, but as you well know, a fool
cannot wait. And as this is the club's two-
hundredth year, Chef has created a double
Cointreau fool to mark the occasion."

Personally, I can't think of anything
more likely to go amiss than a glorified
trifle of cooked fruit and whipped cream on
top of two American bourbon whiskies. Blunt
came to my rescue. "My good man, we are not
suffering fools this evening."

Michael beat a quick retreat with the
rolling cart. Really, where do they get
these people? The two of us seemed to have

formed an alliance based on necessity and an indifference to sweets. Now for the question uppermost in my mind. "Tell me, Anthony, have the Russians ever made use of the letter?"

He pursed his lips in thought. Then he said, "You know how they operate. The right-hand Ivan never knows what the left-hand Ivan is doing. I'd have thought possibly Suez, but now it seems that was the Americans' doing. Last year's cock-up with that hideous Profumo and a Russian sharing the same bit of fluff—they might have unleashed the dogs over that. But"—he gave me one of those palms-up shrugs the French use to mean, who can say?—"of course, they don't confide in me."

"Humble pie isn't your dish, Anthony. Of course they confided in you. You were the linchpin of their little plan." I'd be damned if I'd let Anthony think he'd got one over on me. I exhaled and made a perfect smoke ring. "As a good little English Communist, you didn't decide to do this forgery business on your own, did you?"

The smoke ring had drifted toward Blunt. He put his index finger into the middle of it and broke it up, saying, "You're the one blowing smoke." The icy übermensch had returned.

I was the HMS *Relentless*. "The war was ending, governments were falling all over Europe, and Moscow decided to give ours an extra push. Yes? To do that, Moscow would have to take down their old, sworn enemy. Yes?"

"And who might that have been?"

"Churchill."

Blunt dabbed at his mouth with his napkin and then tossed it on the table. "Your imagination has always been your best quality."

I plowed on through cruel, uncaring seas. "Winston's the one who saw the Iron Curtain descending. Coined the term, in fact. Winston was the great defender of the monarchy, of our whole way of life. So, tar the King's brother and you feather Winston. Do it while he's still in power, and you might bring down more than the Government. You might bag the whole system."

"If you say so." There was that one eyebrow again.

"I do say so. But time was of the

essence, and I'm guessing you ran out of it. This is what I think: the Kremlin and Whitehall are more like each other than either wants to admit. Factions, study groups, more study groups—by the time they knew what they'd got in that letter and how they wanted to use it, poof! We'd held our snap election, Winston and the Conservatives were out. Atlee and Labour were in. You'd missed your chance. The people's party are running the show, Winston's packed off to write his memoirs, and no one's left in Government to use the letter against."

Blunt had been leaning back in his chair throughout my tirade. Now he pressed forward. There was a ruddy colour in his face I hadn't seen before. "Why are you going on so about this? Look, it's over and done."

"I said there's no one left *in Government* who knows about the letter. That's the whole point of blackmail, isn't it? Someone has to know you know a dirty secret about them. The only people who fit that description now are the Royal Family."

"Damn the Royal Family!" Blunt said it in

a hoarse whisper but too loudly. The old
Tory behind him gave me a murderous look.
Why me? I hadn't said it, so I tried to
deflect the accusation by discreetly
pointing my index finger toward my drinking
companion. Unaware of the high drama around
him, Anthony took out a handkerchief and
dabbed at invisible perspiration on his
forehead before going on. "All right, I
believed in a cause, the People's cause.
You believed in one too, while it lasted:
liberal democracy. 'Our way of life,' you
called it. And Windsor, wasn't he a
believer? In Fascism. Racial purity. Anti-
Bolshevism. Whatever it was. Pure rot, but
he believed in it all the same. Who's to say
who was right? You? Me? Why not leave the
deciding to history?"

The passion had drained away as quickly
as it had come. He leaned back again, his
voice almost a whisper. "I told them they
had to act fast. That the minute the
Germans surrendered, all the common man
would want to hear about would be jobs and
housing and getting on with life. Put the
war and everyone in it behind us. Them. But
I was just an upper-class fop. What could a

man of my station possibly know about the
common man and his wants?" He raised his
voice a bit as the bile came up. "You learn
more about a man lying naked next to him
than all the economic theorists will
ever . . ." He left the thought unfinished.

The County type sitting at the table
behind Blunt gave us a look that announced
he had heard the bit about naked men; that
no right-thinking clubman would ever think
such a thought, let alone utter it aloud;
and that if one did, one should recant or
rethink one's membership. All in one
look.

In a few minutes we rose from the table,
said our good-byes, and parted at the door,
Blunt for Portman Square and I for a late
supper with Ann. The next evening I
received the above document, which
I bequeath to you. It should vouchsafe the
authenticity of the Duke of Windsor's
letter to Hitler.

Anthony has proved himself unorthodox
indeed.

CHAPTER 50

WINSTON S. CHURCHILL

·⟨✦⟩·

THE
SECOND WORLD WAR

VOLUME I

THE GATHERING STORM

inquisitive

For my dear, Ian.
Valentine would have been
proud.
With true affection,

WSC

CASSELL & CO. LTD

LONDON · TORONTO · MELBOURNE · SYDNEY

WELLINGTON

PROVENANCE

For the last ten days I've been holed up in
my room, typing like a madman. Ann and I are
leaving for Goldeneye tomorrow, and I've
wanted to have this finished before we go.
The only break I've given myself has been
to go round one morning to see my godfather
at Hyde Park Gate, number 28. He recently
took the decision not to stand for
reelection from Woodford, making this only
the twelfth year this century he has not
been active in public service. Imagine.

I expected a man in his ninetieth year
to act his age. Not Winston. He hallooed me
into the room with an "Ian, my boy!" and a
thunderclap of a slap on the back. Before I
could take off my coat or get in a word of
greeting, he'd launched into a monologue—
disguised as a question—about writing
habits. He was talking around one of his
perennial cigars, so I thought he said
"riding habits." The nattering served to
let me know he was vigourously engaged in
a new book and was not some round, pink
nonagenarian who'd been put out to
pasture.

Clementine came in with tea and biscuits, clucking over Winston's ill treatment of his guest. She took my coat, enquired into Ann's health, and only then performed the disappearing act she'd perfected over a half century of marriage.

Winston was saying, "Keep to a schedule. That's the thing. Up at Chartwell, I'd have been out on the grounds for the past half hour. The earthenworks don't see to themselves." Winston used the language of trench warfare to describe gardening. "We're on the East Atlantic flyway up there, you know. All sorts of birds on our ponds." He looked out the window towards the park. "Not as many birds in town, apart from the pigeons." He made a ceremony out of flicking his ash into a biscuit tin that had been commandeered for the purpose. "But we few make up for it in being old and tough." He still had that twinkle.

I used the mention of Winston's writing to launch into the reason for my visit. "Sir, I've been doing a little writing lately . . . nonfiction."

He took a pull on his cigar. "One of your travel pieces, eh? Where are the glossies

sending you this time, the Seychelles? No,
I remember, you're a Caribbean man now. You
sent me a picture postcard . . . Anguilla?
Antigua?"

I leaned forward in my chair. "Not
exactly. This one's a history. The nineteen
thirties and forties. You're in it, as a
matter of fact."

"Am I now?" He took the cigar from his
mouth, and I watched his mood go from merry
to suspicious. "Am I speaking with a
competitor?"

I saw where I'd put a foot wrong. "Not
history history. More like a few personal
profiles."

"Nothing too unflattering, I hope?"

"Only a little." I was thinking I should
have just written him a letter. "There's a
bit about Rudolf Hess in there."

"Ah." Winston clamped down again on the
stump of his cigar.

I thought I'd start with an icebreaker.
"I've come across some information about
another someone, and I'm not entirely sure
how to proceed."

"Does this someone have a name?"

"Anthony Blunt."

"Ahh." The drawn-out sound told me I was
back on firmer ground. He rotated what was
left of the Upmann a full 360 degrees with
his stubby fingers. "I presume we're not
talking about his personal preferences?"

"No, his political ones."

"Well then, I can save you a lot of
trouble." He accompanied his words with a
full downward thrust of cigar into the
biscuit box, followed by a grind of ash
against tin. Raising himself from the
chair, he called to his wife. "Clemmie, did
I bring last year's boxes down from the
country?"

Her voice came from the other end of the
hallway. I always thought I could detect a
note of reproach. "You know you did.
They're under this year's."

Winston pointed to the floor beneath his
writing desk. "Would you be so kind as to
hand me the bottom two tins?"

Everything in the Churchill household
seemed to be contained in, or overflowing
from, cigar boxes and oversized biscuit
tins. I shuddered to imagine his arteries.
He handed me back a mass of papers marked

1963/Personal and went through
1963/Official at lightning speed.

"When you come to be my age, they put you
on the committees no one else wants. Aha!"
He handed me a sheaf of papers stamped
Confidential, saying, "I am taking you into
my confidence."

To make a long story short, the Ministry
of Defence were asking the Ministry of
Pensions (and copying the Parliamentary
Subcommittee on Pensions) to rubberstamp an
action it had already taken "in the matter
of Blunt re: Philby." On the basis of
information presented to it by MI5, the
Crown had approved stopping payment of the
wartime pension of one Anthony Blunt for
reasons described only as "sensitive." The
tenor of the file suggested that further
steps had been contemplated which might or
might not be taken. There were boxes
indicated next to the names of the three-
member Subcommittee who received the
report: a Scottish MP named Gordon; the
Chairperson and Member for Finchley, a Mrs.
Thatcher; and Winston. A blue pen had
ticked the box next to Winston's name.

My godfather took the file back from me
and put it away in the biscuit tin. "If
that's what you're on about, it's already
been seen to."

I was still marvelling at his
omnipresence in all things British when
I found myself with my coat back on,
heading for the door. "Wait a moment, Ian."
The foyer bookshelf held several copies of
each of his books. He took down one of *The
Gathering Storm* and made a thing of telling
me he was signing it, "with my best pen in
my best hand."

I decided to chance it. "Before I go,
sir. You remember that letter I gave you
from Rudolf Hess? Or rather, half a letter?
What did you do with it?"

He didn't answer but kept on writing his
inscription to me. Eventually he said,
"Half a letter?"

"Written in German by the Duke of
Windsor. You said you were going to give it
to the King."

Winston looked up at me over his glasses.
"Then I must have done, mustn't I?"

I couldn't make him out. Was he
dissembling, or had he really forgotten? I

thought he had finished signing the title page, but he went back and added the word "inquisitive" to it before he handed his book to me. "Take care of yourself, Ian."

I left him patting his jacket for another cigar. In the next room, Clemmie's voice rang out. "Not till after lunch, Winston. You promised."

I thought I was done. Jamaica beckoned. The bit you've just read about Winston and his biscuit tins was supposed to be the last, followed by a brief summing-up. And then the day before yesterday a call came through. It was my assistant at the paper (I still like to keep my hand in), telling me a woman had phoned. An old friend, she'd said, without giving her name. And would I meet her for lunch the next day? She'd named a place no one ever goes to and a time, 12:30. Cleverer still, she'd left no number, so I had no way to ring her back and beg off.

Have you seen *Witness for the Prosecution*? It was Wallis playing Marlene Dietrich playing . . . It was a dark, woody sort of place not far from the British Museum. She wore a very blue Chanel suit

and a hat with a veil. It's 1964. Who wears
a veil anymore?

She greeted me with "The Duke isn't
well." Not "How are you?" or "Ian, you
haven't changed," or any of the standard
openings. For her part, Wallis *had* changed.
What had been stylish at forty had become
severe at seventy. The veil's delicate lace
curtain showed her cheeks to be heavily
rouged. She had the large ruby ear clips I
remembered and a peacock or flamingo pin—I
couldn't tell which—that must have cost the
old boy a packet.

"The Duke isn't well, and a little birdie
tells me you're writing a memoir of"—she
gave me one of those looks that were meant
to be significant—"our time together?" Her
sentence ended with a question mark, but it
wasn't a question.

The brittle woman in Chanel had been
served her drink, a Chartreuse. I asked for
my Harper's bourbon, which they didn't
have. I made do with Johnnie Walker and
told my digestive system to make do as
well.

All I said was "Not 'our time together.'
The war. And the years before the war."

She took no notice of my having spoken. She was looking at the menu. "Edward didn't feel up to flying, so he's back at the ranch in Alberta. I've come to town for a little shopping and a little fence-mending. Please don't make this difficult. I've had a rather trying morning with my niece."

Not many people can describe the Queen of England as "my niece." She looked past me. "I'll have the sole." It's one of those throwback, down-at-the-heels establishments where the waiters affect well-worn formal attire and stand back from the table until summoned.

The man said, "And for the gentleman?"

Wallis unnecessarily interjected, "My treat."

I said, "The chop. And bring me the bill."

"Very good, sir."

It wasn't very good at all. "Wallis, how do you know about—"

She was not to be interrupted. "Ian, of course I trust in your discretion. Explicitly. But as I say, the Duke is unwell. Any shock to the system—"

The eight-year-old Scotch was spreading

its warmth, suffusing me in its glow. I was getting over the surprise of seeing Wallis. "Don't you mean 'implicitly'? You trust me *implicitly*. Otherwise, it isn't trust at all."

"I trust you not to write about us, darling."

I don't know how she got the word "darling" through her clenched teeth. She said the next thing in a quite different voice. "An American acquaintance had a thing he said about sex. That it's a sport in New York, a profession in Hollywood, an art in Paris, and a heavy industry in London. What do you think of that?"

"I think it's rather apt."

"Apt? I think it's vulgar. And I would remind you you're speaking to a Duchess."

I tried a flanking manoeuvre. "All right. My wife, Ann, and I are off to our place in Jamaica tomorrow. Ever been?"

"When you spend five years in the Bahamas without seeing anyone of quality, you've had quite enough of the islands."

That's about how the rest of the meal went. Edward's incandescent Sun had sunk in on itself, leaving Wallis a burnt-out case.

What had been wit was now bitter gall.
Afterwards, I put her in a cab. She held on
to my hand even as I tried to close the
door. It was raining, and between holding
my umbrella and Wallis holding on to me, it
was all I could do to keep my balance.

"I hope I've done the right thing,
speaking with Elizabeth about your memoir,"
she said. "But we simply can't have you
printing anything lurid right now, not with
Edward so unwell." Wallis let go of
my hand and pulled the door of the cab shut.
The driver, not the most patient of men,
gunned the motor. And she was gone.

That blabbermouth Winston. Had he really
talked to Wallis?

CHAPTER 51

With the last half-dozen pages still unread, Amy felt the bus slow down and come to a stop just short of its usual berth on Park Avenue between Forty-first and Forty-second Streets. A limo was idling in the No Standing zone and didn't move when the bus driver blew his horn. With the back of his vehicle still sticking out into traffic, the driver chose discretion over valor and opened the doors of his bus. "Grand Central, folks. Everybody out."

Amy was the first one off, her handbag looped over her left shoulder and the computer case atop her rolling suitcase as she lugged it toward the four lanes of Forty-second Street. When she happened to look to her left, what she saw didn't register immediately. Her mind's eye was still on Fleming's long letter to her and what it meant. Then the fact that she'd seen her name, misspelled, on the card that was still stuck in the limo's passenger window came home to her and she started to run.

Or at least she tried to run, but the little wheels on

the American Tourister weren't up to the job, and she found herself dragging thirty pounds of luggage behind her.

The driver was out of the Town Car. "Dr. Greenberg! Wait!"

The light had just turned red against her, but Amy didn't slow down. She reached behind her like one of those relay runners taking the baton and grabbed the strap on her bag and darted into the intersection. By the grace of God and/or amazing luck, all four drivers—two in each direction—who could have mashed their accelerators and wiped out the woman hauling the carry-on bag . . . didn't. Amy made it across the street and looked back. Her pursuer was stuck on the other side of Forty-second Street. She had about a minute.

Amy kept running, through the bank of wooden doors and into the chaos of Grand Central Terminal. Her right arm was coming out of its socket, so she dropped the suitcase on its wheels again and, gripping the extended handle instead of the strap, made a beeline for the information kiosk in the center of the great hall. Well, a drunken bee's beeline.

It was the beginning of the Tuesday homeward rush for New York's commuters. To Amy it looked like one of those training films they show you in high school for driver's ed, filmed through a windshield as cars slam on their brakes in front of you and children chase balls out into the street. Only, Amy was on foot. People kept darting out in front of her: a mother with a kid, absurdly bundled up to the point of immobility on a May day; a guy from Zaro's Bakery trundling a delivery of bread to the shop over by track 36; a couple of Dutch or German tourists—the flattop haircuts and brown shoes were a dead giveaway—pulling bags just like Amy's side by side up the ramp she was running down. She split them like a running back and kept going.

She set her sights on the information booth with the four-sided brass clock directly under an enormous American flag. It wasn't actually her goal, just the midpoint of her run to the escalators going up to the MetLife Building on the north side of the terminal. By now her path had turned into a slalom course around the clumps of people: a handful waiting on line for train or track information; people greeting each other or waiting to greet someone; and the trickiest part of the course—people talking on their cell phones and idly moving around, oblivious to the crowd around them and Amy's desperate need to get by. It was a kind of Brownian motion of humanity, and Amy did her best to navigate it.

When she glanced over her shoulder, Amy saw the man with the mustache from the Town Car running down the ramp from Forty-second Street. He'd made up at least two-thirds of the distance on her. The luggage was slowing her down and making her stand out. She'd be a sitting duck on those escalators across the way. She had to ditch the suitcase.

There's an ornate stairway on the west side of the station that leads up to a couple of restaurants on the mezzanine level and then to the street. Tucked behind the base of the stairway on the right is a water fountain, with just enough space under it to park a bag. Amy darted behind two of the burly army guys they have patrolling the place post-9/11, hoping Mustache hadn't seen her. She grabbed her bulging computer case and left her suitcase behind (wondering if she'd be able to retrieve it later before it set off a bomb scare).

There was a sign next to the water fountain that read, "If you see something, say something." For an instant, she thought of just going up to the soldiers with the guns and saying something. But then she remembered Detective Pinsky's sarcasm. What would she tell them—that some fanatical driver wanted her to ride in a limo? They'd shrug and walk away, leaving her with Mustache.

She took off along the corridor of entrances to the Westchester-bound Metro-North tracks and made an angled left at Zaro's and its aroma of fresh-baked bread. Across the passage there was an escalator down to the Lower Concourse and more trains. Amy had no way of knowing if the guy had spotted her, if he was behind her—even right behind her. All she knew was that she had to get down to the lower level.

Originally, Amy's plan had been simply to get to Scott, who by now should be waiting in the second-floor bar of the Yale Club on Vanderbilt Avenue and Forty-fourth Street, next door to Grand Central. Now she had to improvise. Instead of going up the escalators, out the MetLife Forty-fourth Street lobby and across Vanderbilt Avenue, she'd have to go down to the station's lowest level and up another way she knew about, a World War I–era elevator that went directly into the Yale Club.

When she was a teenager, Chief had shown her the unmarked vestibule and taken her up in the elevator. It was their "secret passage," one that the Yale men on the old New York Central's board had included during Grand Central's construction. They had used it to board their private railroad cars for the overnight run up to their luxurious "camps" in the Adirondacks and then to return to the club weeks later without having to walk among the hoi polloi in the public part of the station.

The end of the private car epoch in the 1960s had

made the Yale elevator's original role obsolete. The westernmost tracks on the lower level, the ones that had serviced those cars, were closed off and the elevator turned into a freight carrier used by the concessionaires who provide food and drink for the Club. These days it stands twenty yards away from the nearest Metro-North platform, enclosed in a drywall vestibule painted the same drab green as the maintenance rooms and electrical closets. Only the heavy five-button combination lock on the vestibule door—permanently set to 3-1-1-1-4, the Yale Club's opening day of March 11, 1914—suggests anything worthwhile is on the other side.

But Amy's plan had at least two possibly fatal flaws. Just to get into the closed-off area of tracks meant going through a metal door with a No Trespassing sign on the parapet above track 117. Sometimes it was locked, sometimes it wasn't, and Amy didn't have a key. Flaw number two: there was another way down here to the Lower Concourse—the stairs where she'd left her suitcase. If Mustache had seen which way she'd gone, he could cut her off by taking the staircase down and make up the ground on her. Of course, he didn't know about the unused tracks and the elevator. Maybe he'd think she was coming down here to lose herself in the crowd milling around the food court. Maybe he'd turn the wrong way.

All the food shops were off to her right. Amy headed left. She almost made it to the ornate entrance of track 117. "Dr. Greenberg!" The voice came from off to her right, and it was close. Damn. She had to throw him off her tail.

Unlike most of the other tracks that have individual access ramps leading down from the Lower Concourse, tracks 115, 116, and 117 share a landing with separate stairs to each track. Now Amy kept on running, right past the locked door on the left side of the landing and down the metal steps. Just at that moment she wished she were Katie, the jock in their college group. Katie *lived* in her Reeboks; this stairway would have been a piece of cake for her. But in these low heels, Amy could barely manage to stay upright with her handbag pulling her left and the computer case pulling her right. She'd have to trick her pursuer and try to buy back the time she'd lost.

Mustache was already at the top of the stairs by the time Amy had made it to the bottom. Her panicked look back showed her his wig had ridden back from his forehead in the commotion. She knew him! But from where?

"Dr. Greenberg! Don't make this any harder on yourself!"

That didn't sound good. He'd catch her if she ran even ten more yards. But the 5:19 to Croton-Harmon was filling up right in front of her. She raced ahead in an all-out sprint and got on.

People were taking off their coats and opening their books and papers as Amy hurtled past and, a couple of times, into them. "Sorry." "Pardon." There was a bathroom at the end of the car. Amy got to it, closed the door behind her, and slid the latch shut.

The smell. Part disinfectant, part the thing the disinfectant was disinfecting. Just one more reason for Amy to hold her breath as she heard feet come running up to where she was. He seemed to wait there. Deciding something? Amy's hands were so slippery with perspiration from running, the computer case she hadn't dared put down on the dirty floor now slipped from her grasp and landed with a soft thud. Had he heard? And then the heavy door at the end of the railroad car made its characteristic open-and-shut sound. He was searching the rest of the train. Amy wanted to give him a minute, enough time to get a couple of cars ahead of her before she made a U-turn back to the stairs and safety.

And then she knew where she'd seen the limo driver before. Hurriedly she rummaged in her purse for her day planner and flipped through the pages to the sketches she'd made of the people at the Dublin bank. With her pencil she quickly added a mustache to the man's face. It was Macken, all right. The Irish bank manager.

This would have been a perfect time to whip out her cell phone and call Scott for help. Or 911 for that matter. *If* she'd brought it with her. She thought about using the pay phone on the train, just a few feet away. But no, it would take too long to punch in her credit card number. Then an announcement on the train's PA system made up her mind for her. "This is the five-nineteen express for Croton-Harmon. Watch the closing doors."

Amy flew out of the bathroom, getting to the doors at the same time as three or four late arrivals who were trying to get on. Push came to shove and Amy broke free, almost bowling over a woman. "Well, I never!" the woman whined to Amy's back.

Her plan would have worked were it not for the conductor's announcement. The problem was, it seemed to have had the same galvanizing effect on Mustache/Macken, who sliced through people boarding the train two cars ahead. He came flying toward her.

She had no chance, but she went for it anyway. Back along the platform, then up the steps. No Trespassing? Not a chance. She pushed on the door and it gave way. There was a narrow platform on the other side, and then more steps down. She knew where to cross the old tracks and their third rails without electrocuting herself. Macken was so close, she could hear his ragged breathing. Or was that hers?

She could see the green vestibule door and the lock with the five buttons. Could she will herself onto the elevator and safety?

CHAPTER 52

No, she couldn't. Amy got to the door all right, but in her haste to push the five numbered buttons on the combination lock her sweaty fingers slipped and she hit the wrong code. The door wouldn't budge. And then came the sharp pain from a five-inch barrel of metal poking into her ribs.

"Turn around . . . slowly." The man gasped for breath. The two of them fought for air as if they'd just run a marathon. They were standing in a little cul-de-sac hidden from even the view of the maintenance people. They couldn't be seen. Or heard.

She could see the underside of the man's toupee and the double-sided tape that had held it on. The man's mustache was ridiculous, clinging to a single spot on his upper lip at a forty-five-degree angle to his mouth.

"Mr. Macken!" Calling a man holding a gun on you "Mr." was dumb, but she'd forgotten his given name.

"If you'd have just gotten into the car." He

reached up and took the wig off and threw it on the ground. "We could have talked. I could have explained my position . . . *our* position."

Amy tried to stay calm, but the gray barrel of the gun aimed at her heart looked enormous. Maybe she could stall. "Position on what?"

The question made Macken testy. Only then did he remember the mustache, and he swatted it off his face. "Why, the Fleming material, of course." He took out a handkerchief and dabbed at his forehead with his nongun hand. "A point-by-point indictment of English treachery. And by an Englishman for once."

The academic in her said, "Fleming was Scottish." That was another dumb thing to say to a sweaty guy holding a gun.

Through the heavy breathing and the perspiration, Macken was still trying to explain. "The point is, he wasn't Irish. So it isn't the old complaint from the old complainers. I'd love to see the face on that pompous old prince when we tell him what we've got."

Who? Prince Charles? Conversing at gunpoint wasn't helping Amy's little gray cells. "But I thought—I thought this was a German thing. Wasn't Kaltenbrunner a part of your—"

"How do you know about Jürgen? What happened at your hotel? Why didn't he get off the plane?" Macken had been dabbing at what remained of the spirit gum on his upper lip, and the hankie made a little adhesive sound every time he pulled it away. Now he stopped and made Amy tell him about Sheridan and the CIA man's using Kaltenbrunner's name. "Your government are in league with them, you know. They call it 'the special relationship.' " He actually spat on the ground. Disgusting. "We could have covered all this in the car. The English are the daemons of the world." Amy was sure he'd said "daemons." "Everywhere they go, everything they touch. Africa . . . look at the Afrikaaners. Egypt. Iraq, Palestine . . . India, the Pacific. What they did to the aborigines in Australia. You Americans forget you fought two wars just to get away from them. This is bigger than just a bunch of angry micks." Macken sought her eyes with his. "Jürgen Kaltenbrunner was a soldier in the fight. His father starved to death in an English concentration camp."

Amy's body was drained by the fear, but her mind seemed to be working off some auxiliary power source. "English concentration camps? C'mon."

Macken was rummaging through the pockets of his jacket with his left hand as he kept the gun aimed at her with his right. "You're a professor, you're supposed to deal in the truth. Look it up. The Isle of Man. Only, they called it an internment camp." He found whatever he had been looking for in his inside breast pocket. It was a photograph. He shoved it in Amy's face. "Here. Look."

Macken was so agitated he had trouble holding the picture steady. Even so, Amy could tell it was of one of the documents from Fleming's manuscript, the one of Hess's dental records. Amy could clearly see the yellow hotel bedspread in the background.

The man with the gun was all-out angry now. "You see? Churchill killed Rudolf Hess, just as he killed thousands of German POWs. The English . . . they . . . they make a desert and call it peace. Fleming found out about this; he must have explained all this." Macken looked down and seemed to remember the gun. "Okay, talking's over. I still need the papers, whether I get them from Jürgen or from you."

Amy tightened her grip on her computer case. If only she'd gotten the door's combination right. "Look, Mr. Macken." His name came back to her. "Milo. I've read the whole thing. It's not about English treachery. It's treachery, all right, but one man's—the Duke of Windsor. And he was helping the Germans, like your friend Jürgen's father."

Macken actually smiled. "A teacher, but so much to learn. You're confusing a people with its leaders. The former English king was helping Hitler and sell-ing out his people. We know something about that in Ireland. Now, the papers. Hand them over and no one gets hurt."

What do they say about muggers? Give them what they want. It's not worth getting killed over. And then, behind her assailant, the light flickered. As if the naked bulb lighting the cul-de-sac were about to blow. Or the shadow of a tall someone had noiselessly moved between the light and the wall for just an instant. Amy needed a little more time.

"How did you know what Fleming left me? How did you know to have the maid take the pictures?"

Macken rose to the bait. "In my father's day it was common knowledge Fleming knew dangerous things. Rumor was, he'd written them down. And then, as it happened, with the bank failing, I asked Colleen O'Beirne to give me the list of the people I needed to contact about their boxes. The owners. By mistake, she also gave me the old list of purchasers, and Fleming's name was on it. I had to know for sure what he had, so we set a few things in motion."

"Colleen O'Beirne's accident. Did you set that in motion?"

"Actually, that was your doing. Your clumsiness with the box, all those papers you dropped. Unfortunately, it's all on videotape these days. Can't have any loose ends."

"Am I a loose end?" Amy's heart was beating at an all-time high. To protect it, she instinctively held the computer case in front of her. "I promise I won't say anything. You said no one would get hurt."

Macken took his handkerchief and wrapped it around the muzzle of his Glock 9. "I lied. If there's one thing I've learned, it's don't trust anyone. Now, if you'll just put the case on the floor. Wouldn't want to bloody any of the—*unnh*!"

CHAPTER 53

Milo Macken fell forward so violently, the computer case was trapped between their bodies. In no more than five seconds, he really was a body: it was horrifying for Amy to learn just how fast a human being can die from a knife wound in exactly the right place.

Brian Devlin calmly picked up Macken's gun from where it had fallen. Amy was nauseated at having a second dead man lying on top of her and simultaneously euphoric at being rescued from imminent death. She wanted to hug her rescuer, and would have if Macken hadn't come between them. At the same time, her intuition told her—screamed at her, actually—that Brian Devlin wasn't the cavalry, no matter how good his timing.

Ever the English gentleman, Devlin peeled Macken from Amy and deposited him on the ground in such a way that he wouldn't be seen easily from the cul-de-sac and yet wouldn't keep the green door with the lock on it from opening. He unwound the damp handkerchief and used it to clean the blood off the blade of his stiletto. Then he pocketed both the gun and the blade and stuffed the handkerchief into the dead man's chauffeur's jacket. Finally, he smiled that too-even smile of his. "That was a close thing." Like balancing his tea on his newspaper, he'd done this before.

"Thank you." It didn't seem enough under the circumstances, but it was all she could manage.

The question going through Amy's brain must have been visible in her eyes because he answered it. "I knew he was following you, so I followed him. Caught up to him at the light on Forty-second Street. The rest was police work."

"Then you're a policeman. I thought you were a publisher."

"I'm whatever they tell me to be."

"And who are *they*?"

"Now, Dr. Greenberg, that would be telling."

He was charming. She had to give him that.

CHAPTER 54

It seemed only right to offer a drink to the man who had just saved her life. Several, if that's what he wanted. Amy once more bent to the task of tapping in the code that would open the locked door. This time she made no mistakes. The space they stepped into was the hastily built 1980s vestibule, but in three strides they were back in the luxe days of the early twentieth century, before America entered the Great War.

Amy and Devlin found themselves standing in front of brass elevator doors, covered with scenes of old Yale in raised relief. They even had period cars of the New Haven Railroad running past the campus (in reality the tracks were about three miles away, but Amy had always chalked their being there to artistic license). The elevator doors were surrounded by marble, a step up from the material used in the rest of the station. A brass plate held a single button to call the elevator. The brasses and the marble and the elevator cab itself, when it came, had collected decades of tarnish and dust.

All those years of running around the Club as a child made the next part a snap. The elevator was programmed to make freight runs to only three floors: the bar on 2, the athletic courts on 5, and the rooftop restaurant on 22, the three places in the club where food and drink were delivered on a regular basis. Amy pressed the first button, and the old lift started up with a jerk.

A question had been nagging at her. "How did you get to New York ahead of me? I saw you waiting at the airport."

Devlin looked at her, Macken's gun bulging in his left-hand jacket pocket. Good thing the Yalies hadn't gotten around to metal detectors. "The Royal Air Force. We've been watching Macken for some time— had a man right there in the bank."

A man with bad teeth, Amy thought.

"He tipped us that something was going down and then went silent. That's why we tried to keep you from getting on the plane. We found out Macken did a bunk to New York last night, and then we had to double-team his German friend this morning at Shannon. So I hopped a ride on a Harrier to catch up with this one. But the best-laid plans . . ." He let his words trail off as if to say, "all in a day's work."

Another little jolt told her they'd arrived at the second floor. They made their way along the short service corridor that had once been a regular entrance to the Club's main bar. Nowadays, people hiked up the staircase from the lobby or took one of the row of modern elevators. Scott was sitting at a table, nursing a beer. Amy saw him and ran the rest of the way.

He wasn't a big man, but he was tall, with long arms. And now they encircled her in a ring of protection. He tried to kiss her but all she wanted to do was to hold on tight and be held in return. It made a nice tableau for the other members, the early crowd that like to get their drinking in while the sun is still up. It hadn't been this way before coeducation. For the older ones, hugging and kissing in the bar was probably a novelty.

It was a good minute before Amy looked up at Scott and realized he was eyeing the stranger in the nice but bulging suit.

"Oh, forgive me. Mr. Devlin, this is my fiancé, Scott Brown. Scott, this is Brian Devlin. I think he's with Scotland Yard. He saved my life."

Devlin held out a manicured hand. "Special Branch." There were those pearly whites again.

Scott seemed no more taken with Mr. Devlin's incisors than Amy had been, but that could have just been male territoriality. He got out the words "Nice to meet you" and gestured for them all to have a seat before motioning the waiter to come over. "A glass of red wine, Amy?"

She nodded.

"And for you, Mr. Devlin?"

"Brian."

"All right, Brian, what's your poison?"

"I think a Dewar's and water, thank you very much."

Scott pointed to his beer. "And another of the same for me."

"Thank you, Mr. Brown." When the waiter walked away, Scott leaned over and kissed Amy on the cheek. "So, Brian, you 'saved' Amy's life. Did you give her a lift or something?"

Amy put a still-trembling hand in Scott's. "Honey, he literally saved my life."

Scott put down his glass of beer so abruptly it made a little bang on the wooden table. "What are you talking about? The man who died on the plane . . . ?" He looked at Devlin. "Did you kill him? Was that why—"

She hesitated for a moment, unsure just where to begin. All that came out was, "No, no . . . that was another . . ."

Devlin leaned back in his chair. "Sorry, old man,

but I think you've got the wrong end of the stick. Miss . . . I mean Dr. Greenberg was followed from the airport. There was an attempted robbery, and I happened to intervene at the right time."

Scott brought Amy's hand up to his lips and kissed it gently. "I had no idea. A robber?"

Amy nodded. Suddenly her mouth was dry as a desert, and her vocal cords had stopped working. The shock must be hitting her.

Their drinks came. Amy took an unladylike gulp of the cabernet. No one said anything for a surprisingly long stretch. Scott seemed to be taking it all in and Devlin had the look a man has after sex. When you knifed someone to death, was there an afterglow?

Scott broke the silence. "Shouldn't you be calling someone?"

The question seemed to take Devlin by surprise. "Whom?"

"The cops. NYPD. You broke up a robbery, you've got his description, the guy's probably still in the area."

Devlin had no sense of urgency. "Oh, he's still in the area all right. On the floor downstairs. Quite dead."

Scott finally understood. "You—you really did save her life. I'm enormously grateful." He thought for a moment. "But don't you have to call the cops anyway? The morgue? Somebody?"

It was funny. For the last couple of minutes, Amy had had the feeling that Devlin was inching his chair closer to hers, that he was leaning in next to her. What was he doing, making a move on her, right in front of her fiancé? In the bar at the Yale Club?

"Oh, I'll be making a call," Devlin said. Amy had been concentrating on Scott, to see how he was handling the news of Macken's death. So even though she shouldn't have been surprised at the nearness of Devlin's voice, it startled her. His mouth was right next to her ear. "But not to the morgue. That is, if you do exactly as I say. Do you see what's in my right hand?"

Amy looked left and down and so did Scott. Under the table, the stiletto in Devlin's right hand was half an inch from Amy's kidney.

Then he did the strangest thing—swung his right leg over Amy's left, obscenely immobilizing her. People at the other tables who couldn't see their legs would think *he* was the fiancé, just sitting a little too close.

Scott got pink, then red in the face and started to get up. Amy could see what Scott couldn't: that Devlin had Macken's gun in his left hand. It too was under the table, and it was pointing right at Scott's crotch.

"Scott, don't! Sit down!" Amy had finally found her voice.

Devlin was all sweetness and light. "That's right. Sit down. If anything happens here, you two will be dead and I'll be the man from Scotland Yard, working on a case of the highest security."

Amy finally understood that smile. It was evil.

"And speaking of a case, we want those papers in yours, Dr. Greenberg." He'd spoken softly, so no one in the surrounding hubbub of the bar could hear. Now he dropped his voice even more, so Amy could barely make out what he said. "Tell your fiancé we wouldn't want anything to go amiss on your wedding night."

Scott sat back down. He couldn't see the gun under the table, but he knew he couldn't get to the knife fast enough to save Amy. Meanwhile, Amy leaned to her right to pick up her black nylon case from the floor next to her chair. Devlin's leg was pressing down on hers, hurting it.

Devlin had left the blade of the stiletto exactly where it had been, so when Amy straightened up again with the computer case in both hands, the metal point stuck into her blouse and broke the skin. He grinned, enjoying the pain it caused.

"If I give this to you," she said, "how do I know you'll let us go?"

"You don't. But look at it my way. Some damaging material has been out in the open for twenty-four hours and it was my job to retrieve it. Now that I have it"—he looked at his watch, twisting his gun hand to read the time—"and my colleagues have by now purged the bank's records and erased the video-tape, you have no proof of anything. Except that a man tried to mug you and you killed him somehow. Without the papers, who's going to believe you? All the Irish bankers are dead. Still, if it makes you feel any better, I'd rather *not* kill you. I'm a sentimentalist when it comes to marriage."

Amy wanted to see it his way, and what choice did she have? A professional with a gun and a knife beat anything two amateurs could come up with. She opened the computer case and took out the thick wad of papers.

Devlin looked at the cover sheet. "*Provenance*, by I. Fleming. Too bad for you it *wasn't* written by Ira Fleming."

He took the manuscript from Amy with his right hand and stood up. The stiletto was already back in his pocket. "Now, if you'll excuse me. The RAF don't like to be kept waiting."

He was still holding the gun in his left hand, but now the hand was hidden in his jacket pocket. He jiggled the pocket a little to call attention to it. "I'm walking right out the front door of this place. Don't try to follow me, or I really will use this on you."

And then he was gone. Scott made a move to go after him, and it was all Amy could do to hold him back, literally. The waiter was at their table. "Will there be anything else?"

CHAPTER 55

Sign the check." Amy heard the harshness in her voice and made a mental note to work on that when they were married. "Please, Scott, let's go." She looked at her watch. The next train to New Haven would leave in a quarter hour. Too much time.

Scott finished paying and saw that Amy had her coat on and the somewhat slimmer computer bag slung over her shoulder. "What's the rush? We're practically in Grand Central already."

"Don't ask questions. Hurry." She hustled them out of the bar and back along the service corridor and around a partition to the old elevator. She pushed the button as hard as she could, to make it come faster. It was still there from the trip up. The doors opened right away.

Once they were heading down, Amy blurted out, "I'm worried about him coming back." Some explanations don't explain anything.

"But why?" Scott asked.

The elevator came to a stop and Amy pushed

through the door into the vestibule. "I'll tell you when we're safely on the train." The vestibule door is always unlocked on the Club side. Amy turned the knob and they were back in the station.

Macken's body hadn't gone anywhere, still crumpled in a corner to her right. She couldn't look, but Scott did. "Oh my God! Is that the guy? Oh my God!"

Scott must have had no idea how loud his voice was, reverberating off the tunnel walls down here. Now every homeless person living in Grand Central would know something was up. "You're sure he's dead?" Thankfully, Scott had lowered his voice. "Maybe we should—"

"He's dead! He died in my arms. We've got to go!" For the second time in about an hour, Amy thought her right arm was going to be dislocated as she pulled her reluctant fiancé away from Macken and toward the public part of the terminal.

They made their way across the tracks, onto the abandoned platform and up some more steps to the No Trespassing door. It opened and Amy and Scott were back on the parapet above track 117, back in the world of commuters.

From here, they could see several trains with wide blue stripes running the length of the cars. These were bound for either central Westchester along the Harlem Line or the county's river communities on the Hudson Line. The trains they wanted weren't blue but the red of the New Haven Line.

Back on the Lower Concourse, Amy searched the departures monitor. The 5:38 express to New Haven was on the upper level, leaving two minutes ahead of a train to Stamford.

"Scott, I'm going upstairs to get my suitcase. I'll meet you inside the entrance to track twenty-five. *Inside* the entrance."

He just stood there. "I'm not letting you out of my sight."

Amy was getting impatient, and she knew it was irrational. Scott just wanted to protect her. "Sweetie, there's something I need you to do. Outside the station, across the street where the airport buses stop, there's a limo with my name in the passenger window. At least, there was an hour ago. I need you to get the card: it may be the only proof we'll have that any of this happened."

"Should I ask the driver for it?"

"He's the dead guy."

Scott still wasn't moving. "Shouldn't we call the police? At least to get the body?"

Scott seemed to be getting agitated and Amy

couldn't tell if he remembered her instructions. "Please, sweetie, the card. We'll call the police from the train."

"All right." Just like that, Scott was off at a run, taking the stairs up to the main level two at a time. Amy headed in the opposite direction, toward the escalators. Less conspicuous.

Three minutes later, Amy Greenberg was standing next to her American Tourister bag just within the imposing arch that announced Tracks 25 & 26, out of view of any prying eyes in the enormous main hall of Grand Central. Five minutes. Seven minutes went by. A watched Scott never comes. And then there he was, out of breath.

"It must have been towed."

So much for that idea. "Thanks anyway, dear."

Amy was holding the handle of her suitcase, but Scott took it from her. "Let me."

They hurried toward the train. Straight ahead was a platform a couple of city blocks long. The wide red bands running along the train cars on either side created in Amy's mind's eye a kind of forced perspective, mentally leading all the way out of the terminal eighty miles to the end of the line at New Haven. The vanishing point.

The New Haven express on their left was filling up fast, though there were plenty of people getting on the Stamford train as well. Scott hurried ahead of Amy, peering into the windows of the 5:38 for two seats together.

It was all Amy could do to catch up to him. "No, honey, the other train."

"But—" Now Scott was totally confused. "This is the one going to Yale. I checked the monitor in the station."

She commandeered the suitcase with Scott still holding it and executed a 180-degree turn across the platform. "I know. That's why we're going to Stamford. Get in here, quick." She seemed to have spent the last quarter hour just giving Scott orders.

Scott had never known Amy to be so insistent, so abrupt. But he let her hustle them onto the 5:40. There were still seats together facing forward, but Amy dropped her purse and computer case on the window seat of a pair that faced back toward the station and sat down with her face as close as possible to the glass.

Scott shoved the suitcase onto the luggage rack over their heads and sat down beside her. "What are you looking for?"

"Not what. Who." Amy pointed with her finger, jabbing the heavy glass of the window. "Him."

Scott leaned toward her to see what she saw. Brian Devlin was frantically running past the train across the way, peering into the windows as Scott had just done. He had almost reached the spot where they had been standing when the conductor called, "All aboard!"

Devlin took another look back along the platform toward the terminal, then up toward the head of the train. There were four more cars he hadn't checked. Then, unexpectedly, he pivoted and looked behind him, right toward Amy and Scott. She pulled the man she loved away from the window a little too hard.

Devlin still had the manuscript in his hand and the bulge in his jacket pocket. Amy prayed for him to get on the other train. And he did.

As it pulled out of the station past them, Amy could see Devlin walking a little awkwardly up the aisle toward the head car, keeping his jacket pocket forward and looking left and right. They'd dodged a major bullet.

Scott was speechless. Or at least, stuttering. "How— What— How—?"

Amy realized she'd been holding her breath. She let it out with a gasp. "The manuscript I gave him at the Yale Club?"

"Yes?"

"It wasn't the real one."

Now Scott was beyond speechless. He was stumped. "You mean . . . what? It was forged?"

She took both of his hands in hers and stroked them gently. "Not forged. Copied." She opened her black bag and showed him Fleming's papers inside. "These are the originals."

Scott's eyes went from Amy's face to the papers and back again, like a child's. She went on. "When I called you from the Delta Lounge, I saw that they have Xerox machines there next to the phones. Ten minutes and I had a copy. Then I switched the title pages, so the real cover sheet was on the copied documents. And that's what I handed to Devlin." She took the papers from her computer case and showed him the photocopied cover.

"But why make a copy at all?"

"Sweetheart, the man who died next to me on the plane? He was there to protect me, protect the pages, I think. And someone killed him. A stewardess—who maybe was the killer—tried to steal them from me. I think the dead man back there in the station wanted to give them to the IRA to blackmail the English with. And Devlin and the British have some secret they don't want even their allies to know. They want to destroy the manuscript to keep its secret. This thing is sending out a signal: "Come and get me." Making a second manuscript was the only plan I could come up with. And it would have worked . . . as long as Devlin didn't have a chance to inspect what he had. But if he did, he'd know they were phonies . . . and that we'd be on that train."

"How would he know that, exactly? And what's the big secret, anyway?"

Amy paused. After all the conspiracy theories she'd developed in her mind, was Scott really an innocent in all this? "Macken said it's all about Churchill killing Rudolf Hess and a lot of prisoners of war. But I don't think so." She touched her computer bag. "Macken didn't know about all the stuff on the Duke and Duchess of Windsor in here."

Now Scott really looked lost. "The Duke and Duchess of . . . huh?"

"I'm still trying to figure it out. I haven't finished reading everything."

"Then just tell me this," Scott asked. "How did Devlin know we'd be on that other train?"

"I told him at the Dublin airport that I teach at Yale. If he's any good at detecting, once he knew the pages were copies, he'd have enough time to come after us. So now, we'll go the slow way and change at Stamford for the next New Haven train."

By this time Scott had reversed roles and was rubbing her hands. They were ice cold. "Darling, you're amazing. You've thought of everything."

Amy looked out the window. They were still in the tunnel under Park Avenue. "As soon as we can get in cell phone range, we'll call the Metro-North police. Because if they don't stop him, he'll be up at Yale waiting for us."

CHAPTER 56

All three Metro-North rail lines climb out of the Park Avenue tunnel at Ninety-seventh Street, and Scott's phone acquired a signal about ten seconds later. Within a minute, his call to 911 had been answered by a police operator and routed to the transit cops, the unit responsible for Grand Central, Penn Station, the surface trains, and the subways. The man on the other end of the call listened to Scott. Then he said, "This guy you say was stabbed in Grand Central? You sure he's dead?"

Scott didn't have to look over at Amy. "Positive."

"Then you don't want us. You want Homicide. Hold on."

This time, the original dispatcher listened long enough for Scott to describe "a dead man in Grand Central Station" before transferring the call again. Twenty seconds of dead air—no ringing, no hold music—and Scott was sure the call had been dropped. They were just leaving the Harlem station at 125th Street.

"Homicide. Spezio."

It was a woman's voice. For just an instant, Scott wondered if "spezio" was street talk for "speak." You never know in this country. "Detective Spezio, a man has been stabbed to death."

"It's *Officer* Spezio, but thanks for the upgrade. Name?"

"I don't know his name. Wait and I'll—"

"No. *Your* name."

Amy had been listening, her ear next to the phone across from Scott's. Now she looked him in the eye and silently mouthed, "No."

Officer Spezio waited a moment before saying, "Caller ID is showing you as Brown comma Scott. Mr. Brown, I need you to confirm that this cell phone hasn't been stolen."

"I'm Scott Brown."

"That's better. Location?"

"I'm on a train."

"No, the body. Where is it?"

Scott told her and added, helpfully, "There's a No Trespassing sign on the door."

"No Trespassing. I see." Was she entering this into a computer?

"The door wasn't locked."

"I see." Scott could hear typing. "And where are you now?"

"We're on the train to—"

Amy clapped her hand over Scott's mouth so suddenly it stung her hand. She realized she could have accomplished the same result by covering the phone instead of Scott. So she did. "Sweetie," she whispered, "don't say where we're going."

Scott gave her a questioning look as Officer Spezio came back on. "Never mind, Mr. Brown. I'm showing that this incident has already been called in. Units are responding as we speak. Hmm. Are you traveling with an Amy Greenberg?"

Amy reached over and pressed the End button, squishing Scott's pinky finger in the process. He didn't seem to notice, saying, "It was already called in."

Devlin. Amy's mind was off to the races again. "Do the police phones have that satellite system, that tracking thing, you know . . ."

"GPS. Global positioning system." He said it like an objective, technological fact. "The *Times* had a story on it . . . I think they call it 'Enhanced' nine-one-one." Scott didn't see the implications.

Amy did. "Only one person knows I'm with you."

"Oh." Scott was catching up.

"What if he said I . . . we . . . did it? Killed

Macken? He's Scotland Yard and we're . . . nobody. And they know we're on a train."

Scott came to life. "Damn, the phone." Amy had only ended the call; now Scott shut off the phone. They both watched the little Samsung window go dark. Amy was thinking, And he's up ahead of us with a knife, a gun, and a badge.

CHAPTER 57

They were just leaving the Rye station in Westchester on the way to Stamford. Scott had been clutching Amy's hands in both of his the whole way. It was sweet, but it made it impossible for her to reach into her bag and pick up the manuscript so she could read it. She made a little move to take her hands away from his and thought better of it immediately. Isn't this what she had wanted, had prayed for? A man to hold her and make her feel safe?

The little movement she'd made must have registered with Scott, because he turned slightly to her and started to speak. "Sweetheart, there's something I have to tell you."

Amy burrowed her hands more deeply between his. "Don't. Not now. I just want to stay this way. With you."

They stayed exactly that way until the train pulled in to the Stamford station. No police were waiting on the platform. Maybe they hadn't got their act to-

gether. Maybe they were farther up the line. Amy
turned to Scott. "How much money do you have?"

"On me? About forty-five dollars."

She opened her purse. She still had three twenties
she'd never changed into Irish euros. And some sin-
gles. "Let's splurge."

A couple of cabs were waiting to take local commuters home. Amy tried to get the first guy to drive
them to New Haven.

"Sorry. I got an airport run in half an hour. No
can do."

The second cabbie, a woman, was more obliging.
"Fifty each way. I'll be driving back empty."

"Sold." Amy got in with her computer bag and
purse while the woman popped the trunk lid and
Scott dumped her American Tourister on some dirty
rags and tire irons.

When they pulled away from the curb, the cabbie
said, "Call me Sonja. Mind if I smoke?"

Scott talked to Sonja's image in the rearview mirror. "As a matter of fact, we do."

Sonja went on. "It's about fifty minutes up Ninety-
five from here. How 'bout I grab a butt around
Bridgeport while you two get a coffee or something?
I'm a two-pack-a-day girl."

So Scott and Amy found themselves having vending machine coffees they didn't want at an Exxon

just off the interstate. The machine's lighted graphic showed a pot pouring steaming coffee into a cup through the words "Happy Motoring Café." It didn't feel like happy motoring to Amy. Not with the night coming on and Brian Devlin out there somewhere ahead of them and an addict of a cabdriver hunched over, huffing a cigarette about ten feet away while they drank warm brown water. Amy was calculating whether she could read Fleming's final pages by the light from the vending machine when Sonja abruptly yelled, "Let's go."

Back in the car, Scott took Amy's hands and kissed them, gently. He didn't let go until they reached the Yale exit off I-95 and Amy needed to point out the way to Edgewood Avenue, just north of the campus. Their house was one of the "painted ladies," the Victorians that line both sides of the street leading out to the Yale Bowl. Her grandparents had lived in the house for forty years, and now it would be hers and Scott's.

Sonja saw them first. "Cops."

Two men were sitting in an unmarked Chevy across from her house. Amy said, "Keep going." She wanted to talk it over with Scott, but not with Sonja right there. "Take a left on Howe and a right at Elm Street." Scott understood. They were going to the library.

Amy grabbed a pen and ripped a sheet from the trusty day planner she took from her purse. She wrote, "If they're at the house, they could be at our Art History offices too," and showed it to Scott. He nodded.

Sterling Memorial Library is often mistaken by visitors for Payne Whitney Gymnasium. Both are mammoth neo-Gothic structures that take up most of a city block. Both are filled morning to night during the school year with sweating Yalies—one group working on their abs, the other on psych and English lit. Once final exams are over, though, the main library goes on "summer hours" and at five sharp locks up tight. (Unless, of course, you grew up at Yale and have a few tricks up your sleeve.)

Amy had the money out before Sonja had reached the High Street intersection. "Thanks. We'll get out here."

The cabbie popped the trunk so Scott could retrieve Amy's suitcase. The woman, who looked to be a couple of years younger than they were, seemed to have adopted them. "Okay if I smoke on the way back? You're paying for the ride."

Stressed as they were, they had to smile. Scott said, "They're your lungs." He was pulling the handle out of the bag so he could roll it onto the sidewalk.

Amy hurried around to the driver's side. "To get back to Ninety-five, stay on Elm and follow the signs."

"Got it, thanks. And one more thing." Sonja started the engine. "I'm pretty sure that same Chevy from your house just pulled in a few cars behind us." She moved out into traffic. "Good luck."

CHAPTER 58

When her grandfather died, no one wanted to intrude on the family's grief with a petty request like the return of his university keys. Later, no one remembered that they hadn't asked.

Amy and Scott were standing under the sixty-watt bulb that lit the area in front of the side door to Sterling Memorial Library. Amy was fumbling for the key that would open the old-fashioned Schlage lock. Funny how most of the locks at Yale aren't Yale locks.

In a minute, the thick wooden door heaved inward and they were inside. It was dead quiet, like a monastery. Without the lights on, the place looked and felt monastic too, with its vaulted ceilings and huge spaces.

There would be security guards making their rounds. Guards with walkie-talkies that could summon . . . who, Devlin? All Amy wanted was a ten-minute piece of all this quiet so she could finish the papers. Then maybe she and Scott could figure out what to do next.

They were quietly moving past the entrance to the stacks when a siren set up its wail directly outside the library's main doors on High Street. Amy and Scott could see the red light from the dome of the squad car as it intermittently illuminated the one-eighth inch of space between the huge central doors. She could hear footsteps somewhere above them, running along the narrow balcony that looks down on the card catalog area: one of the guards was reacting to the noise.

Still holding on to her suitcase, Amy ran over to the nearest elevator and stabbed at the button. She couldn't remember if it set off a ringing sound somewhere. It didn't seem to. The problem was, the elevator itself rumbled on its way down and threw in a few extra thumps when it stopped and opened. Still, with all the noise outside, most likely no one would know where they'd gone.

That was until the guard burst out of the stairwell and switched on the lights. Once the man had crossed in front of the circulation desk, he had a perfect view of the two of them in the open elevator, standing stock-still and looking straight ahead like a Grant Wood portrait, but with an American Tourister two-suiter. The elevator door closed.

Even before they got to the second floor, they could hear the noise a lot of people make when they run into a library at night. Was this the time to go back down and explain? Probably not.

Scott took Amy's suitcase and got off the elevator as soon as it opened on two, but Amy stayed behind to push all the buttons to the top floor. Maybe it would confuse the police. Maybe it would just delay the return of the elevator to the main floor. Maybe.

Amy knew that she and Scott had the home court advantage. Only people as familiar with the library as they were—which naturally included the security guards but not the city cops—would know you can't reach the mezzanine floor from the main elevators. Either you run up the little stairway from the second floor as they were doing at the moment, or you use the back elevator.

Next branch of a Fleming decision tree: hide up here among the PQ–PZ books and hope nobody follows you, or keep going and try to take the back elevator down before anyone takes it up? Scott decided for both of them by picking up the suitcase in his two arms and running even faster. "Come on!"

Scott, who was a little gawky when he walked, was beautiful when he ran: head held up, long legs rhythmically interchanging with each other like those of the gazelles on the Discovery Channel.

Amy promised herself that if they ever got out of this, she would exercise every day. And floss. And—

"Come *on*!" The door to the back elevator was open and Scott already inside, the suitcase still in his arms. His flight response had kicked into overdrive. The door started closing even as Amy was getting in.

Scott pressed L, for the lower level. This elevator was a good deal older than the ones in the main section of the library and it made more noise on its descent. There was an eight-by-ten-inch rectangle of safety glass in the door, so Amy could see how much the car shook from side to side as it dropped. Worse, anyone looking in from the outside could see *them*. They squeezed themselves into the front corners to minimize their visibility.

Scott reached up to unscrew the naked light bulb from the old sconce in the elevator cab's ceiling. It was hot. "Bloody hell!" He briefly cradled the scorching bulb in the material of his jacket and then laid it on the floor so he could put his burned fingers into his mouth. But at least it was dark.

Coming down to the main floor, Amy had only a split second to see the top of a man's head come into view—one with slicked-back, almost black hair—and for her to recognize him: Brian Devlin. And even less time to realize that, if he had pressed the down button, their goose was cooked. The elevator would open and it would be row 39 all over again. Nowhere to run to. Nowhere to hide.

But no. They sailed right past him on their way to the lower level. Devlin must have pressed just the up button. Amy and Scott could hear him clearly yell, "What?" as they dropped beneath him. And then, "Where does this thing go?" And, "No, you two stay here."

There was only one thing to do. As soon as the elevator door opened, run as fast as they could for the door leading to the Cross Campus Library. And that meant keeping the computer case and ditching Amy's suitcase, leaving it behind to the tender mercies of the New Haven police.

Cross Campus is the ten-acre greensward that is the main intersection of Yale University life. Beneath a good part of it is a busy collection of reading rooms where the most-often-read books are housed—the Cross Campus Library. Ventilation shafts and stairwells bring the light and air (and students) twenty feet underground.

The Cross Campus is usually open later than the main library to accommodate the nocturnal studying habits of the locals, and it's connected to its big brother on the other side of High Street by a thirty-yard-long tunnel. Amy and Scott ran through the tunnel, leaving behind them the warren of vending machines the students called Machine City and hearing only the sounds of their own running footsteps and ragged breathing.

And then other footsteps were echoing off the corridor walls. One man's. Who else?

Almost out of breath, Amy and Scott could see the subterranean reading room just ahead and— Thank God for graduate students! Now that Yale College finals were over, the undergraduates had all cleared out, leaving a skeleton crew of graduate students working on their dissertations, playing video games on their cell phones, or just plain sleeping. The librarians had gone home for the day, but at least if anything happened, there'd be witnesses.

Running past the librarians' desk and then past the shelf of atlases, Scott and Amy came to the Arts and Languages area. Scott was carrying the computer case so Amy could run faster, which by now wasn't very fast. All over the place there were tables and chairs and stacks of books and backpacks to negotiate. A couple of the students looked up in surprise at the two middle-aged people trying to sprint past them.

Amy and Scott had just reached the narrow interior stairs that lead down to the History and Social Science level as well as the copy machines when Devlin's voice came from behind them. "Stop or I'll shoot." He was aiming Macken's gun directly at Amy, and he said the words so matter-of-factly, a few people may not have heard them. But Scott knew they had to stop and so did Amy. It was all over.

CHAPTER 59

No it wasn't. As Devlin started to walk toward them, all hell broke loose. The students in the probable line of fire tried to take cover under the tables. Others ran for the exit. A few people screamed. And Amy and Scott got a major piece of luck: one of her students from the previous year chose that moment to amble up the stairs from the copiers, holding a couple of art books and totally engrossed in the copies he'd just made. Jordan Something-or-Other. A big guy. Jordan looked up and saw only Amy. "Oh, Dr. Greenberg, I hoped I'd run into you." Without realizing it, he'd walked exactly between his teacher and the man with a gun: Jordan the human shield. "I've hit a bit of a snag and—"

Scott yanked Amy's arm and pulled her around behind the Romance Languages bookcases. The two of them took off for the fire exit, followed immediately by three of the people who had been crouching under one of the tables. Amy could hear the disappointment in Jordan's voice as he said, "It's only a little snag. No biggie . . . ," which Devlin drowned out with his shout of "Stop or I'll fire!"

The fire exit on the east side of the sunken library has twenty-four steps leading up to street level. The students behind them were stampeding Amy and Scott upward, but still shielding them from Devlin down below. If security people were monitoring the library, each step was probably leading them closer to the waiting arms of the police.

When they reached the top, they saw that they had come up maybe twenty yards from the main Cross Campus entrances, on the south side of Berkeley College, one of the undergraduate residences. A knot of cops had gathered around the main west stairwell. Apparently, the first reports of a man with a gun had come from the panicked students who'd stumbled out of that side. Good. Two of the people who'd been running behind them, a young man and a woman, now sprinted ahead and up across High Street. A couple of policemen who'd been guarding the entrance to Sterling Library took off after them. Better.

There was a low stone wall nearby. They crouched behind it, totally spent. Music was coming from the college behind them, suggesting some sort of function was under way on this nice spring Tuesday evening. Or maybe just someone's stereo was turned way up. The deepening shadows were enough to keep Devlin from catching sight of them when he ran up out of the library an instant later. He *did* see the cops running after two people on High Street and joined in the chase. Another reprieve.

The craziness of their situation wasn't lost on Amy. She had a sheaf of papers in her computer case—some of them original documents of historical importance—that Devlin wanted and obviously would do anything to get. Maybe if she hadn't been an art *historian*, it wouldn't be such a big deal. Then again, she couldn't just ditch them somewhere, like behind this stone wall, because Devlin wouldn't go away without them.

What would Chief have wanted her to do? Just stop and hand them over? Scatter all the pages from the tallest building? Above all, she wanted it to be her choice and not some bully's. But it wasn't shaping up that way.

Then again, what debt did she owe Ian Fleming, that she should put herself and Scott in harm's way? What debt did she owe something as abstract as History, for that matter? What if the world never finds out that the Windsor family had a black sheep? What if they just let sleeping sheepdogs lie?

Across Wall Street, another of those city byways that were closed to vehicles within the Yale campus,

Amy could see that the security floodlights on the roof of the administration building had just come on. There was enough light to read by, if you stood right next to the corner of the building. So, two minutes later, Scott was standing guard as Amy, still out of breath from all the running, read Fleming's final words.

CHAPTER 60

FORENSIC REPORT PREPARED FOR
MR. I. FLEMING, 12 JANUARY 1964

DEAR MR. FLEMING,
I HEREWITH SUBMIT THE REPORT OF TESTS YOU ASKED ME
TO PERFORM ON THE ABOVE DOCUMENT. AS YOU SUSPECTED

(CONTINUED)

<u>PROVENANCE</u>

I'm typing this final chapter on my
portable in the gazebo here at Goldeneye.
When I'm done and on my way home in a couple
of months, I'll tuck the whole thing under
my arm and see it securely to rest in a
vault I've picked out in the Emerald Isle.

Now, for my news. I was quite out of
sorts after my lunch with Wallis and I
tried to clear my head by walking around
the British Museum. It seemed to me, as I
stood planted in front of the Elgin
Marbles, that too many of the wrong people
had found out what I was doing and might try
to impeach these pages' authenticity. My
whole intention, as I've said, has been to
present you with a time capsule that you
will open a half century from now in the
certain knowledge that all the players
concerned have left the stage. I want you,
little Amy, to be free to act as your heart
and mind direct you.

After a quarter hour or so of staring at
them, it dawned on me that the Marbles were
trying to tell me something. Not the usual
story of ancient Greek gods and heroes. It

was something else, something they had in
common with the Duke of Windsor's letter.

In 1806, while Greece was still under the
thumb of the Ottoman sultanate, our own
Lord Elgin declared himself the protector
of the marble statuary of the Parthenon,
claiming it as part of our priceless
Western heritage. With the sultan's
connivance (and the payment of a hefty
bribe) he helped himself to half the
pediment and a good chunk of the frieze,
literally sawing marble blocks in two. Then
he had the sculptures loaded on ships for
England. Well, one of the ships sank during
a storm and the marbles had to be pulled out
of the Mediterranean after two years under
water. So, unlike their Greek cousins still
sitting in Athens, the pieces I was looking
at now in the Museum had gone through many
hands to get here. Just as the Duke of
Windsor's letter had been passed from hand
to hand.

It suddenly occurred to me that though I
had tested Blunt's forged copy for
fingerprints, I had never asked Q to
examine the actual, authentic left-hand
side of the note, the one that we'd

originally lifted from the Friedrichshof
that night almost twenty years ago. The one
Ann purloined from Blunt's bank. Would it
reveal any prints that hadn't appeared on
its right-hand twin? Did I know everything
there was to know?

That was a couple of days ago. This
morning, within the past hour, I received a
trunk call from my old friend Q back in
London, with the report of the one last
test I had asked him to conduct.

Q had been his irascible self when I had
given him the sheet of notepaper. "Haven't
I already tested this thing for you? We
know the results; I've got them right
here."

I was at some pains to explain that what
he had tested previously was a forgery, and
that this was the genuine article. He gave
me a lifted eyebrow every bit as
accomplished as Blunt's had been before he
relented. I was to expect his oral report
within forty-eight hours. Ann and I were
flying that evening to Jamaica, so I gave
him my telephone number here on the island
and asked him to reverse the charges.
Which, ungraciously, he did.

The connection wasn't a very good one. Q was in a state such as I have never heard before. His first words were almost shouted down the line: "I think I may have one of the prints!"

Well, that didn't seem awfully remarkable. There must have been many prints on the page. Windsor's, Hitler's . . .

"No, Ian, I may have one of the Prince! A partial thumb and a bit of forefinger. I can't be sure, there's so little print to work with. Only a five-point match. Not enough for a court of law, but UNIVAC says it's Prince Philip Schleswig-Holstein-Sonderburg-Glücksburg."

"And just who is Prince Philip Schleswig-Holstein-whatever-you-said?"

Q's voice lost its hysteria and assumed its customary tone of disapproval. "Really, Ian, pay attention. He's Philip, the Prince of Greece and Denmark. The Earl of Merioneth. The Baron Greenwich."

I'd heard that litany before, but I was slow to put two and two together, so Q did it for me, his excitement rising again with every syllable. "Philip, the Royal Consort.

The Duke of Edinburgh. The Queen's husband, for God's sake!"

Oh, that Philip. Prince Christophe's brother-in-law, the one with all the sisters married to . . . Nazis. Now that I thought about it, I was pretty sure I'd seen him years before. A tall teenage British naval cadet who had spent time in France and was back on leave in 1939 Paris at Wallis's Christmas party. And even earlier, as the fifteen-year-old who had been dragged along by his princely parents to Wallis's wedding at the Château de Candé. Was *he* the one who had tipsily sung along with Chevalier and Coward? The one who had seemed to know Charles Bedaux? If so, *that* Philip's eyes had read . . . and fingers had handled . . . and fingerprints had been deposited on . . . the note the English ex-monarch was sending to Adolf Hitler telling him he'd be glad to go back to being King after the Germans won.

Amy, I don't presume to know what the world will be like in the year 2014, when you read this. But I do know, if I've calculated right, that all the people with an interest in this matter will have gone to their reward: Winston and all the members of his Government, Blunt and his friends, that Hess stand-in in Spandau prison, the Queen and Prince Philip, the Duke and Duchess themselves, and, of course, your grandfather and me. Which will leave you free of any but the interests of history and your own conscience.

Edmund Burke is supposed to have said, "All that's necessary for the triumph of evil is for good men to do nothing." May I add a coda to that thought: the wicked haven't won a blessed thing while there's one good man (or in your case, woman) to bear witness to their crimes.

Now it's up to you.

CHAPTER 61

Amy had had to read Fleming's final words through twice. She was still playing mental catch-up. Prince Philip? The figurehead at the Queen's side? If he had been Bedaux's go-between . . . Amy flipped back to the document itself, the incriminating letter to "Lieber Herr Hitler" covered in fingerprints. Right here, this was proof. Real proof. She put the pages down.

Scott was saying, "So what is it? What's the secret?" but Amy didn't hear him. She had glanced up at the stone carving that ran along the top of the administration building, Woodbridge Hall. It was the university crest with its Latin motto, *Lux et veritas*. Light and truth.

What a random way to have a decision made for you. Of course: bring the truth to light. If you couldn't do that here among the cloistered walls, where could you do it? Amy realized it was no longer a decision of *whether* but simply one of *how* to make the truth known. But first they had to survive the evening.

Then she had a brainstorm: if she and Scott could make it to the *Yale Daily News* building, Amy could do the right thing and hand the manuscript over. Devlin would be forced to go home empty-handed. The trouble was that the Oldest College Daily, as they liked to call it on the masthead, was on the other side of the Cross Campus Library and the police. Okay, she'd give them a call. "Scott, I need your phone."

Scott was looking at her instead of reaching into his jacket pocket and handing it over. "I can't. I dropped it in the library when I pulled you away from Devlin."

Damn. If they'd simply gone to the newspaper office in the first place, they'd be home free all now. All right, they'd just have to hoof it. Amy got up, and Scott was asking for the third time what she had learned from Fleming when they saw the young couple from the library, the ones who'd been such good sprinters. The woman shouted, "There they are!" to someone Amy couldn't see. Amy and Scott changed course and were making a full-blooded dash away across the empty space of the plaza by the time the woman called again, "I saw them!"

There was no place to hide. Off to their right Amy could see an artsy sculpture garden, sunken a full story below grade and part of the courtyard level of the Beinecke Library complex, the easternmost of the trio of Yale libraries and the one devoted to rare books. A low wall ran all the way around it. Too low. It would have to be the library itself if they were to hide from their pursuers.

About five minutes before the eight o'clock closing time, a cluster of scholars was filing out past the security guard, holding briefcases open for inspection and shielding Scott and Amy from the guard's view as they stumbled in through the revolving glass doors, huffing and puffing.

Like a high-tech jewel box, every nook and cranny of the Beinecke Rare Book and Manuscript Library has been created to preserve the priceless materials kept there from the ravages of air, light, and thieves. The building itself is made of rectangular one-and-a-quarter-inch-thick panes of translucent Vermont marble, designed to filter daylight so that rare materials can be displayed without damage. And there are video cameras everywhere: above the main entrance, over the sliding doors to the sculpture garden in the lower courtyard, across from the access to the stack of books itself. In fact, cameras have all but replaced human eyes.

Amy was thankful the dim lighting would make it hard for anyone viewing a monitor to recognize her and Scott as they slipped away from the little knot of people filing out and made their way to the lower level.

A bell began to sound and a guard called down, "Closing time, people," to all the slowpokes who were walking up the stairs as they were hurrying down. Amy and Scott had the idea at the same time: hide in one of the bathrooms until everyone had gone. Stupidly, they tried to drag each other into different bathrooms. Amy was trying to steer him into the men's, because it was closer, and Scott was pulling her toward the women's because "the guard's a guy and he won't be as comfortable checking out the ladies' stalls." Scott won.

The police chose that moment to burst into the library. The acoustics were garbled, but Amy and Scott could make out at least two newcomers with raised voices. Whatever was said, a pair of footsteps went up to the mezzanine and another pair was coming down the stairs to this, the courtyard level. The descending footsteps grew louder as the fugitives huddled in the next-to-last stall, Scott on the closed toilet seat and Amy sitting on his lap. A man's voice called, "Everybody needs to leave! Now!" The voice wasn't Devlin's.

They could hear a faucet run in the men's bathroom next door and then shut off again. They heard a door open and the same cop asking, "Anyone else in there?"

"No, I'm it" was the barely audible answer, just before the straggler headed up the stairway.

It was possible to hear the guard or policeman or whatever he was moving around in the reading room on this level; he was opening and closing things wherever he went. And then he was outside the ladies' again. The door banged open. Scott had had the foresight of raising his feet off the floor and wedging them against the stall door. Now anyone looking for them would have to make a door-to-door search to find them. This guy didn't do that. He could have, he should have, but he didn't.

It was another five to ten minutes, well after the last muffled voices had faded away, before Scott even dared to drop his feet to the floor. He jostled Amy off his lap. "My legs are asleep!"

Okay, the object so far had been to hide from their pursuers, and they had succeeded. Now what? For the next few minutes, the two of them stood in the tiny space with the toilet between them, Scott alternately standing on one leg and then the other like a stork. When all his limbs were again functioning, he opened the stall door.

This was the opportunity Amy had been hoping for. They had the library all to themselves except for the cameras, one of which was fixed over the entrance to the reading room and aimed at the heavy sliding-glass door to the sunken sculpture garden outside.

Tonight, Noguchi's huge marble pieces representing the Earth, the Sun, and a cube that was meant to be Chance could be seen in bold relief, thanks to a floodlight several stories up on the library wall. Amy and Scott were sitting again, cross-legged on the floor in the hallway just outside the reading room and the prying digital eye's field of vision. From here, you could see over the granite retaining wall above the courtyard to a small section of the evening sky. It was romantic if you squinted a little and tried not to notice you were sitting on the floor.

"Scott, do you love me?"

He turned to her, openmouthed. "Are you serious? Are you kidding?"

She wasn't kidding. "Do you love me? Tell me."

Scott was getting huffy. "Would I have proposed if . . . Of course I love you."

"Say it without the 'of course.' "

"I love you, Amy. You must know that by now."

She twirled the temporary ring again and again around her finger, half taking it off each time. "Right now I'm not sure what I know."

Scott was reaching into his pocket. "Then let me prove it." Now he had something in his right hand. "I was waiting for a quiet moment, but there haven't been any." He opened the small, dark blue box in his hand.

Her *real* engagement ring was a perfectly clear diamond flanked by two smaller ones in a simple white gold setting. Amy took the ring out of the box and read the inscription. "For AMG from SHB. Always." It was absolutely beautiful. For once in her life, words failed her.

Scott said, in a soft voice, "Now you'll never have to ask me that question again. Because you'll always have my answer. Always." He kissed her, just as softly, on the cheek. Right where the first of her tears had paused on its way down her face.

She hadn't expected the tears. Funny, wasn't "Always" the word Ribbentrop was supposed to have written on all those florist's cards to Wallis? "Scott, sweetheart, I've been thinking. If we have children—"

He gently put his finger to her mouth. "When. When we have children."

"All right. When we have children . . . in the Jewish religion you can't name the son after the father if he's still alive."

"So no little Scott Jr.? That's okay."

Amy had to keep going. "So if it's a boy, let's name him after the grandfather."

Scott smiled. "Raymond Brown? He sounds very serious. How about Chief Brown?"

Amy took both of his hands in hers. "I was thinking of his *paternal* grandfather. Anthony Brown." She pronounced it like *Antony and Cleopatra*.

Scott tried to withdraw his hands but Amy held on tight. "How . . . how did you know?" he asked.

"Your mother, the famous art historian, is Margaret Harcourt Brown. But years ago, at the Courtauld, she was just Maggie Brown. Right? And then she married Anthony Blunt, who made it possible for her to have you. And that made it possible for *me* to have you."

Amy had never seen Scott tear up, let alone cry. Then the whole story came tumbling out. The one he had tried to tell her on the train. The day he had graduated from University, his mother had decided he was old enough to know that she wasn't the widow she had claimed to be, raising her only son on an art historian's salary and an army pension. That there had never been a Major Harry Brown, only a boyfriend who had refused to marry her when she had gotten pregnant. And that the well-off benefactor who'd agreed to be named on Scott's birth certificate as the father was her employer, Sir Anthony Blunt.

"The thing is," Scott continued, "Anthony Blunt died in the early nineteen eighties, before I ever really had a chance to know him. Mother told me of this wonderful thing this man had done for her, for us— even as all the horrible things he had done by spying for the Soviet Union were beginning to come out.

"Three years before he died, the new prime minister, Mrs. Thatcher, was asked a question in Parliament concerning the identity of the Fourth Man, the Cambridge spy who had never been caught. She outed my stepfather on the spot, the cow. They stripped him of his knighthood and his Cambridge fellowship. Mother said that one time he had even been booed out of a cinema in Notting Hill."

Amy tried to stroke Scott's cheek, but he gently moved her hand away. "I've been wanting to tell you all this, but up to now I didn't know how. About my stepfather . . . Near the end there was a glimmer of hope. To keep going, he'd had to go out and find rich people who would continue to underwrite his work and have him appraise their purchases, the way the Crown had done previously. One of these wealthy patrons had a daughter, a girl named Diana Spencer."

Amy gave him a look. Scott went on. "Yes, that Diana. When it was announced that she would marry Charles, the Prince of Wales, my stepfather tried to use the connection, the influence of knowing her father, the Earl of Spencer, so well. To obtain a royal pardon, perhaps even a rehabilitation. A real long shot. But without his honors and his pictures, my stepfather had nothing to live for.

"He was writing and phoning Diana with no reply. Mother tried to talk him out of it, but he made quite a thing of his wartime service and the 'unfair' revocation of his military pension. And then he made this awful blunder. He wrote Diana that he had 'devastating information' concerning the family she was about to join. That he 'might not be able to remain silent' about it. All about some secret wartime mission he took with Ian Fleming and an American driver named Greenberg, the one man alive who could vouch for what he said."

Scott shifted his position a little on the floor. "The thing is, Diana *did* meet with him then, after the honeymoon. But only to tell him she had pled his case with her husband, Charles, and had been turned down cold. Well, Anthony Blunt was not one to take no for an answer. So he told her Fleming had assembled a file of incriminating information about the royal family, things that had happened in the nineteen thirties and forties. And that he, Blunt, knew where it was. The last part was an enormous lie, of course.

"Diana must have gone back to the family again, because this time, it was the Queen who responded. She sent a note, politely but firmly asking him to 'cease all further communication with the Princess and the family.' Mother still has it. In the end, it didn't matter. He died within the month."

"Naturally I was shocked down to my toes to discover that my father wasn't a deceased army major after all but a notorious Russian spy. That my whole life had been a lie. That evening, to celebrate my leaving University, we had a little dinner at home. I remember I was still sitting at the kitchen table when mother laid a little journal bound in blue cloth on it. It was Blunt's."

Where there had been tears, there was now a determined look in Scott's eyes. He needed Amy to know the truth. "Anthony Blunt wrote down everything he knew about the Duke of Windsor's letter, how he had made two copies of it and kept the original, what Ian Fleming had told him—all of it. He gave it to my mother for safekeeping."

Amy said quietly, "So Maggie knows everything."

"Everything Blunt knew. Not that she could ever prove any of it. When he died, she decided to keep quiet, for my sake. Until she thought I was old enough to understand.

"Well, I already had my A levels in art history, and

I made a rash decision. To find out what this big dark secret was that my stepfather had been going on about, and maybe to somehow clear his name. And mine."

"And so you came to America?"

"A retired American officer named Raymond Greenberg was not hard to find, not for a young man like myself used to researching things. And then to discover we were in the same field! It was kismet or something. So I came here to America to study under Dr. Greenberg. And, to be honest, find out what he knew."

"And what did my grandfather tell you?"

"Nothing. He drove a couple of guys in a car up a mountain and down again. He never knew why."

"Chief never told me any of this."

"I think he knew how attracted I was to you, and I guess he didn't want to spoil it. I hope I'm not spoiling it now. But when you received that letter from the Irish bank about a secret bequest, naturally I was curious . . ."

Amy kissed him on the nose. "I understand."

Scott got up. "My legs are starting to cramp again. We really have to figure out—" He made one of his cranelike movements and seemed to duck his head even as he was getting up. "Sweetheart, step back, would you? Now?"

Amy was nonplussed. "What—?"

Scott took her by the arm and pulled her back from the doorway while raising her to her feet. "He's out there. Up there."

"Who?"

"Devlin."

Amy was just on the verge of an involuntary scream when Scott clapped his hand over her mouth. When she looked at him, he said, "I owed you one."

As she retreated, she glimpsed a man leaning over the sculpture garden wall and peering down at them. Then he was gone. If it really *had* been Devlin, they were up against a pro who was armed to the teeth. A Special Forces killer against a top-notch hide-and-seeker and her boyfriend. Amy heard the desperation in her voice as she shared with Scott her last-ditch plan to stay alive, the one she'd come up with while hiding in the library's bathroom.

The crash behind them told her all bets were off. Brian Devlin must have shot out the glass in the sliding doors. They looked back and saw him standing on top of the sculpture garden's retaining wall, looming over them. He had peeled off his jacket and thrown it down. She could see Macken's gun in his right hand. And then he jumped.

Devlin had aimed his leap so he would land on one of the sides of the angled cube of Chance, apparently rolling the dice that he could land on his butt and slide down to the ground in one piece. His intended victims didn't hang around to see if he'd make it. They were already scrambling up the stairs to the main floor.

This was it. Devlin had knowingly set off the alarm, so he must be figuring he could quickly neutralize them and confiscate Fleming's manuscript before witnesses arrived. They had seconds . . . a minute at the most.

CHAPTER 62

Brian Devlin stepped over the broken glass of the sculpture garden doors and made a hurried reconnaissance of the reading room. Then he checked out each of the bathrooms and storage areas on the lower level before returning to the stairs that led up to the street-level lobby. There was a camera in a corner above his head. As he started up the stairs, he smiled for the camera and the security people, off in their control room in the main library.

Amy saw him smile. Scott had run up ahead to the public gallery on the mezzanine, but when Amy looked back, she had caught sight of Devlin's image on the black-and-white monitor at the security desk in the lobby. She shivered at the sight: all those predatory teeth.

There was the sound of more glass breaking upstairs. On the monitor, Devlin heard it too. His grin widened even as he methodically mounted the stairs with Macken's gun held out in front of him, slowly swinging it in a continuous arc. Amy turned and scrambled to join Scott as fast as she could.

From the Beinecke entrance area, a double stairway rises to the mezzanine level, a public gallery of free-standing exhibits on two-foot-wide by four-foot-high pedestals. A sign at the foot of the stairs announced that the current traveling exhibit was of writing instruments: sharpened quills used by various signers of the Declaration of Independence and fountain pens belonging to more modern authors, even a whole desk set of Faulkner's. Less than thirty seconds later, Devlin had finished inspecting the lobby area and had moved past the sign and up the stairs to the mezzanine.

From where they were hidden, Amy and Scott could hear him stop at the top of the staircase and then walk away from them, along the south side of the promenade that rings the massive glass tower of books. At the far end, the same deliberate footsteps took him along the west side of the library. And now he was coming back along the building's north wall. On permanent display in the northeast corner stood one of the five complete Gutenberg Bibles in the United States, the one Amy remembered so fondly from childhood. The one she was hiding behind now.

Scott looked over to where Amy was hiding. He could see a bit of the fabric from her skirt sticking out from behind the display case. His legs were starting to cramp again. The long wait in that awkward posture in the bathroom must have done something to his circulation. He needed to change position, but he musn't. As it was, he was just skinny enough to be hidden by one of the narrow concrete stanchions that protruded from the wall, between the glass case holding a first edition of *The House of the Seven Gables* and the one with *The House of Mirth*. Wedged in two exhibits away from Amy, with the case he had broken into off to his left and the Bible to his right, he knew that any movement, even by so much as an inch, would give the game away.

Near the ceiling, a video camera was trained on the case with the Bible in it. Scott could see Devlin now as he raised the gun and took aim. Not at the lens, but at the power cord leading from the back. From an angle under and a little behind the camera, Devlin fired. Bull's-eye.

The explosion was still reverberating through the cavernous building as Devlin spoke in one of those voices children use at games. "Dr. Greenberg . . . ready or not, here I come!" It sent shivers shooting straight up Scott's back and into the hairs on his neck.

On the floor below, someone had unlocked the main entrance and was coming through the revolving doors. More than one someone. The locals. Now

Devlin was less than ten feet from Amy. He didn't even have to raise his voice. "Stand up and give me the papers."

She was still crouching with her back to him under the big Bible. His voice echoed a little in the vastness of the library. "Slide your computer case over to me. I only want to see what's in it, the material. No one's going to get hurt. Once I have it, I'll let you go."

Amy Greenberg said nothing. The people downstairs were making enough noise for all of them: "Police! Show yourselves!" And "Who fired a weapon?" And "Commander Devlin! Where are you?"

Devlin had the stiletto out. From where he was, Scott could see it in the man's hand, the slightest gleam of silver in the dimly lit space. This wasn't in their plan. Devlin wasn't waiting to make sure Amy had the Fleming papers. The professional had noiselessly crept forward and now he was right behind her, about to bring his arm forward to deliver the fatal cut.

When William Faulkner's onyx desk set, with pearlized pen and pencils in their onyx holders, crashed through Devlin's parietal bone just above the occipital, it nearly cleaved the two hemispheres of his brain. Scott had probably used more force than necessary. He had the fleeting thought that two pens were definitely mightier than one sword.

CHAPTER 63

That evening the bedlam that had engulfed Yale's Sterling Library security room packed up and moved about a mile away to the headquarters of the New Haven Police Department on Union Avenue.

When the campus cops, and later the city cops, had charged up the stairs of the Beinecke Rare Book Library, they had discovered that a man was violently dead and two Yale professors—one of whom was wanted for a murder earlier that day in New York City—had done it. The dead man was apparently a law enforcement officer, which made it a capital offense. He was also a foreign national, which meant embassy and State Department involvement. To top it off, the victim had been working on a case of international terrorism, so by law the pair in custody could be held incommunicado without due process. And then there'd be, potentially, a press conference down the road with FBI and National Security brass. For a small city police chief like Felicia Williams, who knew nothing about baseball, it was like hitting one over the fence with the bases full in game seven. Oh, and there was the destruction of university property.

She'd had the strangest phone call. Thirty-some-odd calls, actually, in the hours since the arrest. But one phone call Captain Williams would remember for the rest of her life. Some kind of priority call from a military operator. An Englishwoman, who hadn't given her name, had started right in about a bunch of papers the vic was supposed to have had. Important papers. When the captain had said no, there was a gun and a knife but no papers, the old lady had ordered—ordered!—her to give each of the suspects "a thorough going-over." The captain should obtain the papers, hold them till someone flew over from England to get them, and under no circumstances enter them into evidence. Some bush-wah about them being the "property of the Crown." The nerve. And then the call was over and she was gone.

If there *had* been any papers on Brown or the Greenberg woman, her people would have found them. And then they would have been duly turned over to the property clerk in the basement for processing, like any other evidence. But no, all they'd found was a computer in a computer case, a handbag with the usual woman's stuff, and a suitcase they'd recovered in a library elevator. A sketchpad, but no papers.

The next call had been from Yale's president. He'd been awakened by the campus cops, and he was swearing up and down that "his people" couldn't possibly have done a thing like this. The captain could expect Yale's lawyers to be filing motions bright and early in the morning.

Nothing like town-gown crap to lift your spirits at one in the a.m. Still, everything would keep. Her guys wouldn't be done with the crime scene for another couple hours and her best interrogator, Obst, would come on with the morning shift. Williams had been up for about twenty hours straight. She had to get some shut-eye. But it had been a great day.

CHAPTER 64

The Beinecke was closed indefinitely for repairs. The huge glass doors on the lower level had been specially designed by Gordon Bunshaft, the building's architect, to be everything *but* bulletproof. The company that had constructed them was long out of business and a replacement would have to be shipped in by truck from a factory in Wisconsin. The display case too would have to be made to order and installed.

An hour after the homicide, the police had cordoned off the library's northeast corner with their signature yellow Crime Scene Do Not Enter tape. It stayed up for days while fingerprints were lifted, blood spatter was collected, and the bullet that had shot out the surveillance camera's power supply was retrieved. A forensic photographer from the FBI took pictures of every surface Amy or Scott had been suspected of touching, from every conceivable angle. Meanwhile, before the staff members who'd been on duty that evening could be permitted to leave on their summer sabbaticals, the department's detectives interviewed them and then screened every pixel of video from all the cameras with them. They watched Amy and Scott rush into the Beinecke, saw Devlin shoot out the glass and leap down into the courtyard. They tracked first one teacher and then the other running past the display cases. The man, Scott Brown, had stopped in front of one of them and hunched over it before smashing it with his shoe. Destruction of property. They could see him take the murder weapon—if, technically, it *was* murder—and hide. Soon after that, the camera had died. When they'd screened it all, they debated what it meant and screened it again. With one thing and another, big and little, it was a couple of weeks after the "incident," as Devlin's death was now being called, before any civilians were allowed back into the damaged jewel box.

The day the yellow tape came down, a Lincoln Town Car was discovered at the parking impound lot next to the West Side Highway in Manhattan, known to its employees as the Fun City Garage. It still sported a card in its passenger window with the name "Dr. Greenburg." When the vehicle's owners, the McDonough Brothers, were contacted, they came down to pay the accumulated parking and towing charges but insisted the car had been stolen off their lot in Long

Island City weeks before. And they knew no one named Greenburg.

Meanwhile, Special Branch of Scotland Yard was now denying that Devlin had been on assignment to the States. They claimed to have been awaiting his return from a training exercise in Dubai when he had "disappeared from our radar." A review of Delta Airlines' records showed Devlin had been booked to travel from Dublin's airport to New York on the same flight as Amy Greenberg but had never boarded. And finally, Interpol had helped determine that the dead man in Grand Central was not a New York limo driver, as his clothing suggested, but an Irish banker who at some point had been wearing a false mustache and a wig. And that two of his colleagues had been killed in a suspicious traffic accident the day before his death.

It all meant that the case against Amy and Scott, piece by piece, was falling apart, much to Captain Williams's chagrin. Louis Obst, her five-foot-four-inch Boston terrier of a detective, had taken separate statements from Amy and Scott, and then had taken them again forty-eight hours later, hoping for inconsistencies. They held to their story: that a limo driver with an Irish brogue had accosted Dr. Greenberg at JFK, trying to bundle her into the stolen Town Car before menacing her in Grand Central. (Why anyone should fixate on this particular woman Obst couldn't imagine.)

Macken's bank was failing in Dublin. Could be he was on the verge of losing his job. Maybe he'd just gone off his rocker. But if he had, why stalk Dr. Greenberg? There was nothing in the bank records about her, and thanks to her Yale lawyers, she and her boyfriend weren't volunteering anything. (The summer break had freed up a couple of the big hitters from the Law School faculty to do a pro bono thing, and they'd clamped down on the grilling before it really got started.)

Brown was in the clear anyway for the Grand Central killing: he'd spent a crucial half hour conspicuously sitting alone and drinking beer in New York's Yale Club. Of course, witnesses had put the woman and Devlin up there too later on. From the chief's point of view, nothing about this case added up. All she knew was, her press conference with the DC heavies was going bye-bye.

And then came the clincher. From the start, it was clear the knife found near Devlin's body was a match for the wound that killed Milo Macken. Now forensics determined that at no time had either Amy or Scott handled it. (Or the gun, for that matter.) British-made, the knife proved to be standard issue to UK security field forces. And the kicker: lab tests proved the traces of blood caught between the blade and the hilt were Macken's. Devlin must have killed Macken in some sort of rogue operation and tried—for reasons unknown—to frame the couple in Captain Williams's custody. Case closed.

The charges against Amy Greenberg and Scott Brown were dropped and they were released on a particularly nice late spring day. As a small act of official contrition, the couple was driven back to the house on Edgewood Avenue by police personnel. They held hands wordlessly in the back seat. Everything had already been said.

Looking out the window of the car, Amy could read the headline in one of the *New Haven Register* vending machines along the curb: "Yale Pair Cleared in Library Death." And beneath it, "Grand Central Murder is 'Yard Work.'" Still looking out the window, Amy said, "I'd like Maggie to be my matron of honor." Scott gave her hand a squeeze. It was their new language.

That same afternoon, Mary Clare Capuana, the visiting art historian who had originally curated the damaged Beinecke exhibition, received an e-mail from library.yale.edu at her campus office just off Franklin Street in Chapel Hill. An attachment showed her a photo of the damaged display case just as the police forensics team had left things: a mess, with pens and quills jumbled together and scattered willy-nilly among bits of broken glass, a dog-eared manuscript, and a lot of little white cards—now stained from the fingerprint dusting process—that had described everything. As the summer fill-in librarians weren't familiar with the original installation, would Professor Capuana please suggest a new arrangement for the display? And would she take into account the fact that Faulkner's bloody desk set was still in police custody and would require extensive cleaning after its release?

She studied the picture for quite a while before typing her reply: "The manuscript isn't ours."

CHAPTER 65

For two days, the large package from Ireland had been sitting on the front porch where the DHL guy had left it. Now Amy put on the dress and stood in front of the mirror. Right then and there she decided on a June wedding.

They would have liked a Saturday, but all the Saturdays were booked. So Amy and Scott settled for an afternoon wedding on the third Sunday in June, Father's Day. Appropriate. The groom never would have met the bride were it not for the need to clear the name of his own adoptive father. And then there was Raymond Greenberg, the only dad Amy had ever really known and the one who had attracted Scott to New Haven, to their house, to her. She wondered how he'd have felt about her deliberately throwing a game of hide-and-seek by letting Devlin find her. She decided Chief would have hated the idea.

Scott's mother had flown over as soon as she heard they'd been arrested. Then when they'd been freed, the three of them had talked into the wee hours, crying a little, laughing a little. Now Maggie would be standing next to Amy at the ceremony. It would be the world's smallest wedding outside of a Las Vegas bridal chapel. Scott had gotten a colleague to stand up for him as best man. There'd be Susan and Blanche and, yes, Katie all the way from Australia. That made seven. Add a couple of husbands and boyfriends and a few pizza-loving members of the History of Art Department and the whole group would still rattle around inside Yale's Battell Chapel.

It wasn't lost on Amy that here she was, a Jewish girl, marrying an Anglican boy. A Jewish girl who loved the *Book of Kells*, a crucial pillar of the Roman Catholic faith, and who might yet cast her own two eyes on its possible explicit (now promised by Shields in a week or so), bringing happy news to a billion Catholics while giving her own career a nudge. A girl who was at the moment writing her own vows (and doodling a sketch of herself and Scott at the altar as she struggled to do so) that would be uttered in a brief nondenominational ceremony in an all-comers house of worship. Was she an American, or what?

On the Friday before the wedding, the Beinecke Library issued a press release describing "a major find in the field of modern British scholarship." "Find" was the operative word. The immediate beneficiaries of the announcement were the two big Connecticut papers, the *New Haven Register* and the *Hartford Courant*, the only publications that were given the story for their Sunday editions. Yale had put a forty-eight-hour embargo on it for everyone else, part of their I'll-rub-your-back-if-you'll-rub-mine goodwill policy with the local press.

By the morning of the big day, the lurid interest in Amy and Scott had pretty much worn off. They had had their fifteen minutes in the spotlight. So just before noon the couple climbed into the Dodge Caravan Maggie had rented at the airport, without incident and without observing any of the usual wedding superstitions. (The Girls had already ridden off to the church ahead of them.) Amy was striking in her Irish wedding gown, and Scott benefited from the aura tuxedos bestow on the lanky and portly alike. They were adults, theirs was a mature love, and had Amy's dress not been as long and heavy as it was, they would have floated the six blocks to the chapel together on love. As they drove away, the lovers had eyes only for each other. So the man hiding in the shrubbery went completely unnoticed.

Even as the intruder was watching the bride and groom leave the house, his colleague was strolling across the Yale campus a half mile away with the Sunday edition of the *New Haven Register* under his arm. Ramesh realized he had uttered only four words all morning, two of them being the "Thanks, pal" he'd forced himself to say with an American accent when he'd picked up the newspaper at the front desk of his motel out on Whalley. The paper served as camouflage, a prop for the nondescript man in the nondescript suit. But soon it would serve another, more important role: when placed on the wooden ledge that ran the length of the front of the choir loft, its four-inch Sunday thickness was just enough for Ramesh to rest his elbow comfortably on it with the gun barrel clearing the brass railing. Always inspect your shooting stand the night before. Always, always, always.

He looked at his phone for the fourth time in the last ten minutes. Nothing yet from Simon Pure. Not for the first time he wondered what sort of gits named Pureton would christen a son Simon. What chance did the boy have in school, in life? The phone vibrated with an incoming text message. One word: "In." First step accomplished.

The spot in front of the minister where the bride and groom would say their vows was directly in front of and below Ramesh. An empty choir loft, a reasonably thick American newspaper to lean on, a Ruger 24/7 Tritium sight for fast target acquisition in low light situations and a Sausage McMuffin (the other two words he'd said) in one's pocket—still in its tinfoil wrapper—if one were delayed . . . What more could a marksman ask?

Even among the cold-blooded killers of his government's security forces, Ramesh stood out for his varied skill set. He was a dead shot with any sort of weapon; he had an acrobat's strength and wiry frame (the better to hang off the back of a speeding motorbike); and he had a head for whatever sort of high-tech toy came along, like his Luminox night-vision goggles and his SureFire light gun with its 460 beautiful lumens. Today's job, though, would be very low-tech. Once Simon Pure secured the document that Briefing had assured them was in the Greenberg woman's house, the rest would be up to Ramesh and his modified Remington. Nothing trendy, just a good American rifle. Small caliber, but deadly enough— dependable and common as dirt. He would make it sing, as he had on those other occasions. Poetic justice, he thought, that the singing should come from the choir loft.

A young man, possibly a student, was shuffling through sheet music at the organ. Ramesh couldn't see them, but he could hear one or two wedding guests conversing as they took their seats beneath him. Were it a Church of England wedding, it would be nineteen minutes precisely to the first clear shot, with the opening hymns out of the way and the father having deposited the bride at the designated spot. As a boy, Ramesh had relieved the boredom in his father's church by timing all the ceremonies with the same watch he was wearing now. The one his father had given him.

He sighed inwardly. Anglicans were nothing if not predictable. But these mix-and-match, thrown-together American affairs—all à la carte, with people facing each other and reading their vows off pieces of paper and musicians breaking in at odd moments—threw timing right out the window. He'd have to be in the ready position the whole way; hence, the cushioned arm rest. Bring the gun up at the last moment. Ramesh had worn the unfashionable brown suit so the rifle and its wooden stock might rest, butt down, against his leg without contrasting with his clothing. He needn't have bothered. No one ever gave him a second look. He sighed again, knowing his English father must have had the stronger genes to have given him such an un-Indian appearance. The upside was, it served him well in this line of work.

He looked at the phone again. Simon had been in the house for twelve minutes. It would take him no more than fifteen, twenty at the outside, no matter how well they thought they had hidden it. This one would be a good case study for the first-year trainees: go in when the targets were known to be occupied for a predictable amount of time away from the premises; locate and retrieve the package; communicate to the shooter when you were clear, and disappear.

He wondered what the trainees would make of Devlin's death. It was incomprehensible, an experienced field agent neutralized by two amateurs. Had it been the woman, some scruple about killing her? No, that didn't compute. Devlin had killed an unarmed woman and her boyfriend before. Ramesh could see him now, crouching there in that Paris tunnel and holding the joystick of a brake box as Ramesh and Simon Pure had sped past him on the motorbike. No, killing a woman had been no problem for Devlin.

The thought started him down the same old unpleasant byways in his mind. Why wasn't he, Ramesh, more troubled about killing? Killing female civilians, at that? He had helped his employers "take out" a princess in Paris. Such a loaded expression. Most of the pros he knew drew the line at women. Was it something to do with his mother?

Of course, the Irish woman in the car . . . That had really been about the bloke sitting next to her, the government accountant with the crazy teeth. It was Ramesh's incredibly good fortune that the bank manager had wanted to eliminate the woman at the same time that his Service had received the contract on the man. Ramesh had seen to it, freelance. Ramesh and his very popular photon-light gun.

The first chords of organ music startled him and made him lift his elbow just enough so the heavy newspaper started to slide to the left. Ramesh tried to catch it, but he couldn't really turn his body because he had to keep his right leg pressed against the gun so it too wouldn't fall. Several sections of the paper fluttered to the floor.

The music, reverberating up here in the loft, was loud enough to cover any sounds the falling newspapers were making, but he looked over the railing anyway. The gawky groom, Brown, was already standing in place next to his best man. Three bridesmaids, in three mismatched styles of dresses, were chatting together on the other side of the minister, who was signaling the organist to begin "Here Comes the Bride." Ugh, Wagner.

Ramesh was careful to retrieve and fold each section before sliding it in among the others. First, the classified adverts, including a separate insert for cars and trucks. Then sports and the cinema listings. The last section Ramesh picked up was headed "Local." He was about to restore it to the main body of the newspaper when his eye was caught by the lead article. "Yale Library Announces Major Find." Well, they *would* lead with a Yale story in the local news.

He turned his attention back to the scene in front of him. The groom was smiling as an older woman approached him and veered off to the left. And then there was the bride, tall, determined, moving deliberately into her predestined position. Apparently there was no father to give her away, to block—even temporarily—the execution of their plan.

The minister stepped forward. Until he stepped back again, Ramesh wouldn't have the targets where he wanted them, side by side. He let his eyes drift back down to the paper. The organist was making a meal of the final fat Wagnerian chords as the bride finished her march. Ramesh debated bringing the gun up now, but he thought better of it. You don't want to stay in the ready position overlong. Contracted muscles can freeze or twitch involuntarily. Bad for business. Something in the first paragraph . . .

"Yale University's Beinecke Library announced today the acquisition of a previously unknown memoir by Ian Fleming, the popular novelist who served with British intelligence during World War II. The memoir is believed to have been written . . ."

Something was nagging at the edges of his consciousness. Ramesh was famous in the British Secret Service for his focus, his ability to block out everything, including the details of other team members' assignments, so he could better concentrate on his task: the kicker teeing the ball up after a try, building his little mound of earth before putting the leather oval down. The crowd may yell, nerves may scream. Still, you "do your thing" and aim for the uprights to the exclusion of everything else. But . . . hadn't there been something about a manuscript? What was the package Simon was after? And where was Simon, anyway?

No new messages. He didn't like doubt. He didn't like half of one thing and half another. Ramesh was an all-or-nothing man. That's what was so satisfying about his profession. It was hit. Or miss. Life. Or death. Nothing relative, nothing subjective. A binary function, like a switch. On or off. Yes or no. Shame or glory.

"Dearly beloved, we are gathered together in the sight . . ."

At least the opening was conventional. It lifted Ramesh's spirits a little. If this train would only stay on the rails, he could be out of here by half past at the latest. A filling on the bottom right was starting to give him trouble. He'd have to see Dr. Choudhry when he got back. The Congregational minister— odd choice for a woman named Greenberg, no?— seemed to be settling in for a while.

". . . in the holy bonds of matrimony."

He slid the Local pages back into the rest of the
Register, but he must not have nested them properly
into the other sections because about three inches of
text stuck out the bottom. "Yale announced it had
already begun circulating the memoir, for purposes of
authentication, among other experts in the field,
many of whom are based in Europe. In describing the
find . . ."

His phone trembled in his pocket. Ramesh looked
at the screen. "No sale." It was shocking not to see
the "Pkg received" he'd expected.

"Do you, Scott Harcourt Brown, take Amy Mar-
cia Greenberg . . ."

Ramesh was pushing the buttons on his phone as
fast as his fingers would allow, forwarding Simon's
message to Homing Pigeon. (The staff guys got code
names. Even the assignments had code names they
made you memorize. Meanwhile the field men—who
took all the risk—had to work in the clear. Was anyone else as irritated about it as he was?)

". . . to be your lawfully wedded . . ."

Homing Pigeon's response was immediate. "Proceed." Ramesh had to admire the man's decisiveness.

". . . to have and to hold, from this day forward . . ."

Almost there. The moment they'd trained for.
When he would put down the phone and pick up the

gun. When the spheres came into alignment, when the man would lift the woman's veil and kiss her. The moment for the kill.

". . . as long as you both shall live."

He put down the phone but he didn't pick up the gun. Something wasn't right. Reasonable doubt was all right for juries, but he had to be beyond all doubt. Want to be a robot? Join the regular army. Ramesh was thinking. The Service was the thinking man's force, and the twenty or so G-9s saw themselves as entrepreneurs. Civil servants who were at the same time free agents of a kind. He was thinking about the piece in the paper. About Simon's failure. About the mission, its code name, everything.

"The library's Executive Director, Dr. Ralph Confessore, called it 'Terribly well-documented. Though Fleming is popularly known as the creator of James Bond, we believe *Provenance* will have major repercussions within and beyond the fields of military and diplomatic scholarship, and . . . cont. on page three."

It wasn't doubt that made him pick up the phone again and dial 101-#. It was certainty. The voice on the tie-line said, "This is a priority call. It will be terminated in exactly forty-five seconds."

Forty-six seconds later, Ramesh had aborted Operation James Bond. He sent a text message to

Homing Pigeon, "No sale," and put the safety back on the gun before returning it to its place under the loosened floorboard for Post-Ops to retrieve later. He rose and, before going, looked back at the happy scene.

"You may kiss the bride."

AUTHOR'S NOTE

Some people who have read this book before publication have asked me how much of *In Secret Service* is fact and how much fiction. First off, it's a novel and not a history. So I've felt perfectly free to start with the actual life stories of several dozen real people—among them King Edward VIII and Wallis Simpson, Winston Churchill, Anthony Blunt, Rudolf Hess, and, of course, Ian Fleming—and work around or extrapolate from the facts to create the tale I wish to tell.

For instance, Winston Churchill really did write that encomium to Valentine Fleming; Wallis really did have an Aunt Bessie and Uncle Sol; Anthony Blunt really was outed in Parliament by Margaret Thatcher; there really was a group of FDR's friends that met in The Room, a furnished apartment in the house at 34 East Sixty-second Street in New York that made the front page of all the New York papers when it was blown up by its last owner in the summer of 2006.

On the other hand, all the modern characters are made up, as is Fleming's entire, lengthy (I know, I know) letter to Amy. I have no idea if there ever was an entrance to the Yale Club directly from Grand Central Terminal. There ought to have been one. And I don't have firsthand knowledge, nor do I have anyone else's firsthand knowledge, of Wallis Simpson's sexual equipment. Androgen insensitivity syndrome is merely one of the guesses people have made to account for Wallis's stunning success with men, one I decided to go with, as I did the contents of Wallis's China dossier.

I am greatly indebted to Martin Allen, whose book *Hidden Agenda: How the Duke of Windsor Betrayed the Allies* revealed the existence of a letter the Duke of Windsor wrote to Adolf Hitler in 1939. I reimagined the contents of the letter to make it more overtly sinister, so it might function as my MacGuffin, the Hitchcockian thing everyone is chasing after. I also benefited from Mr. Allen's research into Charles Eugene Bedaux.

Then there are the things that are neither definitely factual nor fictional. Edward and Wallis might have bumped into Ian Fleming in Austria in the winter of 1935. They were all there at the time. King George VI really did authorize Anthony Blunt to retrieve a damaging letter from a German castle at the end of World War II. Possibly Fleming went along, though probably not. Guy Marcus Trundle really was a London car dealer who was romantically linked to Wallis. Perhaps he was helping Churchill. Prince Philip grew up in St. Cloud outside Paris. He might have been home on leave at Christmas in 1939.

How and why did Princess Diana really die? What was Rudolf Hess doing stumbling out of a burning plane in Scotland one night in May 1941? What kept Anthony Blunt safe and secure more than a dozen years after his cover was blown? *In Secret Service* is my Theory of Everything Mysterious, a connect-the-dots picture with hundreds of real dots and hundreds more of invented ones.

For the reader who is as much of a history geek as I am, I include a short bibliography:

Martin Allen, *Hidden Agenda: How the Duke of Windsor Betrayed the Allies,* New York: M. Evans & Co., 2002.

Andrew Boyle, *The Fourth Man: The Definitive Account of Kim Philby, Guy Burgess, and Donald Maclean and Who Recruited Them to Spy for Russia,* New York: Dial Press, 1979.

Charles Higham, *The Duchess of Windsor: The Secret Life,* New York: McGraw-Hill, 1988.

Jon King and John Beveridge, *Princess Diana, The Hidden Evidence: How MI6 and the CIA Were Involved in the Death of Princess Diana*, New York: S.P.I. Books, 2001.

Andrew Lycett, *Ian Fleming: The Man Behind James Bond*, Atlanta: Turner Publishing, 1995.

Kirsty McLeod, *Battle Royal: Edward VIII & George VI: Brother Against Brother*, London: Constable and Co., 1999.

John Pearson, *The Life of Ian Fleming*, New York: McGraw-Hill, 1966.

Joseph E. Persico, *Roosevelt's Secret War: FDR and World War II Espionage*, New York: Random House, 2001.

Susan A. Williams, *The People's King: The True Story of the Abdication*, New York: Palgrave Macmillan, 2004.

ACKNOWLEDGMENTS

First, thanks to my family, Ellen, Sloane, and Perry, for suffering through this book with me. Thanks to Robin and Peter Jovanovich, who graciously put up with my reading aloud to them; to Fred and Barbara Cummings, for their legal and literary help; to Dennis Soohoo; Tania Chamlian; Richard Butt; Steve Forcione; Davidson Gordon; Allen and Whitney Clark; Katie Brown; Bill Gedale; Steve Otis; Claire Tisne; Mary Charles Von Canon Sisk; Shelly Coon; Ed Lamance; and my brother Ken, the nonpareil art historian. Thanks to my editor, Trish Todd and everyone at Touchstone. Thanks as well to my editor at Pocket, Kathy Sagan, editorial director Maggie Crawford, publisher Louise Burke, associate managing editor David Logsdon, and Kate Moll who managed to make the documents fit on the page. Thanks to Brad Meltzer and Lee Child for the nice words, and to Jim Patterson, Ted Bell, Dick Marek, and Jim Othmer for the helpful ones. A big thank-you to Larry Kirshbaum and everyone at LJK Literary. And, of course, a bouquet to the person who made that possible, Martha Otis. Cheers!